Four Kilos

PHIL NOVA

ISBN-13: 978-0692366271
ISBN-10: 069236627X
Five Borough Publishing
New York

CHAPTER 1

Craig Hill, a six-foot tall carpenter with yellow skin and eyes from jaundice, stepped out of the green plastic portable potty where he had been vomiting for the past fifteen minutes.

He wiped his mouth with a piece of toilet paper and noticed that the sound of construction had stopped and the first floor was empty. The other workers had already gone to lunch.

Just as he was about to emerge from behind a stack of sheetrock and metal studs, he heard yelling outside in the street, and then what sounded like a gunshot.

A pale white man in a pair of shorts and a Hawaiian shirt raced into the building with a pistol in one hand and a square black object in the other hand.

Craig stepped back, behind the stack of construction material, and watched.

At the front of the building, the man slipped the square object into a four-inch cavity between a half-finished sheetrock wall and an exterior block wall behind that.

Someone outside yelled, "Stop! Police!"

The man darted toward the back of the building.

Two cops bolted into the building with their guns drawn.

Craig stepped back a little farther. He heard a gunshot and wondered if a stray bullet could penetrate the stack of sheetrock and metal studs he was hiding behind.

Another gunshot echoed throughout the construction site, and then another.

The smell of gunpowder drifted toward Craig as he backed up until reaching an unpainted metal staircase. The gunshots continued like fireworks on the first floor while Craig made his way up the stairs to the second floor.

Sirens became louder outside.

He didn't have the strength to run all the way up to the eighth floor, but he wanted to get a little higher than he was.

The gunfire stopped as quickly as it started.

While Craig stood on the staircase between the second and third floors, a herd of workers stampeded down the stairs. A few plumbers asked what was going on. Craig shrugged and followed them down.

Back on the first floor, Craig pushed his way through the crowd until he could see what had happened. The man with the Hawaiian shirt lay dead on the concrete floor with bullet holes in his torso and legs. One of the two cops that had chased him into the building lay dead on the floor while the other cop held his bleeding shoulder and gazed at his partner's corpse.

A dozen more cops entered the building. They told the construction workers to go outside and stick around for questioning.

On his way out the front door with the other workers, Craig snuck a glance at the half-finished wall and wondered what was in there.

CHAPTER 2

Police barricades and patrol cars with flashing lights blocked the intersection and surrounding streets while uniformed cops kept curious pedestrians out of the way.

An unmarked gray police car pulled up and parked in the middle of the street.

Victor Cohen, a short, stout, half-Puerto Rican, half-Jewish, homicide detective with a thick black mustache and a cheap wrinkled suit stepped out of the car on the passenger side.

He slipped a stick of gum into his mouth while looking down the block at the five-story brick apartment buildings on both sides of the street and noticing that the gym he had gone to as a teenager was now just an empty storefront covered with plywood and graffiti.

Detective Rosie Li, a short, thick, American born Chinese woman stepped out of the driver's seat wearing a loose-fitting pants suit.

Victor and Rosie approached a group of NYPD crime scene investigators in the middle of the street examining a dead white man wearing shorts and a Hawaiian shirt. The man was face down with two bullet holes in his back. It looked as if he'd been running.

Victor asked a uniformed sergeant, "Where's the other three?"

"Two of them are on the sidewalk." The sergeant led Victor and Rosie across the street.

Behind a parked van, they found another crime scene unit

examining another dead white man in shorts and a Hawaiian shirt and a dead Dominican man in street clothes with a bullet hole in his forehead.

Victor looked around at the upside-down coffee cups everywhere. The cups covered bullet shells and slugs, and there were quite a few of them. "This was like an old western shootout."

Rosie said, "And no one saw anything?"

"Of course not," said the sergeant. "That would be too easy."

Victor looked down the block. On the corner of Avenue A stood an eight-story luxury apartment building under construction, The Howell Building.

An exterior hoist on tracks sat on the ground. At least forty construction workers waited outside the beige-brick building, under the sidewalk scaffold. Uniformed police officers questioned them one by one.

The sergeant said, "The other guy with the Hawaiian shirt ran into that building. Internal Affairs is in there now questioning the cop that survived."

Victor said, "So the two beat cops were coming down Avenue A when they heard shots here on Sixth Street. A man with a gun and a Hawaiian shirt ran across the Avenue, into that building under construction, and the two cops chased him inside. And now one cop is dead."

The sergeant answered, "That's right."

Rosie said, "We better get in there and check it out."

Victor and Rosie proceeded up the block. The humidity increased while big drops of rain hit the ground and then instantly evaporated. The sun was still shining overhead.

Victor said, "New York is turning into Miami."

Rosie said, "I hope not. That would mean more bugs."

While crossing the Avenue, Victor noticed that new luxury apartment buildings and hipster coffee shops were popping up every week. It didn't look like it did when he grew up here, in the days of heroin, crack, and ten dollar hookers.

Victor and Rosie showed their gold shields to the uniformed cops at the door and then entered The Howell Building.

The floor was bare concrete. Finished and unfinished sheetrock walls separated rooms while wires and pipes were still visible in the ceilings. The smell of gunpowder mixed with dust filled the hot, steamy air.

Despite the temporary lights hanging overhead, the first floor was dark because most of the newly installed windows were covered with plywood.

Victor had worked construction one summer in high school and he hated it. The money almost tempted him to stay, but he always knew he wanted to be a cop.

Smelling as if he'd poured a gallon of cologne on himself, Detective Carillo from Internal Affairs approached Victor and said, "If it isn't the Jew-Rican."

Victor had heard that nickname all through junior high and high school and somehow it had followed him to the force.

He reached his hand out to Detective Carillo, and while shaking it, Victor squeezed Carillo's hand, hard. Victor hadn't lifted weights in six months, but he still had a grip like a vice. He knew Carillo was in pain as he squirmed and tried to act like he wasn't.

Rosie must have noticed what was going on because she reached her hand out to Carillo and said, "Hi. I'm Rosie Li."

Victor released Carillo's hand and walked away. He approached the sectioned off area at the back of the building and looked down at the dead cop and the dead Hawaiian shirt man. "Where's the other one?"

Carillo said, "Getting patched up. Where you been?"

"We were on our way uptown when we got the call. You know how traffic is at this time." Victor said, "So I guess you're here because of the dead cop."

"You're getting' smarter in your old age, Cohen."

"At least they didn't send Edmunds."

Carillo said, "I'll tell Abby you said hello."

"Yeah, thanks." Victor squatted down to get a better look at the dead man in the Hawaiian shirt.

CHAPTER 3

Work had stayed on hold while cops questioned workers and crime scene techs collected evidence. Most of the workers spoke among themselves, speculating as to what happened and wondering if they were still on the clock.

Late afternoon, when the dead bodies and the army of cops were finally gone, the workers wrapped up their tools wherever they were working and secured their areas before leaving for the night. Craig Hill felt just as tired as if he'd worked all day.

He followed the other carpenters down the stairs from the third floor to their shanty on the second floor. He didn't have any tools he wanted to leave there, so he kept going, down the stairs to the first floor.

Steamfitters, electricians, tile setters, and others, made their way down the stairs from higher floors.

On the first floor, police lines blocked access to the back of the building.

Craig looked over at the half-finished wall at the front of the building. None of the cops had looked anywhere for anything other than bullet shells and stray slugs. He wondered if the cops even knew that the man in the Hawaiian shirt had hidden something. Whatever was in that wall was worth killing for, and worth dying for. He had to get it.

Still wearing his hardhat and work gloves, Craig slipped into the portable potty where he waited while most everyone else went home.

It took forever for everyone to leave. A few people trying to get into the portable potty knocked on the door. Craig had to tell them he was sick and make fake vomiting noises. He knew everyone was afraid of him, and he knew that would give him the privacy he needed to wait as long as he needed to.

Finally, when he was certain they were gone, he stepped out of the potty and hurried to the wall with the package in it. He stood against the wall holding his backpack and tried to stay out of sight while waiting for a chubby laborer sweeping the floor down the hall to turn the corner.

He knew he could probably wait until tomorrow, but it would drive him crazy all night. And, assuming it was something valuable inside that wall, he worried someone else might come looking and find it. He wanted to know what was in that package, and he wanted it now.

Just as the chubby laborer stepped out of sight, Craig bent over and slipped his long, skinny arm in between the sheetrock and the exterior block wall.

He couldn't get down far enough, and he couldn't see what was in there. The package must have dropped all the way to the bottom.

Wondering how many more people were still working, and hoping for a little more time, Craig tried for a few more seconds in vain to force his arm farther down.

It was taking too long, and it wasn't working. He looked around to make sure no one was coming around the corner and then he retrieved a long serrated sheetrock saw from his backpack, which he then pushed into the wall, hoping he was in the right place.

He remembered seeing an electrical box, but because he was far away and everything happened so fast, he couldn't be sure about the exact measurement. It looked like it was probably about a foot away—he hoped that was right.

He quickly sawed through the sheetrock while constantly glancing both ways to be sure no one was coming. White dust accumulated on the floor below.

After cutting a six-inch line, he turned the saw and began cutting a large square hole. That's when he realized a round hole would have been quicker, but he was trained to cut square holes, it was just habit.

He heard banging around the corner. Craig grabbed his saw and backpack and headed toward the door. The carpenter's shanty was already locked and he didn't have an excuse for still being there. He knew if anyone questioned him, he could always play the sick card. One look at his yellow eyes and skin and most people didn't need to be convinced.

Just before reaching the front door, Craig peeked around the corner and didn't see anyone. He looked back and still didn't see anyone.

He thought it might be rats coming up from the basement for a party, now that most of the humans had gone.

Craig decided it was safe enough to continue what he'd started. He headed back to the wall and finished cutting the hole.

Before reaching in, he looked around again and didn't see anyone.

He slipped his hand into the hole and felt around until his fingers brushed over something. It was square and hard and wrapped in plastic. He touched it, but couldn't get a grip on it. At least he was close enough to get it.

Craig forced his hand and wrist down at an angle, breaking the sheetrock below the hole, just enough to reach in a little farther and grab the package, but he had to break the sheetrock more to make the hole big enough to pull it out, and at the same time, trying not to make any noise.

Finally, with the hole big enough, Craig grabbed the package and pulled it out of the wall. It weighed about ten pounds. Before he could look at what he was holding, he heard something fall in another room.

He grabbed the package and his backpack and hurried behind a finished wall into what was one day to become a kitchen, a long skinny room with capped pipes protruding from the unpainted walls and new cabinets on the floor waiting to be installed.

He stood against the wall and waited. After a few minutes, when he didn't hear or see anyone, he decided to check out what he found. He moved away from the entrance to the back of the room.

Starting from the corner of the package, Craig carefully removed the black plastic covering. It felt like four bricks stacked on top of each other.

Under the outer layer, each brick was wrapped separately in clear plastic. It was yellowish white. He knew right away what it was—cocaine—a lot of cocaine.

Someone behind Craig said, "Nice."

Craig spun around, his heart slamming against his rib cage.

Robby, a skinny laborer wearing dark safety glasses and a black skull and crossbones bandana on his head stood behind him. Everyone called him Robby the junkie because he was high on methadone half the time and high on heroin the rest of the time.

Robby said, "I knew I saw you take something out of that wall."

Craig froze.

Robby stepped closer and said, "That's a lot of coke, bro. Now the whole thing with the cops shooting up that guy makes sense."

"That dope is fucking up your head. You're imagining things. I bought this from someone." He held it in his hand, ready to put it into his backpack, but the backpack was still zipped up.

Robby laughed. "I just saw you take it out of the wall, bro. You didn't even hear me following you until I dropped my broom. I want half or I'm going to the cops."

Craig knew this coke might go for enough money to get his liver transplant and the hepatitis medicine he needed. He wasn't going to give that up for some greedy little junkie. "Come on, Robby. You know I'm sick and I need a liver transplant. This could be my life."

Robby scratched his skinny, tattoo-covered arm and said, "That's not my problem, bro. I want half."

Craig said, "I'll give you a quarter of one of these bricks. Come on, Robby. That's still worth a lot of money. Imagine how much dope you could buy."

"I see four bricks there. Imagine how much dope I could buy if you give me half. I want two bricks or I'm going to the cops."

Craig didn't have much strength left, but he knew he still had a chance against this skinny little junkie. "Get the fuck outta here or I'll kick your junkie ass." Craig raised his fist.

Robby stepped back. "Have it your way, bro." He took another step back. "I'm going to the cops."

"Wait." Craig couldn't let him go to the cops, but he couldn't give him half of what he found either. He lied. "Okay. I'll give you two bricks."

Robby smiled while stepping back into the room.

Craig glanced at the hard hat hanging from Robby's belt and then he looked up at Robby's face while stepping toward him. He was happy he couldn't see Robby's eyes through the dark safety glasses.

Craig pretended to separate the bricks while his heart pounded harder and harder. He snatched the utility knife from his belt and slashed Robby's throat. Craig knew it wasn't deep enough to kill him, but he hoped it would be enough to keep him from screaming and alerting the other laborers.

Robby grasped his bleeding throat while gasping for air.

Craig placed the package onto a five-gallon bucket, unzipped his backpack, retrieved the dusty sheetrock saw from his backpack, and lunged toward Robby, sinking the metal blade into Robby's stomach.

Robby hunched over onto Craig, blood spurting everywhere. He was so close, Craig could smell the sweat and body odor emanating from Robby's clothes.

Craig stepped back and yanked the saw out of Robby, releasing more blood.

Robby grabbed his bleeding stomach and tried to yell, but he had no voice.

Craig grabbed Robby's head, pulled it back, and stuck the sheetrock saw into Robby's neck. Robby choked on his own blood while Craig sawed Robby's throat open. The tool was meant for sheetrock—it was a lot harder cutting through flesh, even though he had a knife cut to follow.

Blood sprayed everywhere while Craig tried to keep Robby's convulsing body steady and at the same time, pull the saw out of his neck.

Craig could smell the piss and shit exuding from the twitching corpse as he dragged it behind the row of new cabinets.

Upon turning around, Craig was surprised when he saw how much blood covered the newly installed tile floor.

Looking down at himself, he noticed the blood on the front of his old gray sweatshirt and faded dark blue jeans. Even though it was ninety degrees outside, Craig always felt cold, and he always wore a sweatshirt over his T-shirt. He removed the bloody sweatshirt, rolled it into a ball, and stuffed it into his backpack along with the bloody saw and his other tools.

He couldn't take off his pants, but luckily, his jeans were much darker than his sweatshirt, and there was not as much blood on them.

After peeking around the corner and ensuring that the first floor was still empty, Craig grabbed a small cardboard barrel and dragged it into the unfinished kitchen.

His hands trembled as he reached into the barrel, pulled out handfuls of green dust, and sprinkled it all over the blood-saturated floor and wiped a little on his jeans. He knew that if anyone caught him here doing this, he would have to kill them too.

When Craig was certain he'd covered everything, he took his backpack and made sure no one was around before sneaking out of the unfinished kitchen.

Just outside in the hall, he was about to make his way out of the building when he realized he forgot the coke.

Craig's heartbeat increased as a cold sweat ran through his body. There was no one around, so he hurried back, grabbed the four bricks of coke, and stuffed them into his backpack.

Before leaving the room for the second time, Craig once again peeked out to see if anyone was there. The chubby laborer was back, turning off circuit breakers against the wall.

One by one, sections of the building instantly went from light to dark, the darkness getting closer.

Craig waited while trying to control his breathing and thinking about the blood on the front of his jeans. He didn't know if he could do it, he certainly didn't want to, but he would kill the chubby laborer if he had to.

He knew if he didn't forget the coke the first time, he would already be halfway down the street. What a stupid mistake. He slipped his still trembling hand into his backpack and retrieved his hammer from his tool belt while wondering if he would have enough strength to kill a man twice Robby's size.

A tall laborer with earphones on and a blunt in his hand approached the chubby laborer.

Craig stepped back and exhaled. He waited for the two laborers to finish turning off the power and disappear from sight, then he made his way to the entrance with just a small amount of sunlight coming in through the tiny space along the edge of the front door.

The security guard wasn't in his booth, but he had to be around somewhere.

The temporary plywood door had the chain and lock on it, but the lock was still open. Craig pulled the chain off and dropped it to the ground before heading out into the street.

He didn't run just in case anyone saw him leaving the building. He slipped off his bloody work gloves and stuffed them into his backpack along with all the other evidence.

CHAPTER 4

It was late afternoon, but the blazing sun was still high above beating down on the crowded Manhattan streets and sidewalks.

Victor Cohen and Rosie Li had just left the scene of the crime and were driving toward their precinct. Even though the air-conditioner was on, Victor couldn't stop sweating. He retrieved a handkerchief from his front jacket pocket and wiped the sweat from his forehead.

Rosie glanced over from the driver's seat when Victor's cell phone beeped. It was a text message. He slipped a stick of gum into his mouth while reading it, then turned to Rosie and said, "Lab says there had to be seven guns."

"Seven?" Rosie glanced at Victor before turning the corner. "There were the two cops, the dead Dominican guy. . ."

Victor added, "Plus the three dead guys in Hawaiian shirts."

"That's only six." Rosie stopped at a red light and turned to Victor, "That means . . ."

He finished her sentence, "Someone got away."

"I wonder how many there were. I wonder if any of them were shot." Rosie pulled into a parking lot and parked.

Victor pushed himself up out of the car and closed the door behind him. "See what you find on the corpses. I'm going to see the guys in the lab."

"Got it."

They exited the parking lot, then waited for a couple cars to pass before crossing the narrow street and entering a six-story limestone faced building with an American flag hanging from a pole protruding from the third floor. Six-story brick apartment buildings flanked both sides of the precinct.

Victor opened the heavy steel and glass door and held it open for Rosie as she entered the air-conditioned building that smelled of coffee.

"I'm going to visit the little boys' room."

"Good idea."

"I'll meet you on the third floor." Victor turned and followed a dreary blue hallway to the men's restroom.

He relieved himself then washed his hands and his acne scarred face while another man finished washing and then left the room.

Victor opened a prescription bottle, fished out half a Vicoden, put it in his mouth, cupped his hand, and swallowed the pill with some water from the sink.

After drying his hands and straightening out his wrinkled suit, Victor headed out of the bathroom and down the hall toward the elevator while passing patrol officers and other detectives. Many of them glanced twice at Victor as he passed. News of the dead cop must have already spread. He knew he had to solve this one quickly, but it wasn't going to be easy.

The sterile smelling forensics lab had recently received a fresh coat of bright white paint, but the blue cabinets and gray countertops were still in need of replacement.

Victor examined the shells and slugs that the crime scene techs had collected. A female technician in a white lab coat described the markings and explained why there had to be seven guns. Three of the guns found had not been fired and the slugs found in the man face down in the street didn't match any of the other three guns that they did have.

Back on the third floor, Victor approached Rosie at her perfectly organized desk and asked, "Anything?"

She finished scrolling through a list on her computer. "The Dominican guy was Rene Ortega. He was easy to find. He's got an assault, a couple possessions, and one sales on his record. Spent a little time on Riker's but never went upstate."

"What about the prints on the Hawaiian shirts?" Asked Victor.

"Nothing here in New York. Waiting to see if the FBI gets a match."

Victor sat at his cluttered desk and leaned back in his chair. "Well, there were definitely seven guns. Three of the guns we do have, weren't even fired. I figure, if the Hawaiian shirt guys outnumbered the Dominican guy four-to-one, then why would one guy run?"

"So, you think the Dominican had a partner?"

"Probably."

Rosie said, "I got a long list here just to get us started. I'm sending it to the printer now, Ortega's known accomplices and most of his family members. And they just told us no more overtime."

"Well, if they want the case solved."

Rosie took off her reading glasses and rubbed her eyes.

"I'll get it." Victor stood and crossed the noisy room full of detectives at their desks, then after waiting a few seconds for the list to finish printing, he retrieved it from the printer and headed back to Rosie at her desk. "Family first?"

CHAPTER 5

Dressed in a light gray Armani suit with a white cloth napkin tucked into his shirt as a bib, sixty-year-old Enzo Nattichioni soaked up some tomato sauce from his plate with a piece of meatball on his fork in his favorite Italian restaurant.

Scenic paintings of Italian landscapes hung from preserved brick walls while waiters in tuxedos brought drinks from the bar to people's tables. The smell of roasted garlic filled the air.

Enzo glanced over at his cell phone as it rang on the table.

His forty-three-year-old, fake-blonde mistress, Layla, slid the phone closer to Enzo and then took a sip of her white wine.

Enzo put his fork down and answered the phone. "Yeah."

A man on the other end spoke, "Someone's here to see you."

"Do I know him?"

"You do."

Enzo glanced at his diamond bezel Rolex and said, "Fifteen minutes."

"I'll tell him."

He hung up the phone and turned to Layla. "I can't stay for coffee, baby."

She looked away from him. "What else is new?"

"Cazzo. You like driving that Benz? I can't pay for it if I don't work." Enzo inhaled the last few ravioli on his plate and glanced over at the barely touched piece of fish on Layla's plate.

She sipped her wine and asked, "You staying with me

tonight?"

He looked at her ample cleavage and wished he could stay the night with her. "Sorry, baby. I can't tonight." He swallowed the last of his red wine, threw a hundred dollar bill on the table, stood, and kissed Layla on the cheek. "I'll see you tomorrow. And don't give me that look."

She sipped her wine but didn't pay any attention to Enzo as he left the restaurant. He didn't care. If she gave him too much of a problem, he would just dump her like he did the last one. As long as he still had his family.

Enzo had been married for thirty-nine years. He and his sons were planning a big party next year for his fortieth anniversary. Enzo and his wife also planned to retire to Arizona in a few years. They had been there recently on vacation and both of them felt relief from their arthritis due to the hot dry desert air.

Enzo stepped out of the air-conditioned restaurant and onto the hot sidewalk. He bit off the end a cigar, put the cigar into his mouth, and lit it, puffing on it while strolling down Arthur Avenue passing a fruit stand, a bakery, and a Salumeria.

Enzo had lived in The Bronx until he was thirty, then he and his wife moved to Yonkers. He worked in a factory until sixteen years ago when a machine took his left pinky off.

He collected disability and hung out at his friend's bar in The Bronx for a couple years before learning he could make a good profit from lending money.

When business picked up, a local mafia captain, Peppino, approached Enzo. Enzo paid Peppino a monthly protection fee, which he didn't mind because he knew no one would try to stiff him now that he was connected.

He usually lent his own money, but when the order was too big, he edged off some of the loans to Peppino, and still made a percentage for himself.

Enzo took a couple more puffs before putting his cigar out, then he waved at a few people on the other side of the street before entering a bar on the corner. Just as he was about to step inside, he noticed a few raindrops splattering on the sidewalk here and there.

Inside, the wood-paneled room was dark and cool. A few people sat on stools at the bar and a few people sat at tables. Adriano Celentano played in the background.

Enzo looked toward the back of the bar and saw a young nervous Dominican man with a pencil thin mustache and goatee sitting at a table and sipping on a drink: Sammy Ortega.

Enzo asked the bartender, "Where's Ray Ray? He just called me."

"Said he'll be back in ten. Scotch?"

"Give me a glass of red, and another of what the kid in the back there is having."

Enzo approached Sammy's table in the back, shook his hand, then sat in the chair across from him. Even in the dark, Enzo could see Sammy's swollen eyes. He knew Sammy had been crying. "What's wrong kid?"

Sammy said, "They killed Rene. Motherfuckers killed my brother."

Enzo looked around and told Sammy, "Cazzo. Not so loud. There's ears everywhere."

Sammy glanced at the other people in the bar, then lowered his voice. "We got jacked, Enzo. And, they killed Rene."

"Who's they?"

"I don't know. We came out of a coffee shop in the city. Our connection already left a few minutes earlier. We came out of the restaurant with four keys and then some motherfuckers in Hawaiian shirts snuck up on us."

"Hawaiian shirts?"

"Yeah, Hawaiian shirts. Three of them. One on each side and one in front. It's like they came outta nowhere. The guy in front pointed his gun at Rene's face and told him to give up the package. We knew we were fucked, I guess that's why Rene just gave it up so easily."

Enzo motioned for Sammy to stop talking as the bartender brought Enzo's wine and another rum and coke for Sammy.

"Thanks Joe." Enzo handed the bartender a twenty-dollar bill, then waited a moment for him to walk away. He turned to Sammy and said, "So, the guy took the package from Rene. Then what happened?"

Sammy continued. "He already had the package, but the motherfucker shot Rene anyway. Right in the forehead. He ran up Sixth Street with the package. I grabbed my pistol from my waistband and shot the guy on my left. The guy on my right pulled his trigger, but his gun jammed. He didn't even try to fix it, he just started running, so I started shooting. I hit him in the back as he ran across the street. I went after the guy with the package, but the cops were already chasing him into some building under construction. So I got the fuck outta there."

Enzo asked, "He still had it with him when he went into the building?"

"I'm not sure. He was too far to tell."

Enzo swallowed half a glass of wine and said, "I'm sorry to hear about your brother. I always liked Rene."

Sammy sat quietly and looked down at the table in front of him.

Enzo said, "We gotta find that package. I only put up forty grand. The other hundred came from to Peppino."

Sammy looked up at Enzo. "I'm gonna find that motherfucker and I'm gonna kill him."

"You trust the people you got it from?"

"I don't know. My brothers have been dealing with them for years. It seemed like Rene trusted them."

Enzo said, "Don't count nothing out. You do what you can to find out who robbed you, and I'll talk to Peppino. I'll try to get you some time and maybe some information if he knows anything."

Sammy nodded and gulped his drink.

"Please understand if I can't make it to Rene's funeral."

Sammy looked at Enzo but didn't say anything.

Enzo took a roll from his pocket and stripped off two one-hundred dollar bills. "I don't mean to be rude, but I'd like to get a nice flower for your brother. He was a good kid."

CHAPTER 6

Victor took the M-train from Manhattan into Queens and then stopped at a small grocery store on the corner of Queens Boulevard to buy a half-gallon of milk and some crackers.

Outside, he kept his suit jacket on to avoid having to carry it, but he unbuttoned the second button on his shirt, hoping that would help.

Even though the sun was on its way down, the air was still hot and stale. The streets and sidewalks were wet, but quickly drying. Victor was thankful he hadn't been caught in the rain, and hoped it wouldn't rain again until he was home and settled in.

He strolled three and a half blocks along tree-lined streets that consisted of small two-story houses guarded by brick apartment buildings on the corners. Kids played in the streets and on the sidewalks. The trees had all their leaves out absorbing the last of the day's sunlight.

Victor and his wife had just moved into the neighborhood six months ago, one week before their daughter was born. They had bought a house in a short sale. It needed some cosmetic work, but was in overall good shape. The mortgage was high on their two-story house, but now that his wife was back to work, they were able to get by.

As he arrived on his block, Victor passed his faded blue house and knocked on the door of the little white house attached to his.

A Jamaican woman in medical scrubs answered the door.

"Hello, Victor."

"Hello, Alesha." Victor entered the warm, stuffy house and closed the door behind him. He followed the nurse through a dark living room full of preserved antique furniture to a kitchen where he found an old woman at a table eating a small plate of beans and chicken. "Sorry to interrupt your dinner, Mrs. Lopez."

"No mind that." The woman spoke Spanglish. "Come eat something."

Alesha sat down to another plate of food next to the old woman.

"I can't" Victor bent over and kissed Mrs. Lopez on the cheek. "My wife has dinner waiting for me." He placed the milk into the refrigerator and the crackers into the cabinet.

"She better. Or I might take you away from her."

Victor and Alesha both laughed.

Mrs. Lopez said, "I'm kidding. She's a good woman. She came by with the baby today to see me."

"Finally."

"Don't be like that. She's a good woman. She goes to work and takes care of the house."

"I know." Victor took the garbage bag out of the can and tied it. He had always thought of his mother when he saw Mrs. Lopez. He knew she would have been just like her, if she hadn't died of breast cancer at forty-four-years-old.

Victor washed his hands, then asked, "You need anything else?"

"Another kiss?"

Alesha chuckled and said, "You old tramp."

Mrs. Lopez snickered.

"Just don't tell my wife." He kissed Mrs. Lopez on the cheek one more time before leaving the house with her garbage.

Outside, Victor threw the bag into a garbage pail and then entered his house next door.

He proceeded through the sparsely decorated living room while following the smell of food cooking and the sound of pots and pans in the kitchen.

Victor's wife, Evelyn, a short, thick woman with curly black hair, stood at the stove stirring something in a pot. She turned around and said, "Hey, Babe."

Victor kissed her, washed his hands, then lifted the lid on the pot. "Beef stew. When will it be ready?"

"You have more passion for the stew than for me."

"That's not true." He grabbed her by the hips and pulled her close. "The stew is just fuel, so I can give it to you good later tonight."

She laughed and turned back to the stove. "Fifteen minutes."

He kissed her on the back of the head, then gave her a light slap on the butt. "I'm gonna jump in the shower."

Victor glanced at the baby monitor on the table to be sure the battery light was on then he headed out of the kitchen, up the stairs, and into his bedroom. A picture of his mother sat in a frame on his dresser along with loose receipts, change, and other junk that his wife was always asking him to clean up.

After turning the bedroom air-conditioner on low, Victor tiptoed to a crib against the wall and checked on his sleeping six-month old daughter, Sofia. He reached down and placed his finger in the palm of her hand. Even in her sleep, her little hand curled up and squeezed his finger. He loved when she did that, and he knew he had to enjoy it while he could.

Victor was a late bloomer in the police force when it came to having children. Most of the cops his age were dealing with unruly teenagers at home, and Victor had heard the war stories.

Sofia let her grasp go while moving in her sleep. Victor waited for her to stop moving, then kissed her lightly on the head and stepped away from the crib.

He took off his clothes and threw them in a hamper on the other side of the room before heading into the hallway.

While passing the small bedroom across the hall, which would soon be Sofia's room, Victor glanced inside and noticed that his wife had done more decorating. Flowers and butterfly stickers now covered the pink walls.

He smiled and headed to the bathroom where he took a prescription bottle out of the medicine cabinet, removed a Vicoden, snapped it in half, and swallowed it with some water from the sink. Then he took a shower.

While drying off, Victor opened the window to let some steam out. He hated sweating just out of the shower, so he usually took his time drying off and getting dressed with the window open before going into the air-conditioned bedroom.

Evelyn yelled from downstairs, "Victor! Food is ready! And

bring Sofia down, she slept long enough!"

"Okay!" Victor went into the bedroom, dried off, and got dressed quicker than he wanted to. After turning off the air conditioner, he picked up his daughter without waking her and carried her downstairs where he placed her into a high chair at the table and kissed her on the cheek.

Evelyn shook Sofia lightly, "Come on, Sofia. Time to get up." She looked at Victor and said, "I shouldn't have let her sleep that long."

While his wife tried to wake their daughter gently, Victor loaded both their plates with food, poured two glasses of soda, then broke off a chunk of Italian bread.

Sofia was awake, but out of it.

Victor laughed and said, "She looks drunk."

Evelyn laughed too, then sat down at the table and opened a jar of baby food. She alternated feeding herself and Sofia while Victor ate as if he'd just gotten out of a concentration camp.

After dinner, Evelyn washed the dishes while Victor went into the living room and sat on one of two recliners in front of the TV.

He swallowed a Percocet, which he didn't have a prescription for, then he placed his soda glass down on the small table next to his chair.

While reaching for the remote control, Victor glanced at the faded beige walls that surrounded him and felt guilty that he had never got around to painting yet. He had the paint in the basement, along with a stack of pictures he hadn't hung up yet because he hadn't painted yet. Evelyn didn't nag him about it, but she did make an occasional sarcastic comment.

Work had been so busy lately, and he didn't want to turn down any overtime while it was still available. He kept promising his wife he would get to the painting, but never did.

The carpets were in good shape when they bought the house, so they had a company come in and steam clean them just before moving in.

Victor reviewed his case files while the TV played in the background.

Just when the Percocet began to perform its function, Evelyn barreled into the room yelling and screaming words that sounded garbled.

He slowly rotated his head.

She threw a handful of photographs at him. "You bastard! Why do you still have these?" She threw another handful at him.

While shielding his face from the oncoming photos, Victor glanced at a few pictures on the floor, pictures of himself with his ex-girlfriend from six years ago.

"You still love her! You pathetic fucking loser! She dumped you! Get it through your thick fucking head!" Victor's wife tossed the last of the pictures into the air and then threw the empty shoebox at Victor's face.

Sofia began to scream and cry from the kitchen.

Evelyn took their daughter and stormed out the front door while saying, "I can't believe I married such a pathetic loser."

Victor fell to his knees and began scooping up the photos and placing them back into the shoebox. How did she find it? He had hidden the box in the back of the coat closet behind some scuba gear that he had bought years ago and never got around to learning how to use. He hadn't looked at those pictures since they moved into the house.

He held one in his hand and stared at it. It was a picture of him standing on the beach in Puerto Rico with his lost love, Jennifer Rivera. He remembered sucking in his belly for the picture. They had travelled to Puerto Rico many times, sometimes to visit relatives, but they usually preferred to stay on their own in hotels and just enjoy the beaches and nightlife.

After two and half years of perfect happiness, Jennifer dumped Victor. She had thirteen-year-old twin boys who started getting into fights in school and letting their grades slip. When the boys were only eleven, they liked Victor, but as they got older, they became jealous of him. Jennifer told Victor she couldn't see him anymore. She said she needed to focus on her children.

Victor had tried to convince her that many kids got like that during puberty, especially boys. He also said they could see each other every other weekend, when the boys were with their father. Jennifer told Victor that was not enough. Victor pleaded with her, but she was stubborn.

He couldn't believe that after saying she loved him twice a day, every day, that she could just turn her back on him so easily. After all the times she told him how special he was to her, and how happy she was to have him in her life, how could she just turn it off like a switch and treat him like a stranger? Victor had asked himself those questions millions of times and he knew the mental stress had affected his health in a negative way, but he just didn't know how to erase her from his mind.

Even now, six years later, he still thought of her and sometimes dreamed of her at night.

Pressure began to build in his abdomen, then floated up through his esophagus and into his head and face. The pressure in his face forced tears out of his eyes. He tried to hold them back, but they poured out. He felt angry and ashamed that he still loved a woman that wanted nothing to do with him.

When Victor met Jennifer, he had already been taking Vicoden prescribed by his doctor for back pain, but after the breakup, he took more and more. When the doctor refused to increase his dosage, Victor went elsewhere. Being a New York City cop, he knew where to get what he wanted.

He stayed with Vicoden and then Percocet for about a year and a half until finding out that Jennifer Rivera was getting married. She married a man from her mother's church. That's when Victor needed something stronger: OxyContin.

More than a year after Jennifer's wedding, Victor and his ex-partner found themselves involved in a shootout with a murder suspect. Victor, high on Oxy, moved slower than he should have and took a bullet in the calf.

When the police department found out he was using drugs without a prescription, Victor spent one year in drug rehab and then one year on desk duty. He's been back in action now for ten months. He was sorry that he had put his ex-partner's life in danger, but he was also thankful he didn't lose his job and his pension.

Evelyn was a secretary in the precinct. They had known each other for a few years, but they got close while Victor was on desk duty. Fifteen months ago, she missed her period. They were married right away and then started looking for houses in Queens.

Other than the two Vicoden a day that the doctor had prescribed for his three slipped disks, Victor was clean during and after rehab. But after recent arguments with his wife about working too many hours and not spending enough time at home, helping to raise their child, he had an excuse to add Percocet to his daily menu. That's what he told himself. Deep down inside, he knew it was really because he still felt the loss of Jennifer.

Victor thought about calling Evelyn on her cell phone and apologizing and begging her to come back home, but instead, he just stayed on the floor and continued looking at pictures of himself with Jennifer until he passed out on the carpet.

CHAPTER 7

Craig had hidden the package in at least ten different places since arriving home in his studio apartment in Brooklyn. Now he was moving it again. This time he stuffed it into his hamper, right in the middle of his dirty clothes.

For just a moment, Craig thought about breaking off a tiny piece for himself, but he could never really do it, not after all those years without it.

He had already thrown his bloody work clothes into a garbage bag, but didn't want to leave it with the regular building garbage, so the bag sat against the wall next to the door. He knew he should dispose of it right away, but he just didn't have any energy left. He decided to wake up a little early, then, before going to work, he would throw the bag into a construction dumpster he'd seen up the block.

A rock ballad from the eighties played through a pair of computer speakers plugged into a laptop on the floor. Craig swallowed two pills: a vitamin C and a milk thistle for his liver. He knew it wouldn't cure him, but any little bit would help.

A box fan on the floor spun around slowly on low, but even that gave Craig a chill so he turned it off, but left the window open to get some air in the musty room.

Exhausted, Craig pushed some old newspapers out of the way, then sat down on his faded brown sofa. He knew he should eat, but he didn't have an appetite. After leaning over and checking some music he was downloading on his computer, he sat back and closed his eyes.

Images of hellfire and torture from the bible flooded Craig's mind. The thought wasn't easy to process, he had killed a man. Murder. He couldn't stop thinking about all that blood and the gurgling sound Robby made while choking on the metal saw blade.

He reached under the couch and pulled out a flat wooden box. The box once contained chocolate covered nuts that his sister had given him a few years ago as a gift. The chocolate covered nuts were long gone. Now the box contained Craig's weed and paraphernalia.

He opened it and lit one of the many joints that he'd already rolled earlier that week. The smell of weed quickly filled the small apartment. After placing an old towel along the open space at the bottom of the door, he opened his only window and placed the fan in front of it to blow the smoke out.

While smoking, Craig noticed his supply was getting low. He tried to think about his normal routine, but his mind was obsessed with the four kilos of coke in his hamper and the man he'd killed earlier.

Craig usually only smoked half a joint. By the time he realized he'd smoked the whole thing, his mind kicked into overdrive. Every negative scenario he could envision entered his head. Someone could knock his door down at any minute: the cops, the people missing the coke.

After putting the joint out in the ashtray, Craig crossed the room to his bed where he retrieved some clean clothes from a pile that he hadn't folded yet. He had to get the bloody work clothes out of there. He wanted to move the coke too, but he didn't know where, so he decided to leave that for now.

He powered off his computer and plugged it in to charge, then threw on some jeans and a heavy sweatshirt with a hood. From under the mattress, he retrieved his 38-caliber revolver, just in case.

Craig had bought the pistol a few months ago when he knew he didn't have much time left to live. He had planned to shoot himself rather than die in a hospital bed, but he was never able to go through with it.

He also thought there might be a chance—maybe the lottery or some other miracle—that he could come up with the money he needed for his transplant and medicine. Now, he hoped the coke in his hamper was his miracle.

Standing at the door with the garbage bag in hand, Craig surveyed his undecorated, messy apartment. The sofa had a couple holes in it that were getting bigger every week and the dresser had two broken drawers that didn't come all the way out. He stared at his two fat goldfish and the thick algae build-up on the ten-gallon fish tank on the kitchen counter and wondered what his ex-wife would say if she saw him living like this.

Craig checked his pockets for his keys, but they weren't there. He wondered if he left them in his work pants. He looked around the apartment first, but didn't find them.

Finally, he untied the garbage bag, and tried to remove his bloody jeans without getting himself dirty. Inside the pocket, he found the keys.

While stuffing the bloody clothes back into the bag and tying it, Craig wondered how he could have been so stupid. Dizzy, he sat on the floor next to the door. His stomach growled for food, but he knew he wouldn't be able to keep anything down. Maybe a protein shake.

Consciousness began to fade as he drifted into sleep.

It was only a few minutes before dreams of stabbing Robby jolted him awake.

After a quick protein drink, Craig undressed, then set his alarm clock before clearing the clothes off his bed and lying down with the pistol in his hand.

Tomorrow was another day. He stared at the ceiling, unable to sleep, while memories of murder haunted his thoughts.

CHAPTER 8

It was almost midnight when Enzo Nattichioni stepped out of the bar and onto the brightly lit street. Even at that time of night, it seemed like the middle of the afternoon. People were still eating and drinking at restaurant tables on the sidewalk across the street and teenagers were still hanging out on the corners talking and laughing.

Enzo headed up the block and then got into the back seat of a white Cadillac sedan parked next to a fire hydrant. A man with a scarred face and a head like a boulder, put the car into gear and pulled away from the sidewalk.

As they cruised down Arthur Avenue, Peppino, the small old man in the passenger seat, leaned over and turned to Enzo in the back. "Talk to me, Enzo."

Enzo told Peppino everything that Sammy had told him.

Peppino said, "Well, the shooting really did happen. That much we know. How well do you know the kid?"

"Sammy's a good kid. He fought in Iraq. And I know his brothers for years. All of them stand up guys."

"We can give them a couple weeks, but a hundred and forty grand, that's a lot of dough."

"I know," replied Enzo. "I'll tell him. Two weeks. Then the payments begin."

"I put some feelers out. I'll let you know if I find out anything on who robbed those kids. But I'm doing it as a favor. It's not really our problem, Enzo. And I don't want people to think we're in the charity business now. *Capisce*?"

"Yeah." Even if he didn't agree with Peppino, Enzo would never say so. At six feet tall and two hundred and seventy pounds, Enzo looked like a giant compared to the little white-haired man who was giving him orders. Peppino was small and old, but connected and respected. Enzo had heard rumors that Peppino had killed four men when he was only twelve-years-old.

Peppino turned back in his seat, facing forward.

The driver turned the corner and asked Enzo, "Where do you want me to drop you off?"

Enzo answered, "My car is parked on 187th Street."

CHAPTER 9

Craig's alarm rang thirty minutes earlier than usual. It didn't really matter because he hadn't slept most of the night. Every time he started to sleep, dreams of sawing through Robby's flesh had awakened him.

Even though the room was warm, he shivered. He dreaded getting out of bed. A few years ago, he used to lie there wondering why he bothered going to work every day when he knew his union insurance didn't cover his medication. But, that didn't matter now, since the last two years he hadn't made enough hours at work for medical insurance anyway, and his liver was almost already gone.

Today, Craig had another reason to get out of bed. He thought about the bloody clothes in the garbage bag. It really didn't matter if he went to jail. He would be dead in less than six months anyway. But the coke in the hamper might be his salvation.

He was still exhausted after so much stress and not much sleep. He thought about calling in sick, but worried it might make him look guilty when they found the body.

Craig took his computer out of sleep mode and checked the weather before putting on the classic rock collection he'd recently finished downloading.

The music played in the background while he went to the bathroom, got dressed, sucked down a cup of instant coffee, and took two puffs from the roach in the ashtray while standing at the open window.

Before leaving, he closed the window, then thought again about moving the coke, but decided the hamper would be the best place for now.

With the garbage bag in one hand and his backpack in the other, he locked the door and headed out into the hall. Craig hadn't put the bloody sheetrock saw in the garbage bag because he knew it could make a hole and fall out. He had the saw wrapped in plastic and in his backpack.

He was happy he lived on the first floor, he never would have made it up and down the stairs every day, and because his building had only four floors, there was no elevator.

Craig hurried outside and up the block passing a row of semi-attached two-story brick houses. He stopped in front of a four-story building on the corner and scanned the area. The sun was just peeking out over the horizon.

He crossed the street and looked around once more to be sure he was alone before throwing the garbage bag and then the saw into the dumpster. He pushed the saw down deep and just as he was about to try and push the bag down deeper, he heard something.

While stepping away from the dumpster and onto the sidewalk, Craig noticed someone coming out of a house a few doors away. At first, he felt nervous, but after noticing the man's construction clothes, Craig's mind relaxed.

The sun brightened as more cars and people began to materialize in the neighborhood. Craig continued down the block, past the building where he lived, and down another block lined with two-story semi-attached houses to the subway station. He hoped that dumpster would be gone soon. Robby's body, however, was a different story. He wished he could have dumped that somewhere, too.

Craig's train ride to Manhattan was about thirty minutes, then he took a bus to the east side and walked another eight blocks, passing ancient apartment buildings with storefronts on the ground level. School kids yelled and laughed while scrambling up and down the sidewalks. Herds of commuters got on and off the caravan of city buses.

The smell of roasted coffee made Craig stop at a Café and get a cup to go, along with a corn muffin, which he ate while walking.

Despite his early morning activities, he was still ten minutes early.

Inside The Howell Building, he put on his tool belt and inserted an old worn-out sheetrock saw into the missing space. Craig watched everyone as they prepared their tools and equipment and made their way to the floors they were working on. He kept looking over his shoulder. It felt as if someone were watching him.

Before heading to the staircase, he glanced over at the wall that separated himself and everyone else from Robby's body. He hoped no one would work on that kitchen today. Of course, someone would eventually find the body, but he preferred later rather than sooner.

Craig was always the last one up, but his foreman never complained. Craig knew the company was letting him work out of sympathy, especially since he was almost already dead.

On his way up the stairs to the fourth floor, hot and cold sensations took turns torturing him as his mind flashed back and forth between Robby's body behind those cabinets, the four kilos of coke in his hamper, and the garbage bag full of evidence waiting to roll off the dumpster and into the street.

Once upstairs, he stopped to catch his breath, then he got right to work. The other guys all kept their distance, but tried not to show it. Craig appreciated the gesture.

Even though he couldn't do any heavy lifting, and wasn't what he once was with a screw gun, he was still good with measurements and straight lines, so that's how he spent most of his days, measuring and marking up sheetrock for someone else to cut and hang.

He spent the entire morning looking around, paranoid. He was waiting for someone to yell when they found the body, but then realized he would never hear it from this far up.

Craig glanced at the time on his cell phone. He was freezing and losing steam. He needed his coffee. Where was that apprentice?

Craig felt as if he were having a heart attack when a small man with safety glasses and a black bandana over his head stepped out of the portable potty and put on his hard hat. For just a moment, Craig thought it was Robby's ghost. He watched the man walk away, then took a sip from his water bottle and waited for his pulse to return to normal.

After another fifteen minutes of work, Craig turned to the guy next to him and said, "Where's that kid with the coffee?"

The guy turned and looked at the staircase, but didn't say anything.

Craig turned and looked at the stairs and saw two uniformed cops entering the floor while two others guarded the entrance. Craig knew this was it. It was too good to be true. Now he'll never sell the coke, get a liver transplant, and live happily ever after.

As the cops got closer to where he was working, Craig's hands began to sweat and his stomach began to churn. He bent over and spewed vomit onto a wall and the concrete floor. Everyone, including the cops jumped out of the way.

One of the cops checked his uniform while staying away from Craig. "What the fuck?"

Craig's foreman said, "Give the guy a break. He's dying."

The other cop said, "If he's dying, then why is he working?"

An older cop with sergeant stripes entered the floor and said, "What's the holdup here? Let's get these people downstairs."

Craig wiped the vomit from his mouth while all the other workers went downstairs. He knew they must have found Robby's body, but at least he wasn't a suspect. Not yet.

CHAPTER 10

Just as Victor and Rosie were about to leave the precinct and head to The Bronx to question Rene Ortega's ex-accomplices and some of his relatives, a lieutenant approached and told them there had been another murder at The Howell Building.

Heavy traffic blocked the street in front of the precinct as a sanitation truck collected garbage. The Howell Building was only two and a half blocks away, and the sun was still low enough for the air to be comfortable, so Victor and Rosie decided to walk.

While passing a row of sixteen-story apartment buildings, Victor slipped a stick of gum into his mouth and offered one to Rosie. She took it. After turning the corner, the landscape changed from high rises to ancient five-story brick buildings.

Victor chewed his gum while remembering another cop-killer case he'd solved four years earlier with his ex-partner. The media called them heroes, but no one could understand the pressure they were under to succeed. The case had Victor up almost every night. He was mentally and physically exhausted. The stress from that case had caused him to take more pills, more often.

Victor and Rosie followed Fifth Street down to Avenue A, then turned, walked one block, and found a repeat of yesterday. Construction had stopped and all the workers were outside while an army of uniformed cops kept cars and people out of the intersection.

As he entered the building, Victor passed a tall, thin man with yellow eyes and skin wearing a tool belt and coughing. He tried not to get too close to the guy.

Inside, the cops had an area closed off near the front of the building. Victor and Rosie followed the trail of cops and turned the corner into an unfinished kitchen where they found a crime scene unit examining a body on the floor, behind some cabinets.

Victor asked one of the examiner's, "Who is he?"

"Robby McPherson," responded the examiner. "A laborer from what they tell me. Someone stuck him in the stomach with something long and serrated, a tool I'm guessing. But, that's not what killed him."

Rosie asked, "So, what did?"

"Whoever stabbed him in the stomach also sawed his throat open."

"Glad I asked," replied Rosie.

Victor asked, "Time of death?"

"Not sure yet, have to find out how hot it gets in here at night. Probably yesterday afternoon, or evening."

Victor said, "Yesterday afternoon this place was crawling with cops. No one could have killed him then."

Rosie said, "You never know." She turned to the examiner and asked, "What's all this green stuff on the floor?"

Victor answered before the examiner had a chance to. "It's green dust. They sprinkle it on the floor to keep the dust down while sweeping."

"That's right," added the examiner. "And whoever killed this kid tried to use the green dust to hide the blood. Not that it matters."

"So," said Victor. "Now for the big question. Are the two cases connected?"

"Maybe," said Rosie. "We still don't have a motive for yesterday's shootout. And two murders in two days in the same place is a huge coincidence."

Victor looked around at the metal studs, sheetrock, copper pipes, metal-shielded wires, and uncovered electrical outlets. "I worked construction one summer in high school."

Rosie said, "So, that's how you knew what the green dust was for. You are an enigma, Detective Cohen."

Victor smirked and looked at the blood spatter stains on the wall near the door. "Looks like he stabbed the guy here, then dragged him behind these cabinets."

The examiner and Rosie agreed.

Victor said, "I'm gonna take a stroll around the first floor."

He stepped out of the unfinished kitchen and approached the same uniformed sergeant who'd helped him yesterday. They shook hands.

Victor asked, "Still looking upstairs?"

"A lot of ground to cover," answered the sergeant. "We already cleared the top two floors, but it's gonna take some time. Between garbage and construction material, well, you know what they say about the needle and the haystack."

"No stray tools at all?" Asked Victor.

"Only one. A broken wood-handled hammer. Definitely not the murder weapon."

"Thanks sergeant." Victor turned around and saw Rosie typing on her tablet while coming out of the unfinished kitchen.

The sergeant approached the staircase and started on his way up.

Rosie asked, "What's up?"

"Nothing yet. They'll be looking for a while. Maybe all day."

Victor and Rosie strolled in and out of unfinished apartments. They approached the area in the back of the building where the shooting had happened yesterday. Rosie sneezed.

"Bless you."

She sneezed again, a few more times, hard.

"You okay?" Asked Victor.

"Fine." She exhaled, then said, "Just all this dust."

They stayed silent for a moment while looking over everything that they'd already seen the day before, then they headed toward the front of the building.

Victor noticed a partially cut and partially broken hole in a half-fished sheetrock wall. He approached and looked down into the four-inch cavity between the sheetrock on metal studs and the exterior block wall.

Rosie asked, "You see something in there?"

"No." Victor stood back at stared at the hole in the sheetrock. "Doesn't that hole look strange to you?"

"I see holes like that everywhere," replied Rosie as she pointed at various holes cut into sheetrock walls here and there.

"This one is different though. Looks like someone cut a nice clean square hole and then someone else broke the sheetrock from the inside out. Look, there on the bottom."

"You're the construction expert. You tell me."

"I don't know. Just stands out to me."

Rosie continued looking around and asked, "What's going on in that head of yours?"

Victor said, "I don't know. Yesterday we had a shootout at the OK Corral, and today we got a kid covered in green dust with his throat sawed open. Could it possibly be a coincidence? Or is there a connection?"

Rosie looked around and said, "Before we can connect the two, we need a motive for each killing."

Victor said, "Maybe the dead kid we found today witnessed what happened yesterday, and the missing man came back to kill him."

"How could the kid have seen what happened on the first floor if he was working on the fifth floor yesterday? And besides," added Rosie. "Even if the kid did see them, the guys from yesterday all had guns. Why wouldn't they just shoot the kid instead of taking the time and energy to saw his throat open with some kind of tool?"

"I don't know, but the bodies are piling up quick."

Rosie said, "Something's just not right here."

"Maybe it's the building. Maybe the construction disturbed an ancient Indian burial ground."

Rosie laughed. "You really are out there. Aren't you?"

They headed outside and passed the crowd of construction workers hanging out, waiting their turn for the cops to interview them. Victor knew they were all being paid for the day, or they wouldn't have been so relaxed and cooperative.

He stopped on the sidewalk and said, "Maybe the two murders aren't connected. Maybe one of these workers had it out for the dead kid. Maybe he killed the kid hoping we'd think it was connected to yesterday, just to try and throw us off."

Rosie said, "Possible. But a long shot."

"I like to examine every possibility."

"I see that. Just don't put the burial ground thing in any reports yet."

Victor and Rosie headed back up the street going toward the precinct.

"It feels like it gets hotter every summer." Victor loosened his tie and unbuttoned the top button of his shirt while gasping for air as the humidity increased and sweat beaded up on his face and head.

CHAPTER 11

Internal Affairs detective, Abby Edmunds, entered a silent, empty office with a plastic bag in her hand. She approached one of four empty desks and scribbled something on a post-it note: Call me Carillo. You have something I want. Edmunds.

She stuck the note to the computer screen and left the room.

The gray tiled hallway was also silent as she continued toward a door at the other end.

Abby entered a room identical to the first, four desks, but only three of them were empty.

Detective Mangano, a thin young man with perfect hair, sat at his desk, leaning back in his chair while looking at his monitor. He sat up straight when Abby entered the room.

She took a foil-wrapped hero sandwich out of the bag and dropped it onto his desk. "No more lemon Snapple. I got you peach."

"Peach?"

Abby placed the drink on his desk and said, "Give thanks in all circumstances, for this is the will of God."

"Okay. I'll drink the peach."

Abby took her sandwich and a coke out of the bag and sat at the desk next to Mangano. She took her computer out of sleep mode.

She and Mangano were already involved in a case where cops were letting prostitutes go free in exchange for sexual favors, but she really wanted to bag Victor Cohen.

Detective Carillo was running The Howell Building shooting investigation, but he owed her one, more than one, and she wanted the case.

She tore into her hero sandwich while scrolling through pages on her computer. Abby loved taking down drug using cops and everyone knew why. Nineteen years ago, her father, a narcotics detective, entered a dangerous situation with a partner who was high on coke. The dealers killed Abby's father and his partner.

Abby had already been a cop for two years when her father died, that's when she decided she wanted to be an internal affairs detective, and nine diligent years later, she made it.

Three years ago, Abby worked day and night trying to take Victor's badge and his pension. The judge had mercy on Victor because even though he had taken prescription drugs illegally, he had also been taking legitimately prescribed drugs for his back injury.

Abby had never lost a case involving a cop on drugs, until Victor, and she hated him for it. They had sent him to rehab for a year, and then desk duty for a year, but that wasn't enough for Abby. She wanted him gone.

For the past three years, she'd monitored everything he'd done, waiting for him to slip. She wanted to taste his blood.

CHAPTER 12

Enzo had just finished eating Chinese food at a restaurant a few blocks away from Arthur Avenue and was now back at the bar for a drink. He ordered a glass of scotch and drank it straight up while waiting for Peppino's representative to come.

Johnny Napolitano, a fifty-one-year-old hitman with slicked back black hair and dark sunglasses entered the bar. He approached Enzo and asked, "You Enzo?"

"Yes." Enzo extended his hand.

"Johnny." The man shook Enzo's hand.

Enzo asked, "Can I get you a drink?"

"I don't drink."

"Okay." Enzo didn't know what to say. He didn't mind being protected by mobsters, but socializing with them always made him nervous. Especially with guys like Johnny. Enzo asked, "How 'bout a water?"

"I'd like to get right to business, if you don't mind."

"Okay." Enzo swallowed the last of his scotch, then stood and said, "I'm ready."

Johnny followed Enzo outside.

They were going to visit Sammy Ortega and tell him he had to start making payments in two weeks. They were also going to ask Sammy about where he and his brothers bought their drugs. Peppino wanted to know for sure that the suppliers weren't in on the heist.

Enzo felt he could have taken care of things himself, but with Peppino investing a hundred thousand dollars, he wanted someone there protecting his interest.

For just a moment, the thought crossed Enzo's mind that Peppino may have sent Johnny there to kill him.

CHAPTER 13

It was after seven by the time the cops had let everyone go. Craig couldn't believe he walked out of there. He had been on edge the entire time, even though he knew they had no motive and he was confident neither the cops nor his fellow workers noticed his anxiety. He was mostly worried that a fingerprint might have bled through his blood saturated work gloves, and it would have been an easy match since he did have a minor police record from his teen years.

After the bus, Craig took the train to his stop in Brooklyn, then passed his building and continued up the block. There were a few people around occasionally, but the area was mostly quiet. The dumpster was still there, but he couldn't see much else until he got closer.

He stayed on the sidewalk and tried to act normal while passing a young couple having an argument. Craig glanced over at the dumpster. His garbage bag was still there, but now it was covered with some old pieces of wood and other garbage.

Relieved, Craig exhaled and strolled up Sixth Avenue passing row after row of semi-attached brick townhouses with manicured gardens in front, and narrow driveways that led to small garages in the back yards.

After about ten blocks, he stopped and rang the second floor bell of an old two-story brick house. No one answered. His weed guy wasn't expecting him, and Craig knew the guy was sometimes paranoid, so he texted him and told him he was outside.

Craig waited a couple minutes. He was just about to send another text, when someone opened the door.

Riley, a fat man in his sixties with long gray hair and a long gray beard hovered in the doorway and said, "I didn't know you were coming."

"I was gonna call earlier, but didn't get a chance."

Riley adjusted his thick round glasses and motioned for Craig to come in. He shut the door and they both went upstairs to the second floor.

Craig followed Riley down the hall and into his dark apartment. Crooked pictures hung from the walls while empty beer cans and junk occupied large sections of the room.

Riley stepped over to a small air-conditioner in the window and reduced the temperature from 65 to 73. "Take a squat."

Craig sat down on Riley's blanket covered sofa and stroked a half-dead German shepherd lying on the floor. "Hey Max. You still alive?"

Riley turned the volume down on his stereo, just enough to hear it in the background, then sat on his tattered recliner.

Craig asked, "The Beatles? Again?"

"They were the voice of my generation, man."

"That's nothing to be proud of."

"Fuck you, you Ozzy loving freak." Riley adjusted his glasses and used his remote control to change channels on the TV, which was on mute. He flipped through channels until settling on a Met's game.

Craig asked, "You still got any of that white widow?"

"Sorry, man. All out. I got some sour diesel, though."

"I'm tired of sour diesel," replied Craig. "That's all you got?"

"Until next week."

Craig said, "Gimme an eighth of sour for now, then I'll check you out next week."

"Cool." Riley threw some weed onto a small digital scale and adjusted it until it read three and a half grams. He threw the weed into an empty bag and handed it to Craig.

Craig pocketed the bag and gave Riley fifty dollars. He also handed him two CD's in envelopes. "Here's a copy of that movie I was telling you about, and that Led Zeppelin CD you wanted."

"Thanks, man." Riley handed Craig a joint and a lighter.

Craig lit the joint, took a couple puffs, and handed it back to Riley.

Riley didn't take it. "No offense, man. I just don't want to take any chances. Even chapped lips could get bloody." He pulled a half-finished joint out of the ashtray and lit that.

"Don't worry about it. I'd do the same." Craig didn't blame Riley for being scared, but it didn't make it feel any better. He checked out the game on TV while puffing on his joint and petting Riley's snoozing dog.

After a few minutes of smoking and watching the game, Craig asked Riley, "You still get a little coke once in a while?"

"Sometimes. Just a little bump now and then. Why? Don't tell me you want coke. It would probably kill you, man."

Craig puffed his joint. "Just wondering how much it goes for these days."

"What, do you got a girl or something?"

"No. I just came across a little coke, and I was wondering how much I could get for it."

Riley put his joint out in the ashtray and glanced over at the game on TV. "Well, when I get it, I pay about sixty bucks a gram for decent shit."

"How much do you think a kilo would go for?"

Riley's head spun around. He adjusted his glasses and asked, "You have a kilo?"

"No. I was just wondering how much it goes for."

"Why? How much do you got?"

Riley's German shepherd stood suddenly. Craig jumped. He extinguished his joint in the ashtray and told Riley, "You can't tell anyone."

"Tell anyone what?"

"I got a lot of coke. Not sure how much exactly."

Riley stared at Craig while his dog wandered into the other room.

Craig said, "I'll give you a percentage if you help me sell it."

"I'll help you, man."

"What was the last price you heard for a kilo?"

"I don't know?" Riley took a bud out of a bag and began to break it up on his coffee table. "The last I heard it was going for twenty-five thousand a key."

"That's it?" Craig lit his joint back up.

"That was back in the eighties though, man. I'm sure it's higher now with inflation and all that. If I'm paying sixty a gram, it can't be more than sixty thousand for the key, though."

Craig was disappointed. "Probably worth half that, then. Fuck."

Riley finished rolling his joint and lit it while his dog wandered back into the room. "Thirty thousand dollars is nothing to sneeze at."

"It's not enough for my transplant."

"Oh." Riley stayed silent for a moment while flipping through channels on the TV, then he asked, "You really got a kilo, man?"

"I think I have four kilos."

"Four kilos? Holy shit, man. Where the fuck did you get it?"

"I can't tell you that."

"Holy shit, man. And, how much is my seller's fee?"

"Ten percent?"

"Fuck yes. That'll finish off my new boat fund. Fuck yes. I'll help you sell it, man."

Craig sat with his almost finished joint burning between his fingers while staring at the TV, which now showed a cheetah chasing a gazelle.

He knew the coke would probably be worth enough money to buy his medicine, but not the liver transplant. At least if he had a new liver, it would take many more years before the hepatitis virus destroyed the new liver. That didn't matter anyway. His miracle didn't seem as great now as it did before. He put the joint out in the ashtray for the second time.

Riley said, "I heard about people going to China for transplants. All you gotta do is pay off the warden and you can get anything you want from a non-consenting prisoner."

"Those commie bastards will probably sell me off for parts. Or I'll probably catch an infection from the prison hospital. I ain't going to China. Fuck that. I might go to India, though. I read that I can get a liver transplant there for only about twenty thousand."

"India?"

"I would have to stay there for at least six months after, though, for post-transplant therapy and Immuno-suppressants."

"Why don't you just get the transplant there, and come back here for the other stuff?"

That, other stuff, is about a hundred thousand dollars here.

Even with the money from the coke, I still wouldn't have enough after the transplant, airfare, hotels, private nurses, and who knows what the fuck else. I'm just gonna have to learn Hindi, that's all."

Riley chuckled. "You have to join their religion?"

"Hindu is the religion. Hindi is the language."

Riley laughed. "Oh." He handed Craig his small digital scale and said, "Find out how much coke you really got there, then I'll find out what it's worth."

"You need it back tonight?"

"I'll use my old triple beam for now, but don't keep it too long, that little thing is a lot more convenient."

"See you later, Max." Craig stroked the dog one more time before standing and heading for the door. "Thanks, Riley. I'll call you later."

CHAPTER 14

While the sun disappeared behind the horizon, Victor entered his house, turned on the air conditioner, then turned on the TV.

Evelyn was still at her mother's house with the baby. He thought about calling her and asking her to come back, but decided to give her some time to cool down.

Before getting to work on the case, Victor went into the kitchen to nuke some leftover beef stew. As he waited for his dinner, he looked around at the new decorations his wife had hung. It was the only room other than Sofia's bedroom that he'd painted since moving in.

Evelyn had always done a good job of making a house a home. He was proud to be married to such a good woman. He felt guilty for still missing Jennifer. He wished he didn't miss her, but he didn't know how to make it stop.

After scarfing down his dinner and a couple handfuls of M&M's, Victor headed into the bedroom where he took a shower then threw on a pair of shorts and an undershirt.

He looked at himself in the closet door mirrors. His chest, shoulders, and arms still looked muscular, but his stomach and love handles were huge. His legs weren't puny, but they were on the thin side.

Ever since blowing out those two discs in his back and then injuring his rotator cuff, Victor stopped working out. He knew he could probably go back now and lift some light weights, but his ego would never let him do that. Once he was in the gym, the weights had to be heavy. So instead, he looked at his body in the mirror with disgust and then left the room.

In the living room, Victor began reviewing case files. The Percocet he'd taken earlier started to work its magic. He slipped a stick of gum into his mouth. Every time he craved a cigarette, he chewed gum. He'd started that habit six months ago, the day Sofia was born, and he hadn't had a cigarette since. He did put on an extra twenty pounds after quitting, though.

Victor read page after page. Rene Ortega's family was huge. He had two brothers and one sister with the last name Ortega, but his mother had six other children with two other men. Rene's older brother, Juan, was in prison for possession of cocaine. His youngest brother, Sammy, was a veteran of the Iraqi war and now an auto mechanic. His sister was a dental assistant.

While looking through names and rap sheets of Rene's ex-accomplices, Victor started nodding out. His eyes closed slowly, then his head began to drop. He jolted himself awake then tried reading again, only to start falling out again.

He didn't know how long he'd been out when the phone rang. He jumped up and the first person that came to his mind was Jennifer. By the time the phone rang a second time, Victor was awake enough to realize Jennifer wouldn't be calling him. Maybe it was Evelyn.

Victor looked at the number on the phone, but it wasn't displayed. He answered the call on the third ring. "Evelyn?"

"It's Rosie."

"Oh. Hi Rosie. What's up?"

"Were you busy?"

"No, just going over the case."

"Me too. Did you see that kid Robby's sheet? He's a big time junkie."

"So?"

Rosie said, "So? Rene Ortega is a known coke dealer."

"Rene sells coke. And Robby's into dope. The two types of people usually don't mix, except in Hollywood movies."

"I know. Just wanted to know what you thought. Get some rest. That's what I'm gonna do. See you bright and early."

"See you, Rosie."

Victor hung up and started reviewing Robby's files. It's true, he was a junkie, but Victor didn't see how that connected him to a mid-level coke dealer from The Bronx.

He nodded out again while considering Rosie's theory.

CHAPTER 15

Enzo felt relaxed since Johnny had said he wanted to drive his own car to see Sammy. Enzo knew it was more efficient to kill someone in their own car, no cleanup.

He realized he was being paranoid. Enzo made Peppino a lot of money. It wouldn't make sense for Peppino to want to kill him. Worst-case scenario would be Peppino making Enzo responsible for the hundred thousand dollars.

From the passenger seat of Johnny's brand new black Chevy Camaro, Enzo watched out the window as they turned a corner onto Southern Boulevard. Clothing stores, cell phone shops, and fast food restaurants flanked both sides of the busy two way street. Swarms of people were outside enjoying the night air as it cooled down.

Enzo had memorized the address of the building "Turn at the next block."

Johnny turned.

Enzo pointed at a brick apartment building in the middle of the block and said, "There."

Johnny passed the building slowly while scanning the area. Enzo could see Johnny knew what he was doing. He had heard Johnny was ex-military, fought somewhere in South America thirty years ago.

After parking the car, Johnny stepped onto the sidewalk while Enzo struggled to his feet.

They crossed the street and approached the building. Enzo pressed a buzzer on the third floor. No one said anything on the intercom, the door just buzzed open.

Inside the dingy lobby, Enzo headed toward the elevator.

Johnny said, "The stairs. Don't trust elevators."

Enzo knew Johnny was probably right, but with his forty-six inch waistline and Parmesan cheese clogged arteries, Enzo didn't usually do stairs. He tried his best to keep up behind Johnny as they made their way up to the third floor.

Out of breath, Enzo had to stop for a moment.

Johnny reached back and retrieved a big black gun from his waistband, a Glock 10mm.

Instead of slowing down, Enzo's pulse began to race. This was it, Johnny was going to kill him here, that's why he didn't need Enzo's car. But, Sammy was the one who told him to come here. How could Sammy be in on it? Could he be? Enzo asked Johnny, "What's that for?"

"Just in case your boy decides it's easier to off you than to pay you."

Reality came back to Enzo's mind as he caught his breath and stood straight up. Of course, Sammy couldn't be in on it. Enzo knew he was just being paranoid again. He told Johnny, "Keep it close, but I don't wanna go in there like the Gestapo. I know the kid."

Johnny looked at Enzo for a moment. Enzo wondered what he was thinking. Johnny clicked the safety on then placed the gun back into his waistband behind him.

They knocked on an apartment door. While waiting, Enzo noticed Johnny standing off to the side with his hand ready to go for his gun. Enzo didn't like being in this situation. He just wanted to go back to the bar and business as usual.

As an eye looked through the peephole, Enzo thought about what Johnny had said. It would be easier for Sammy to kill Enzo than to pay him. The door opened a little bit and the sound of Merengue music entered the hall. Enzo hoped a bullet wasn't coming next.

A beautiful young Dominican girl wearing one towel over her body and another over her hair opened the door with the chain still on it. She spoke with a heavy Spanish accent. "Can I help you?"

"Sammy here?"

"He is in the shower. You Enzo?"

Enzo nodded. The girl closed the door, took off the chain, and opened it all the way. Enzo went in first, then Johnny.

The music blared from a huge set of speakers sitting on the floor. The well-furnished apartment smelled of incense and weed.

The girl closed and locked the door, then said, "Sammy will be right out." She turned the music down, then headed into the bedroom and dropped her towel.

Enzo stared at her perfect, tight, voluptuous body and wished he were thirty years younger. He always found Dominican women to be the sexiest.

He glanced over at Johnny, but Johnny wasn't paying any attention to the naked girl in the next room, he had his eyes on the closed bathroom door, but occasionally looked around at the rest of the apartment. Enzo wondered why Johnny never took those damn sunglasses off.

He tried not to look, but Enzo couldn't help as his eyes kept drifting back to the naked girl in the bedroom. She pulled a pair of pink panties up over her huge round butt and then snapped on a matching bra. Just as she reached for a tiny sundress on a hanger in the closet, the bathroom door opened.

Enzo turned his gaze as Sammy came out of the steaming bathroom with a towel around his waist.

Sammy said, "Enzo. You're early. I'd shake your hand, but . . ."

"I can wait."

"One minute." Sammy scurried into the bedroom and closed the door.

Enzo noticed Johnny was ready to go for his gun again. Enzo wished this whole thing would be over already.

The door opened and Sammy followed the young woman out of the bedroom and into the living room. Enzo looked at her and thought she looked as good dressed as she did naked.

The girl kissed Sammy and then turned around. Sammy spanked her ass as she sashayed to the door leaving a trail of expensive perfume behind her. She turned around and blew Sammy a kiss, then winked at Enzo before heading out the door.

Enzo knew she had seen him watching her in the bedroom. His heart rate increased as he looked at Johnny and Sammy and wondered if they just saw her wink at him. The girl had him just as nervous as Johnny's Glock did.

"I'm Johnny Napolitano." Johnny extended his hand to Sammy.

Sammy repeated Johnny's name while shaking his hand. Enzo knew by the tone in Sammy's voice that he'd heard of Johnny.

Johnny said, "I'm here representing Peppino's interest in the situation."

"Okay." Sammy took a Newport from his pack and offered one to Johnny. Johnny didn't take it. Sammy lit his cigarette and said, "I told Enzo I need a little time."

Enzo said, "Peppino says two weeks, then regular payments begin. I tried to get you more time kid, but that's business sometimes."

"I'll find those motherfuckers in less than two weeks."

Johnny glanced around the room again and said, "I want to talk to your suppliers."

Sammy looked at Enzo, but Enzo didn't say anything. Sammy looked at Johnny and said, "I don't know. What am I supposed to tell them?"

"You tell them Johnny Napolitano wants to talk to them. That's what you tell them."

Sammy steamed his cigarette.

Enzo said, "Peppino has a hundred grand in on this. He just wants to cover all the bases."

"I'll call them." Sammy steamed the last of his cigarette down and put it out in the ashtray. "I'll call them tonight."

CHAPTER 16

After getting home from Riley's last night, Craig had weighed the coke, brick by brick. Each weighed exactly one kilogram. Four kilos in total. For a moment, he wondered if it could be fake, but then considered the man who died for it, and decided to himself that the coke was probably real.

It had been another sleepless night, and Craig was once again exhausted. The dark circles under his eyes were a huge contrast to his yellow face and eyeballs. Once again, he thought about calling in sick, but decided it was too soon. He knew he was sick enough to get away with it, but he thought it still might make him look suspicious.

Craig got out of bed, turned on his laptop for music, and performed his morning routine.

Once out of the house, he strolled halfway up the block and noticed the dumpster was still there. He knew they wouldn't have taken it at night, but he always hoped for miracles. At least there was a little more garbage stacked on top, which would keep his garbage down.

He turned around and went back down the block, passed his building, and continued to the subway on the next corner.

Once at work, Craig noticed everyone waiting outside on the sidewalk. As he got closer, he saw detectives and uniformed cops questioning everyone and taking notes. Some workers left the building with their tools in hand.

For just a moment, he thought about turning around right there, but he was curious. He knew that if they suspected him, they could have taken all his personal information from his employer and arrested him already.

Craig approached one of the workers and asked, "What's going on?"

The man responded, "They shut the building down. They want everyone to check in before leaving. I guess there's some people they still want to talk to."

"Thanks." Craig turned away from the man and took a step away from the building. He didn't want to hang around and talk to more cops. He was going home.

Craig's foreman saw him and yelled, "Craig!" He approached Craig and said, "You have to stick around. The cops want to talk to everyone again. Don't worry, the company is giving two hours show-up time. If they keep you longer they'll pay the whole day."

"Oh, good." Craig pretended that was all he had to worry about while walking with his foreman toward the building.

CHAPTER 17

While other cops continued their search for witnesses and the missing gun in and around The Howell Building, Victor and Rosie were at the precinct putting on their bulletproof vests and preparing to go to The Bronx to question dangerous felons.

They collected their paperwork and proceeded down the hall to the elevator, then waited in silence.

The elevator doors opened and a few people got out.

Victor froze when he saw a tall, broad, black woman wearing a tight fitting pants suit and a short butch hairstyle strut out of the elevator: internal affairs detective, Abby Edmunds.

Rosie was already in the elevator when she stepped back out into the hall. She looked at Victor and asked, "You coming?"

Victor heard Rosie, but didn't answer.

In her booming voice, Abby said, "Good morning, Detective Cohen."

Victor wondered what the hell she was doing there. "Hello Edmunds."

CHAPTER 18

Abby looked down at Victor and said, "Always a pleasure to see you."

"I'm sure," Replied Victor.

Abby saw Victor's little Asian partner looking at them both, probably wondering what was going on. Abby already knew everything about Rosie Li, but didn't pay any attention to her. She was here for Victor.

"Carillo's case load was so full, so I offered to take The Howell Building shooting off his hands."

"You're a regular good Samaritan, Edmunds."

Abby showed some teeth in a fake smile, then said, "Just think of how close we can get now, Detective Cohen."

"I'm looking forward to it. Anyways, looks like we have our jobs cut out for us."

Abby said, "Have faith, Cohen. For the wrath of God is revealed from heaven against all the ungodliness and unrighteousness of those who suppress the truth."

CHAPTER 19

Johnny drove his Camaro up Mulberry Street while Enzo sat next to him in the passenger seat and Sammy sat in the back. The air conditioner was a little too cold for Enzo, but he didn't dare tell Johnny. Sammy had been silent during the entire ride since leaving The Bronx.

Enzo glanced out the window at the red, white, and green banners spanning from building to building over the street. Italian restaurants on both sides were full of people dining outside at sidewalk tables.

Johnny continued driving north past all the restaurants, then past stores and apartment buildings until arriving at a stone-faced catholic church with a huge stained glass window above a big red gothic door.

Sammy and Rene's coke connection was from the lower east side, but they requested to meet with Johnny and Enzo here. Enzo knew they were playing it safe and he wondered if Johnny had any moral dilemmas about killing someone inside a church.

After parking a couple blocks away, they headed to the church and went inside. Sammy entered first, followed by Enzo, then Johnny.

Enzo surveyed the silent church. Stained glass windows adorned every wall and fluted columns that supported gothic arches separated rows of polished wooden pews. Two women on their knees near the altar prayed in front of the statue of Jesus while a priest lit a row of candles against the wall.

Johnny and Enzo followed Sammy as he approached three men sitting in the last pew off to the side. Two of the men were in their thirties wearing street clothes with big puffy Afros. The third man was older, with a black and gray beard, and wearing a suit as nice as Enzo's.

Sammy slid into the pew first and sat down next to the two younger men while the older man in the suit was on the outer edge. Enzo sat down next to Sammy, but Johnny didn't sit down. He moved along the back of the pew and toward the man in the suit on the end.

The man stood and turned around facing Johnny.

Enzo was ready to stand up. He wouldn't have been able to do much anyway in his physical condition, and especially without a gun, so he just watched.

Johnny said, "Damn, Ricardo. You got old."

Ricardo, the man in the suit, laughed and said, "Women like the gray. They say it's distinguished."

They both laughed and then shook hands.

Johnny asked, "How they hell have you been?"

Sammy, the two guys with Afros, and even the priest turned around and watched while Johnny and Ricardo laughed louder than they should in church.

Enzo wondered what was going on. How did Johnny know this guy?

Ricardo said, "You wanna get outta here?"

"Yeah," said Johnny.

They headed outside and strolled along the sidewalk as the sun disappeared behind a cloud.

Enzo looked up and said, "Thank God for that cloud. The sun is brutal today."

Johnny and Ricardo walked together while everyone else followed.

Ricardo said, "These kids are my brother-in-law's kids. I came in his place when they mentioned your name."

Johnny said, "So, I guess you already know the story."

"I heard," replied Ricardo. "And I assure you, my nephews would never be involved in a set up like that. They know their father works for me, and they know not to fuck around."

Johnny said, "This kid Sammy here lost his brother, and he's looking for revenge."

"I already put the word out. If they're from around here, I'll find out about it. And if I do get them, I'll be sure the kid gets to finish them off himself."

Johnny handed Ricardo his cell phone and said, "Put your number in there. We'll get together for coffee when this whole thing is over."

"Still not drinking? You got the will of a lion."

CHAPTER 20

Craig took the train back to Brooklyn and thought about how lucky he was. He thought for sure when he saw the cops at the building this morning that they would connect him to Robby somehow. Maybe it wasn't really as easy as they made it look on all those CSI shows.

After coming up the stairs from the train station and walking up one block, Craig stood in front of the building where he lived and looked up the street. The dumpster was gone. That was one relief. Now he just had to move that coke.

Inside, Craig checked the hamper to be sure the package was still there. It was. He pushed it back down and added more dirty clothes to the hamper before taking a shower.

After getting dressed, Craig took a vitamin C and a milk thistle and headed out the door with the four kilos in a small plastic bag.

His entire body trembled as he dragged himself the ten blocks to his parents' house. The hot sun was still overhead, but Craig had a hooded sweatshirt on as usual. Despite his cold blood, nervous perspiration covered his entire body. Out of instinct, he occasionally looked over his shoulder, but tried not to, worried about drawing attention to himself.

Walking with the package in the front pocket of his sweatshirt, he didn't look anyone in the eye, but every time someone passed him, his heart rate increased.

Finally, Craig turned off Fourth Avenue and headed up 77th

street passing a row of three-story Brownstown townhouses, many of them with doctor's offices on the first floor. His parents lived in the middle of the block in the same house they'd bought in the late 60's, the house Craig had grown up in. He had the key, but he rang the bell instead, so as not to scare his mother.

His mother opened the door and said, "Craig. Why aren't you working?"

"I thought you'd be happy to see me."

His mother laughed then hugged him. "Of course I'm happy to see you."

They entered the house and Craig closed the door behind him. The parquet floors and antique wood furniture were spotless and polished to a high shine as always.

"What happened to your key?"

"I have it." He followed her into the kitchen where pictures of wine bottles and grapes hung on the walls and a bowl of fake fruit sat in the center of the table. "But I knew you weren't expecting me."

Craig's mother opened the refrigerator and asked, "You wanna eat? I got some leftover lasagna. You're favorite."

"I'll have a little bit. My stomach isn't too good today."

Craig sat at the table while his mother put some lasagna on a plate and then took another plastic container out of the refrigerator.

"You want a couple of meatballs?"

"Just one."

"They're small. I'll give you two."

Craig's mother came from an Italian background. She didn't speak Italian, but she knew all the recipes. She was huge, but full of joy, the exact opposite of Craig's father who was skinny and miserable. Craig's mother made a few Irish dishes that her husband liked, but she mostly made Italian food, which they all liked. Craig resembled his Irish father, tall and thin with blond hair and pale skin, while his two older sisters resembled his mother, short and squat with darker features.

Craig waited while his mother nuked his lunch. "They shut the job down today, but they paid us show-up time."

"Why did they shut it down?"

"The cops were investigating a murder. Some junkie."

"That's terrible." She took the hot food from the microwave

and placed it on the table in front of Craig with a glass of water. The smell of garlic increased his appetite.

Craig ate while his mother poured herself a cup of coffee. He looked around at the china cabinet and the newspaper on the coffee table. He always felt like he was home when he was here, even though he'd been on his own for so many years,

"Where's Dad?"

"Where else?"

Craig knew what that meant. He was at the bar.

"I wanna put some more money in your safe."

"You know the combination."

Craig's father had built a huge hidden safe into the bedroom wall when he first bought the house. He had three hunting rifles in there, which he hadn't used since Craig was a child, and Mrs. Hill had her good jewelry in there, which she also hadn't used in many years.

There was plenty of room, so Craig's mother let Craig keep his savings in the safe after his trouble with credit cards, one of which had his checking account frozen. Craig had about three thousand dollars in the safe that he had saved over the past few years. Now he was going to hide four kilos of cocaine in there.

After eating, and while his mother washed the dishes, Craig hid the cocaine in his mother's safe and hoped she or his father had no reason to go in there any time soon.

CHAPTER 21

Victor and Rosie had spent the day in The Bronx looking for Rene Ortega's best friend and partner in crime, Danny Flynn. They'd already been to Danny's mother's and ex-wife's houses, but had no luck. They also spoke with his ex-parole officer, who couldn't offer any suggestions on how to find Danny, but warned them of his violent sociopathic nature.

Rosie drove the unmarked police cruiser.

As the sun began to drop, Victor's stomach began to rumble. "What do you say we go for a bite?"

"Good idea." She stepped on the brake as they approached a red light. "I just saw a Spanish restaurant a few blocks back."

"I was thinking Mickey Dee's."

"Again?"

"Alright. Let's get some Spanish food."

Rosie switched on the flashing siren and made an illegal U-turn in the middle of the intersection while cars stopped and pulled over to the side.

Victor laughed. "You really are hungry."

She turned off the siren, then after a few blocks, she slowed down and double-parked in front of the small crowded Spanish restaurant. "Must be good. It's packed."

Victor said, "I guess we'll be eating in the car."

Rosie followed Victor inside the building. They both ordered steak with onions and white rice, then waited about fifteen minutes to get it.

They ate in the car while double-parked.

Victor placed his garbage into a bag along with Rosie's garbage and got out of the car. He threw the bag into a garbage can on the corner, then turned around and headed back.

As Victor got back into the car, Rosie said, "You look exhausted. Maybe we should call it a night."

"I'm fine," Replied Victor. "I just look tired because of these pain killers the doctor has me on. As long as you're driving, we're good."

"You sure?"

"Don't I look sure?" Before Rosie could answer, Victor said, "Don't answer that."

Rosie laughed.

Victor said, "Don't worry. I look worse than I feel. Trust me. Let's go around Danny's mother's house again. Everyone eventually goes back to their mother's house."

Rosie started the car and headed down the block. She turned a corner and passed a bunch of screaming kids at a little league baseball game. The sun still had a little left to give, but the baseball field's bright lights were already on.

They turned again passing rows of stores and then apartment buildings.

Rosie double-parked in front of the building where Danny's mother lived. She turned to Victor and said, "If you wanna take a little nap, take it."

"I'm fine. Really."

"Okay."

Victor gave Rosie a stick of gum before unwrapping one for himself.

They sat in silence chewing their gum for a few minutes and then started talking about Rene's family members and other known friends.

After almost an hour, Victor couldn't hold back, he started nodding out.

Rosie said, "That's it. We're outta here."

"What?" Asked Victor.

"Watching you is making me sleepy. This guy isn't coming around here anyway."

"Alright. Let's go."

Rosie started the car, drove down the block, and turned the corner.

Victor said, "Pull over."

"What? Why?"

"I think that's him. Let's see if he turns the corner."

Rosie pulled over to the side and watched in her rear view mirror.

Victor watched through the mirror on his side. Behind them, a man walked down the sidewalk, the opposite way they were driving. The man turned the corner, out of sight.

Rosie reversed the car against traffic as cars behind her slammed on their brakes and blew their horns.

"Very subtle," said Victor.

"You wanna lose him?" Rosie backed the car up until they were blocking the intersection. A car trying to get through beeped at them.

Victor watched as the man entered the building they'd been watching for the past hour. "That's got to be him."

Rosie moved forward and turned at the next corner, circling the block until they were back at the building where they'd started. She double-parked and pocketed the keys.

"Let's do this." Victor stepped outside and looked up at the ancient brick building. He knew Danny's mother lived on the fifth floor, and he could see that her light was on, but because the blinds were down, he couldn't see anything inside.

Rosie approached the buzzer and pressed a few different buttons, but she didn't press Danny's mother's. Victor kept his eye on people walking by on the sidewalk and watching cars as they passed in the street. People spoke over the intercom asking who was there, but neither Victor nor Rosie answered them. Rosie pressed a few more buttons.

Finally, someone buzzed the door open. Victor and Rosie stepped inside and surveyed the empty lobby before moving toward the staircase.

The elevator door opened. Someone came out. It was a tall handsome black man.

Victor knew it was Danny from his mug shots, but he still had to ask. "Danny Flynn?"

Danny smashed Victor's face with his fist and raced out the front door.

Victor lost his balance and felt dizzy, but he didn't go down.

Rosie whipped out her 9mm semi-automatic service pistol and asked, "You okay?"

"I'm right behind you." Victor reached for his 9mm and clicked off the safety.

They bolted outside and saw Danny down the block just as he turned the corner.

Victor said, "Get the car." He raced down the block away from Rosie without saying anything else. He hoped Danny wasn't in as good a shape as he looked.

While making his way toward the intersection, Victor heard tires screech. Rosie peeled out around the corner. She passed Victor while speeding forward.

Victor could barely breathe, but he refused to stop. When he reached the corner, he turned and saw what was happening ahead.

Rosie cut Danny off, screeching to a stop in front of him. As she jumped out of the car with her gun in hand, Danny turned around and bolted the opposite way, right toward Victor.

Victor stopped running, held out his gun with both hands, pointed it forward, and waited. Danny stopped in front of Victor and put his hands in the air. Rosie came up behind Danny and handcuffed him.

After driving him to their precinct in Manhattan, searching him, and printing him, Victor and Rosie questioned Danny in a small interrogation room with faded white ceramic tiles covering the floor and walls.

Rosie pulled out a plastic sandwich bag and waved it in front of Danny. "Don't you know this stuff is illegal?" She opened the bag and counted at least forty smaller bags, each one contained about a gram of cocaine. "Multiple bags, equals possession for sales, equals more prison time."

"I want a lawyer."

Victor said, "You know, Danny. We just wanted to talk to you about Rene. We're homicide. We don't care about that shit in the bag."

Danny glanced at Rosie, then back at Victor. "What do you wanna know?"

Victor asked, "Who would want to kill Rene?"

"Probably a lot of people. I don't know."

"Not good enough," said Rosie while waiving the coke in

front of his face. "More specific."

"Okay. The last time I spoke with Rene, he said some guys from Morris Park were giving him a hard time. That was about a year ago. He didn't tell me who they were."

Victor asked, "What exactly were they giving him a hard time about?"

"They said him and his brother were moving too much shit, and it was cutting into their business. They said they wanted a piece."

Rosie asked, "You're talking about his brother, Juan?"

"Yeah, Juan. These guys sent someone to shake down Juan and Rene. Juan beat the hell out of both of them. I heard he broke one of the guy's noses."

Victor asked, "Did they retaliate?"

"I don't know," replied Danny. "Me and Rene had a falling out not long after that. And we didn't speak since then."

Rosie said, "I thought you guys have been friends for years. What happened?"

"Just an argument, that's all."

"About what?" Asked Rosie.

Danny didn't answer.

Victor said, "A woman."

Danny nodded.

Victor said, "I think we have everything we need. Time to turn you over to narcotics."

"You just said you don't care about that shit in the bag."

"We don't," Replied Victor. "But the guys in narcotics do care. Just be happy I'm not charging you with assaulting an officer."

Rosie glanced at Victor.

Danny asked, "You're not?"

"No," Replied Victor. "Because then I wouldn't be able to do this." Victor cocked his fist back and belted Danny across the chin.

Danny dropped to the floor as blood dripped from his mouth.

Rosie tried to help Danny to his feet while Victor wiped Danny's blood off his fist with a tissue.

CHAPTER 22

Enzo sat next to Johnny in the back seat of Peppino's white Cadillac while boulder head navigated past a seven-story brick hospital connected to another building across the street by an enclosed glass bridge overhead. Enzo glanced at the sweat beading up on the driver's big head and started to feel hot himself.

Peppino leaned over from the passenger seat and said, "If you believe the guy, Johnny. Then we'll leave it at that."

Enzo said, "It could be anyone."

Peppino said, "The guy took the package. The cops killed the guy. The package is gone. See a pattern forming here?"

Johnny said, "The cops."

Enzo asked, "You think the cops took it?"

Peppino turned around facing the windshield and said, "There's a good possibility."

CHAPTER 23

After work, Abby Edmunds drove her ten-year-old Ford to Brooklyn, spent twenty minutes looking for a parking spot, then walked two blocks past young men smoking weed and young women dressed like prostitutes trying to get their attention.

She could have taken out her badge and scolded a few of them, and part of her wanted to, but she knew it could lead to trouble for her family.

After Abby's father was killed, her mother rented an apartment in a private house that belonged to her cousin, and that's where she still lived. The house was on a nice block, but that block was surrounded by bad blocks.

Abby's mother took care of Abby's seven-year-old daughter during the day, but also had two other kids to deal with full time: Abby's ten-year-old niece and eight-year-old nephew. Abby's sister had lost her kids years ago because of her drug habit and lack of a permanent address. Abby helped her mother get custody and since then has also helped financially.

The apartment was crowded and cluttered, but clean. Hundreds of family pictures adorned the walls, some of relatives that Abby had never even met before.

After dinner, Abby and her daughter headed back to their apartment a couple blocks away. Their building was on a busy and sometimes rowdy corner, but Abby always felt safe with her 9mm close by.

Other than a huge cross above both their beds and a picture of Jesus hanging from the living room wall, the apartment was devoid of decorations.

Abby's daughter, Faith, was tall and thick for her age, just like Abby was as a child. After making sure Faith finished her homework, Abby let her watch TV for an hour, then sent her to bed.

Abby tucked Faith in, gave her a kiss, prayed the Lord's Prayer with her, turned off the light, and left the room with the door slightly open. "Goodnight, baby."

"Goodnight, Mommy."

Abby had lived in her small two-bedroom apartment since she'd made IA nine years ago. Her boyfriend at the time had stayed almost every night back then but still kept a permanent residence at his mother's house. Abby knew that's when she should have realized he wasn't serious about being a family man. He skipped out when their daughter was two and was usually behind in child support payments.

The apartment was furnished, but only with the necessities. The off-white walls and brown linoleum floors were the same as when she'd moved in.

In her small living room, stacks of DVD's sat next to the TV, mostly kids movies.

Abby turned off the TV, lay on the sofa, and reviewed the files on The Howell Building shooting.

The dead laborer they found the next day was strange, but that wasn't her problem, that was Victor's. She didn't think Victor had anything to do with any of the murders, she was just hoping to find any mistake he could have made, any little mistake and she could order a drug test.

With the remote control, Abby clicked the stereo on and turned the volume down low enough that her daughter wouldn't hear it. She skipped through the channels and settled on some jazz. It was an old song that she sang when she was younger. A tear came to her eye when she heard it for the first time after so many years.

Abby started singing as a child in the church choir and she was excellent. Her father had always bragged to everyone about her singing, which was embarrassing to her at that age, but she was still happy he did it.

She continued singing in the choir throughout high school, but also entered local singing contests. A producer was interested in Abby and had already started working on contracts with a record company, but Abby stopped singing when her father was killed and she has never sung another word since.

She wiped the tears from her eyes when the song ended and went into the kitchen for a glass of water.

Upon returning to the living room, Abby turned off the stereo and decided to get some sleep. She had to keep her mind on the task at hand. She had to get Victor Cohen one way or another.

CHAPTER 24

Saturday afternoon, Victor and Rosie had already been out since early morning canvasing The Bronx for Rene's cousin who'd been arrested with Rene twice in the past. They didn't find him at his mother's house, or at his baby's mama's house.

After a quick lunch at a local deli, Victor asked, "You want me to drive?"

"I thought you'd never ask."

Victor threw his empty soda bottle into the garbage can before leaving the deli. Rosie followed him out with her bottle of iced tea still almost full.

Outside, as the heat began to pick up, so did the foot traffic.

Victor jumped into the driver seat of their unmarked cruiser and adjusted his seat so he didn't feel like he was on top of the dashboard.

Rosie sat and adjusted her seat. "Jesus. This thing is like a bed. How can you sit like this?"

"I like to be comfortable." He turned the air conditioner up.

"Comfortable? Would you like someone to feed you grapes too?"

"Would you?"

"You wish."

Victor laughed and pulled the car away from the curb. He passed rows of stores, then turned a corner and headed down a block lined with two-story houses.

He slowed down while passing a group of kids playing in a stream of water from a fire hydrant sprinkler.

"Where we going?" Asked Rosie.

"Yankee stadium."

"Feel like catching a game?"

"Remember that call I got while we were eating?"

"Yeah?"

Victor stopped behind a few cars waiting for a red light. "I asked someone to meet me. Hopefully he knows something about the stiffs." The light turned green and he turned onto Jerome Avenue, under the steel-framed subway tracks.

"Who is this someone?" Asked Rosie.

"I met him when I worked up here in The Bronx."

"When you worked narcotics?"

"Yeah." Victor continued down Jerome Avenue as the tracks above turned away and the street they were on opened up to four lanes with apartment buildings on both sides. Victor passed an empty school and then a crowded park before turning down a side street and parking in front of an apartment building.

They waited in silence for about fifteen minutes, then, the entire street vibrated.

A metallic red Cadillac Escalade crawled down the block while the bass from its speakers set off car alarms. The Escalade pulled over.

Victor opened his door and said, "I'll be right back."

"I hope so."

He jumped out of the car, advanced down the block, and jumped into the Escalade.

Inside the car, Victor shook hands with Big Joe, a tall fat black man with a Yankees cap and a gold chain that looked like it weighed as much as his car. "Hey Joe."

"What's up, Victor?" Joe turned the volume down on his Rick Ross CD.

They shook hands. Victor noticed a few gray hairs popping up in Joe's goatee. He had arrested Joe many years ago when he was just a street pusher, but after Victor had saved Joe's fourteen-year-old daughter from a rapist, Joe told Victor he owed him his life. He'd asked him for a little information now and then, but never put Joe on the spot.

Joe said, "Seems like your Dominican friends had beef with

another Dominican gang from Morris Park. Word is, the other gang set up the oldest brother to get busted with a kilo."

"Any names?"

"No specifics. Those Dominican cats usually stick with their own kind."

"Thanks, Joe."

Joe asked, "You feelin' okay?"

"Yeah, why?"

"You look like you need some rest."

"That's what everyone keeps telling me."

They both laughed and shook hands.

Victor opened his door, but before he stepped outside, Joe said, "Victor. Really, be careful."

"Thanks, Joe." He stepped out of the car and headed down the block.

Joe turned his bass pumping music back up and cruised down the block as Victor got back into the cop car.

CHAPTER 25

Neither Victor nor Rosie wanted to do it, but after not being able to find Rene's younger brother, Sammy, they decided to approach him after the funeral.

Both dressed in black, they stood away from the funeral crowd and close to their car parked on the busy street. The morning sun just began to heat the earth.

Victor looked around at all the grass and tombstones and contemplated the afterlife. He remembered his mother's funeral and wondered if her spirit lived on or if she was just gone.

The burial ended and most of the people dispersed, except for three. Victor knew two of them, Rene's mother and sister. He and Rosie had already spoken with them. The third person fit Sammy's description.

Victor and Rosie waited as Sammy and his sister, one on each side, helped their crying mother toward their car.

They both stepped forward, then Victor asked, "Sammy?"

Sammy's eyes drifted toward Victor, but his head never moved.

Sammy's sister yelled, "Don't you motherfuckers have any respect? You already interrogated us, remember?"

"Interviewed," corrected Rosie. "And we didn't get a chance to speak with Sammy yet."

Sammy and his sister continued forward without stopping.

Rosie stepped forward. Victor reached out and touched her

arm so she'd stop. She did.

Victor remembered the empty feeling he felt inside when he lost his mother, and he knew it must have been worse for a mother. He told Rosie, "This was a bad idea, coming here. We can talk to him another day."

They watched as Sammy and his sister helped their mother into the car and took off down the street.

Victor decided to go home early and call Evelyn, and hopefully patch things up. It was their day off anyway, they only got the overtime because of the funeral. "I think I wanna head home and get some rest."

Rosie agreed. "Good idea."

CHAPTER 26

Craig had spent Friday night and most of Saturday smoking weed, sleeping, and watching movies on his laptop. Sunday night was always family night at his parents' house or almost family night as Craig liked to call it because his sisters usually didn't show up.

Craig was happy to be there, though. It seemed the only food he could keep down while sick, was his mother's cooking.

Craig's foreman had called over the weekend and told him to be back at the job, ready for work, on Monday morning.

Now, it was Monday morning, and even though Craig was well rested, he still felt tired as he lay in bed looking at the cracked plaster ceiling. He finally climbed out of bed and headed into the bathroom where he noticed his yellow skin was a little paler today.

With his music on low in the background, Craig performed his daily routine of drinking a cup of instant coffee and taking a couple puffs from a roach in the ashtray before putting on his work clothes and preparing his tools.

While taking the train into Manhattan, Craig wondered if Robby's ghost could still be trapped in the building. He imagined the different ways a ghost could set a man up for an accident. There are plenty of potential traps on a construction site.

While making his way from the train station to the bus, Craig realized how ridiculous his ideas were. He should be worried about the cops, but he had a feeling that if they didn't find anything by now, he was probably in the clear . . . hopefully, in the clear.

The bus jerked back and forth every time it stopped. Craig stood holding the overhead metal bar and began thinking about the coke in his mother's safe. The only other person who knew Craig had the coke was Riley, and Riley had no idea where it was.

Craig prayed to God to protect his mother. He hoped he didn't put her in danger.

CHAPTER 27

Victor and Rosie had already been to The Bronx and spoken with Sammy at his mother's apartment. Fortunately, his sister was at work.

Sammy didn't have much to say. He told them he didn't know anything about the drug dealing activities of either of his older brothers.

Knowing Sammy was a veteran who had never been arrested, and watching the attention that he gave his grieving mother, Victor believed Sammy really didn't know anything. He gave Sammy his business card and offered his condolences for a second time.

While driving back to Manhattan, Rosie asked, "Where you wanna go for lunch?"

"I have to meet someone for lunch today."

"Oh. Okay. I'll see you after then."

"I may be a little late."

"Don't worry about it."

Victor knew she was curious, but he didn't feel like talking about his marital problems.

Back at the precinct, Rosie exited the car and Victor circled to the driver's side and got in. "See you soon."

He took the streets to the Williamsburg Bridge, then crossed over into Brooklyn. He met his wife at their favorite little Mexican restaurant. He was far from formal, but he did press his suit that morning and put on a tie.

Inside, Mexican parkas and sombreros hung from the walls along with scenic pictures of Mexican beaches. Evelyn was already at a table sipping on a Pina Colada when Victor entered. He looked at his watch to be sure he wasn't late. He was five minutes early.

Victor sat across from her and said, "Hi."

"Hi."

It felt as if they were on their first date.

A waiter approached with a menu. Victor ordered a steak burrito and a coke. Evelyn ordered a chicken quesadilla and another Pina Colada.

They exchanged small talk while Victor admired her cleavage. He could smell her perfume from across the table. He wondered how he could be so stupid to mess things up with such a good woman.

While they ate, Victor said, "I'm sorry I kept those pictures."

Evelyn said, "How could you still love her?"

"I don't. I guess I just didn't want to let go. It's stupid. I know."

She stopped eating and sipped her drink. "How could we ever have a life together if you're still holding on to that bitch?"

"I threw all the pictures out."

"Did you?"

"Yes. I really got rid of them this time."

"And you think that's enough?"

He didn't answer.

Neither of them spoke while finishing their food.

After the waiter collected their plates and left their bill, Victor said, "Come home, baby."

She shook her head. "I need some time."

Victor asked, "Can I call you tonight?"

Evelyn said, "Okay, but not too late. You know my mom goes to bed early."

After paying the bill, Victor smiled, then stood and leaned over the table to kiss Evelyn.

She turned her face just a little, so Victor kissed her on the cheek.

"Kiss Sofia for me. And tell her I miss her." He turned and left the restaurant thinking about how hard losing Jennifer was. He hoped that he wouldn't lose Evelyn now.

CHAPTER 28

After checking their firearms and passing through multiple layers of steel doors and bars at Green Haven Correctional Facility, Victor and Rosie followed a corrections officer to a private visiting room that felt like an oven.

With his handkerchief, Victor wiped sweat from his forehead while he and Rosie sat and waited until another corrections officer brought Juan Ortega into the hot, stuffy room.

Juan was of average height, which was still a few inches taller than Victor. He was thin and wore a goatee like both his brothers. Victor could have confused Juan with his dead brother Rene if it weren't for his inmate blues and handcuffs, and of course, the fact that he was still alive.

Juan didn't sit on the chair provided for him and he didn't wait for Victor or Rosie to speak. He just shook his head and said, "Cops? I don't talk to cops."

Victor opened the top button on his shirt to let some air in. "You won't even talk to the cops that are looking for your brother's killer?"

"You think I don't have people on that already?" Juan turned to the corrections officer standing against the wall and said, "Bring me back."

Rosie added, "Three white men with no fingerprints on any database. You think your little friends can do better than us?"

Juan turned around. "Tell me one thing. Were they Italians?"

Victor said, "Looked Irish to me. All pale, like they never been in the sun before."

"*Andeldiablo.* He was right." Juan sat on the chair across the table from Rosie and Victor while the corrections officer stayed back against the painted concrete wall.

Rosie asked, "Who? Who was right?"

Juan glanced at both of them, but didn't answer right away. Finally, he said, "I heard rumors from around the hood that some white boys were involved. I just assumed they was Italians. If I knew they was Irish . . ."

"What do you know?" Asked Victor.

"The motherfucker that set me up is half Irish."

"What's his name?" Asked Rosie.

"Why should I tell you? My guys can take care of it."

Victor said, "What are you gonna do, Juan? Declare war? How many more of your homeboys have to die? Isn't that bad for business? What if they go after your family?"

"Be smart. You have to let us handle this," added Rosie.

After about a minute of complete silence, and what seemed like deep thought, Juan finally spoke. "Nelson Kelley. His father was Irish. His mother was Dominican. His boss sent him to shake me down once, so I kicked his ass. He came back around later with some of his crew, but I had a few of my boys with me, so he bounced. Nothing happened."

"Who does Nelson work for?" Asked Victor.

"No one knows. Nelson is one of the top three in the Morris Park gang, from what I heard. One of them is called Chugo and I don't know who the other one is. I hear all three of them work for someone else, but no one knows who."

"Chugo?" Asked Rosie while she typed on her tablet. "Is that a first name, last name, nickname?"

Victor said, "I'd say it's a nickname."

Juan agreed. "Probably a nickname."

Victor said, "So, tell me about you and Nelson."

"Just like I said, he tried to shake me down, so I fucked him up."

"Can you be a little more specific?" Asked Rosie.

"He came around with one of his boys and said his boss wants fifteen percent of everything we make, or he's gonna shut us down. I don't like to be threatened, so I started swinging. My boy took care of his boy. I bitch slapped Nelson with my pistol and then we left the motherfuckers bleeding on the street."

"And how did he set you up?" Asked Victor.

"I saw a car following us a couple times when we went downtown to pick up. The same car . . . on two different days. I knew they weren't cops, so I figured those Morris Park guys were trying to jack us. We were all packing, but we were still careful, and we lost them. But, by the time we got back to The Bronx and I dropped off my homeboys, the cops were waiting for me."

Rosie said, "And now you're here on your third big possession charge."

"That's right."

Victor asked, "And Rene never retaliated?"

"They wanted to get him at a pool hall where he hangs out on White Plains Road, but the guy is never alone. They said he never even went to the bathroom."

Rosie asked, "Do you have an address?"

"An address? No. It's by Bronxdale Avenue."

CHAPTER 29

It had been a long ride back from the prison. Then, after finishing paperwork at the precinct and taking an extra Vicoden before getting on the train to Queens, Victor was exhausted by the time he'd gotten home last night.

This morning, he slept an extra hour and then, in a text message, he asked Rosie to cover for him while he took a later train into Manhattan. She did. He just hoped she didn't think he couldn't wake up because of the pills. He knew that stigma would remain with him forever.

Rosie was ready to go by the time Victor arrived at the precinct. He only had time for a quick bathroom run before they headed back up to The Bronx to look for Nelson Kelley.

Nelson had one arrest on his record, five years ago. He had done his full two years on Riker's Island due to bad behavior. Nelson's father, a drunken wife beater, had died of a stab wound in prison when Nelson was a child, and his mother now lived in the Dominican Republic. His only sibling was a half-brother who was once involved with the West Side Boys in Manhattan like their father, and now lived in Northern Ireland: Chris Kelley.

Victor had a feeling Nelson's older brother would be the best person to talk to about pale white Irishmen with guns, but he preferred to talk with Nelson first, before requesting a fingerprint analysis from God knows who in Ireland. He knew his captain wouldn't be happy with the red tape involved in making an international inquiry.

The only problem was that Chris Kelley had never been arrested in the United States, and no other records of his fingerprints taken while he lived here.

Victor drove while Rosie reviewed files in the passenger seat. He took two expressways and then headed north along White Plains Road, a two-lane street with two-story houses on both sides. Traffic was heavy going both ways so they saw the same view for quite some time.

Just after passing under a highway overpass and then past a row of stores, elevated steel train tracks turned and followed the same road they were driving on.

Before the first intersection, Victor noticed a billiard on the first floor of a faded white two-story building. He pulled over and double-parked.

Rosie said, "They're still closed."

Victor asked, "Breakfast?"

"Good idea."

They drove to the nearest diner and discussed the case over breakfast. They talked about the possible involvement of the West Side Boys. They speculated as to how Robby's corpse fit into the whole thing. They discussed asking their captain for help, but both decided against it.

After breakfast, Victor and Rosie headed back to the billiard hall and waited for it to open. Rush hour was long gone, but the streets and sidewalks remained busy.

Victor asked, "Why do so many Chinese play Ping-Pong?"

"Because I'm Chinese, I should know this?"

"Sorry. Just making conversation."

They both stayed silent for a while, then Victor broke the silence by talking about Robby's corpse again. They went over many possible scenarios.

It was a few hours before anyone showed up at the pool hall. Early afternoon, a group of high school kids entered the building and Victor wondered if they were still supposed to be in school. An hour later, another group of teenagers went inside.

Victor said, "I think I'll go in. Why don't you go pick us up something to eat? Maybe Mickey Dee's."

Rosie replied, "Thanks for always giving me the important jobs." She got out of the car and circled to the driver's side while

Victor crossed the street and entered the pool hall.

Just as Rosie drove away, a train rumbled along the tracks overhead.

Victor went inside the building and looked around. A few kids laughed while playing pool. Some kids played Ping-Pong, and other kids just sat around talking.

He approached the old man behind the counter and ordered a soda, then crossed the room and sat at a small table against the back wall.

Fake wood paneling covered the walls and a stained carpet that emitted a stale odor covered the floor. A couple bulbs in the dangling pool table lamps flickered as if dancing to the hip-hop playing from an old jukebox against the wall.

Victor swallowed a half a Vicoden with his soda, then took his cell phone out and placed it on the table. He knew that no matter how natural he acted, he didn't fit in, so he didn't bother trying, he just sat there and surveyed the room.

Within a few minutes, two young men with goatees, earrings, and pants halfway down their asses, entered the building. They eyeballed Victor while going to a pool table on the opposite side of the room.

Victor didn't stand, he didn't want to scare them away. He picked up his phone and called Rosie while watching the two young men rack a set of pool balls. One of them chalked his stick while glancing over at Victor.

The phone rang, then Rosie answered, "I'm on my way. Relax."

"Leave the food in the car when you come up."

"What? Why?"

"Two young punks just came in. I think they'd be a lot less intimidated if you approached them. They're at the pool table by the door. I'm sitting down in the back with a soda."

Rosie replied, "Okay. See you in a few."

Victor looked away from the two young men while checking his phone for messages.

By the time he looked up, he saw Rosie talking to the boys playing pool. He didn't even hear her come in. He looked back down at his phone and pretended to send a text.

After a few minutes, Rosie approached and sat down next to Victor. "They're just high school kids, not even Dominican."

"That doesn't mean they don't know anyone."

"I don't think they do. But you're welcome to go give it a shot yourself."

Victor watched the young men as they racked the balls for another game. They did look young. Maybe she was right. He asked Rosie, "Where's the food?"

"You told me to leave it in the car."

Victor stood and said, "I'll get it."

While crossing the room, he glanced over at the boys as they played.

Neither of them returned the look.

Outside, traffic began to pick up as the sun increased its heat.

As soon as he opened the car door, the smell of French fries hit him in the face. He snatched a few from the bag and stuffed them into his mouth before heading back into the pool hall with their lunch.

Victor and Rosie ate and then ordered a couple more sodas while waiting to see who came in. A few more high school kids came in, but that was it.

They sat there until the sun went down outside and then a little longer, but still, no one else came in. Victor knew there had to be a better way to find this kid.

CHAPTER 30

Enzo and Sammy sat at a table in the back of the bar. Enzo had a half-finished drink in front of him. Sammy didn't have anything.

"The motherfuckers had the balls to show up at Rene's funeral. You should have seen my sister."

"Cazzo. Not even the cops have respect anymore." Enzo sipped his drink then held it up. "You sure you don't want nothing?"

"No. I just wanted to tell you about those cops looking for Nelson Kelley. Now I'm going to look for him myself."

"I'll talk to Peppino. See if he can find out anything about those guys from Morris Park."

CHAPTER 31

It was Thursday morning and it had been a week since Craig hid the coke in his mother's safe. He was going crazy. He had been to Riley's house a couple days earlier to buy an ounce of some nice new weed he had just gotten, but Riley still hadn't heard anything back from his coke connection.

Craig was getting tired of waiting. He knew he might have to look for a buyer on his own. He had a couple cousins that used coke, but he didn't completely trust any of them.

He hadn't slept much in the past week, neither.

Craig dragged himself out of bed and performed his usual routine as if he were going to work, but he wasn't. He had a doctor's appointment.

The appointment wasn't until eleven, so Craig decided to go for some banana pancakes at the coffee shop on 5th Avenue. His doctor would be going over his blood work from last week, and he wasn't scheduled for another blood test until his next appointment, so he knew it would be okay to eat.

He watched the young waitress as she whisked back and forth wearing a pair of leggings that were so tight he could see her reproductive organs. Knowing he wouldn't be around much longer, Craig savored the view, and the pancakes, for as long as he could.

After breakfast, he made his way to the subway station and took the train to 9th Street.

Outside the station, he looked both ways to be sure he was going the right direction, then trudged up the sloped street passing stores and restaurants and eventually rows of perfectly-kept three and four story brownstones.

At 7th Avenue, he stopped for a moment to catch his breath, then he turned the corner and crossed the street. He passed Methodist hospital and continued down the block to a six-story brick building which contained medical offices of every type.

Inside, Craig signed his name, then sat on a wooden chair in the carpeted waiting room and watched NY1 on a TV hanging from the ceiling.

An old man with a strip of gray hair circling the back of his head sat half-asleep on a chair on the opposite side of the room.

A little girl with two blondish-red pigtails and a colorful summer dress sat on a sofa against the wall with a big red-haired woman who Craig figured was probably her mother.

The little girl looked over at Craig, and said, "Hi. I'm Deanna. What's your name?"

Craig hesitated then said, "Craig."

The woman next to the girl said, "Deanna, stop bothering people."

Craig chuckled. "I don't mind, really. Most kids, most everyone, is scared of my yellowness."

Deanna said, "That's no big deal. I was yellow like that for a whole month last time."

"Oh." That's when Craig realized the little girl was the patient, not the mother. "I . . ."

The old man on the chair began to snore and Deanna began to laugh.

Deanna's mother whispered, "That's rude."

Deanna covered her mouth and tried to stop laughing. The old man snored louder. Craig started laughing too. Deanna laughed harder. Even Deanna's mother started to laugh.

They must have been too loud because the old man awoke suddenly and stared at them.

A medical assistant called Craig's name. Craig stood and said goodbye to Deanna and her mother before following the assistant down the wallpapered hallway.

He entered a wood paneled office and shook hands with his gastroenterologist, Dr. Zimmerman, before sitting down on a huge comfortable chair. Craig glanced at all the certificates on the wall while the doctor pulled some files up on a computer. He realized that just the desk in this office was worth more than everything in his entire studio apartment.

"So," said Dr. Zimmerman, "there are no changes."

Craig had a feeling that's what the doctor would say. He was always hoping for a miracle, but he knew better than to expect one. "What do you think about me getting a transplant in India?"

Dr. Zimmerman was tall with a full head of thick back hair. Craig knew the man was well into his sixties, and maybe even his seventies, but carried himself as if he were thirty-five.

He stared at Craig for a moment then said, "That would still cost quite a bit of money."

"A lot less, though. A fraction, actually."

"Mr. Hill, I cannot advise you to undergo a surgical procedure in another country, but, if I was dying, I would do whatever I could to survive."

They both stayed silent while the doctor turned to his computer screen and scrolled with his mouse.

Craig asked, "What's with that little girl out there? Deanna."

"Poor thing." Dr. Zimmerman looked up from his computer and directly into Craig's eyes. "She has liver cancer."

"How old is she?"

"She's seven."

"Jesus." Craig felt a sickness inside his stomach. He knew his virus was his own fault. If he hadn't shared needles with those other scumbags in high school, he wouldn't be where he was now. But, that little girl was innocent. Craig said, "Makes you wonder if there really is a God."

"I don't think there is, Mr. Hill. Deanna's father is in prison and her mother works at a diner. People from their church made donations, but they only came up with about ten thousand. Medicaid doesn't pay enough to cover everything. And, since she's developed secondary biliary cirrhosis, that, and her age, makes her a high-risk candidate for transplant surgery. In addition, liver cancer has been known to return even after a transplant. Of, course, I think it's worth taking a chance if it means saving the life of a seven year old. But, it's not up to me. Even if I offered my services for free, they would still have to pay for procurement, hospital fees—"

Craig interrupted, "I know all about it. I have the same price list. Remember?"

They sat in silence for a few more minutes then Craig asked, "How long does she have?"

"Maybe a few months. Maybe a year. You know I really can't say."

Craig's phone beeped. He jumped, then checked it. Riley had sent him a text message: Ready to do it. Tomorrow night. Call me.

Dr. Zimmerman asked, "Everything okay?"

"Yes, fine." Craig slipped his phone back into his pocket and turned his focus back on the four kilos of coke sitting in his mother's safe.

After the doctor's office, Craig went home to use the bathroom and take a little nap, he was feeling sicker than usual. The nap only lasted about ten minutes. He got off the couch and called Riley.

Riley answered, "What's up, man?"

"Same shit. What's up with you?"

"Good news. But, maybe you should come over and talk about it. You know what I mean?"

Craig always thought Riley was paranoid, but this time he appreciated it. "I'll be there in an hour."

"Cool."

After hanging up the phone, Craig made a shake in the blender using milk, a banana, and some strawberry protein powder. When he didn't feel like eating, a shake was perfect to fill his stomach and get his nutrients. He used the last of the drink to wash down his vitamin C and milk thistle.

Craig put on a heavy jacket. The temperature outside had dropped into the low seventies since the sun went down. That would have been comfortable for most people, but Craig was freezing.

He hurried to Riley's house and rang the bell. Riley was waiting for him this time. They went inside, and before Craig even had a chance to sit, Riley started talking.

"It's gonna happen, man. Saturday night. I found some guys that are gonna give you thirty grand a key. That's a hundred and twenty fucking thousand dollars, man. Minus twelve for me of, course." Riley smiled.

Craig said, "I can get an apartment in India and have enough to get my transplant and everything."

"This is it, man. You always said a miracle would come."

"I don't know if I'd have enough left over for the hepatitis treatment, though."

"At least you'll have a new liver. Didn't you say it would take a long time to destroy a new liver? Fuck it. Ten or twenty more years is better than dying in a few months."

"You're right. One hundred and twenty thousand fucking dollars."

"Then when you come back from India, we'll get a couple hot chicks in bikinis and hang out on my new boat."

Craig laughed while Riley lit up a fat joint.

CHAPTER 32

It had been over a week since Abby had taken over The Howell Building case. Her captain had sent her a memo that said that since no police officers could be implicated in any wrongdoing, it was time to close the case.

Abby wasn't happy about it, but knew she couldn't fight it. She could have wrapped the case up a couple days ago, but was still looking for a way to stick it to Victor Cohen. The only thing she could come up with was two small mistakes that Victor had made. He touched one of the guns without gloves and then didn't re-seal the plastic bag properly for storage. She knew it was a long shot, but it was all she had.

With The Howell Building file in hand, Abby entered her captain's office. She handed him the folder. "It's closed, but I'd like to check out Victor Cohen a little more."

Captain Rice, the tall white haired man sitting at his desk, flipped through the pages and closed the folder. "I need you on something else."

"Sir, I believe he may be using again. He made two mistakes that had to do with proper evidence handling, which I noted in my report."

"Because he didn't close the bag right? I need you on your next case, Edmunds."

"I'll look into Cohen on my own time, sir. It will not affect my work. If he's using drugs again, he's a danger to himself and everyone around him. First, he doesn't close the bag right, then what? His firearm misfires and kills an innocent bystander?"

"That's a bit of a stretch. Don't you think?"

"Maybe. Maybe not. People on drugs are unpredictable. Would you rather wait until it's too late? That's why we're here, sir. We are God's workmanship, created in Christ Jesus to do good works, which God had prepared in advance for us to do."

The captain rubbed his temples and said, "You can have access to his files for one week. But, don't go near him."

"This is a slow moving case, sir. Can I have it for two weeks?"

"Ten days. And if this cuts into your other case . . ."

"It won't."

CHAPTER 33

Rosie had taken yesterday off due to a doctor's appointment, so Victor went in late and spent most of the day at the precinct doing paperwork. He'd learned that a member of the Morris Park gang was incarcerated on Riker's Island.

Now, after a quick bagel and coffee, they were on their way. Victor drove while Rosie sat in the passenger seat with her window to let in the cool morning air.

They crossed the Williamsburg Bridge into Brooklyn, then went north on the BQE into Queens. Before the airport exits, Victor got off the expressway and took the streets.

A two-lane residential street with small houses on both sides led them to the Riker's Island Bridge, which looked like a street elevated by columns over the river.

Victor noticed a city bus in front of them full of people on their way to visit inmates. Planes from the nearby airport roared through the sky while taking off and landing.

Corrections officers on the island directed Victor and Rosie to a parking lot and then to a small brick building where they had to sign in. After checking their firearms and filling out the necessary paperwork, another corrections officer accompanied them along with two lawyers to an empty New York City Department of Correction bus, which then took them to a tall, V-shaped, gray building: C-74.

Once inside, they passed through a couple layers of security, more steel doors and bars, then followed a tall muscular officer down a long narrow hallway with blue painted cinderblock walls on both sides.

The elevator took them to the seventh floor where they passed a row of empty cells with blue painted steel bars.

Victor asked, "Where is everyone?"

Their gigantic escort answered, "Working. This section is for the kitchen workers. That's where your boy is right now."

He led them into a large, bright, interrogation room and then stepped outside.

Rosie exhaled and cracked her knuckles while looking at Victor. "We have to get something here."

"You're telling me?"

The door opened and the gigantic officer entered with a fat man in a dirty apron wearing glasses and the same thin goatee as his adversaries. Victor could smell pork exuding from the man's pores.

The man stood.

Victor said, "Sit."

"I have to get back to work. A lot of food to cook. You know?"

Rosie asked, "Do you know Nelson Kelley?"

"Never heard of him, Mami."

Victor said, "He was arrested with your brother a couple years ago."

"So ask my brother."

Victor said, "Tell us where he is."

"Sorry. Can't help you." The fat man turned to Rosie and asked, "So, what are you doing in about 13 months?"

"Nothing you need to know about."

Victor laughed.

The fat man asked Victor, "You hittin' that?"

Victor said, "Have a little respect fat boy."

"Fat boy?" the man took a step toward the table.

Victor stood, ready to knock fat boy on his ass.

The gigantic guard against the wall moved toward the fat man and said, "You better step back."

The fat man showed the palms of his hands and took two steps back. "I'm cool, man. Chill."

The guard went back to his wall.

Victor sat back down and said, "Let's talk about a deal. How can we make your stay here easier?"

"You can get me out."

Rosie said, "Don't be ridiculous."

"Then let me get back to the kitchen."

Victor said, "We can get you extra privileges and extra commissary."

"I'm sorry. I don't know who you're looking for anyway." The man turned to the guard and asked, "Can I get back to work now?"

The guard looked at Victor.

Victor nodded.

The guard took the fat man away.

Rosie asked, "Now what?"

Victor slipped a stick of gum into his mouth and said, "I wish I knew."

CHAPTER 34

Enzo and Sammy sat at the same table in the back of the bar, and this time Sammy was drinking. They both had an empty glass on the table and had already ordered another.

The bartender arrived, gave Enzo an Amaretto with Diet Coke, and then gave Sammy Bacardi Gold on the rocks.

Enzo gave the waiter some money, turned to Sammy, and said, "I hope you're not driving."

Sammy took a slug, then wrinkled up his face and exhaled. "I walked here."

Enzo sipped his drink and said, "So, what's going on?"

"My brothers' homeboys are doing their own thing without me. They said they worked with my brothers, not me. I told them Peppino is holding me responsible for the loan, but they don't care. They said it's not their problem. I could kill those motherfuckers."

Enzo said, "Don't kill anyone, yet."

"Can you talk to Peppino for me? Tell him what's going on?"

"I can try, kid. But, I know the man a long time. Compassion is not his strong point. We lent the money to you and Rene. Now that Rene is gone, that only leaves you. I 'm sympathetic to your situation, but if I go against Peppino's wishes . . . I don't think I have to tell you what would happen."

Sammy looked around and asked, "Where's your shadow?"

"Johnny?"

Sammy nodded.

Enzo said, "Peppino has him out on business. Thank God."

"You're scared of him."

Enzo laughed and said, "You should be, too."

"Why? Because he killed a few people? I killed people in the war."

"It's not the same." Enzo took another sip of his drink. "You seem like a good kid, Sammy. So I'm gonna tell you the truth. If you want to survive this thing, you have to find that coke. Peppino thinks the cops have something to do with it. It's possible, but I don't think so. It sounds to me like the Morris Park boys got it. You have to get it back as soon as possible. At least then you'll have something to show Peppino. I'm telling you this for your own good, kid. You gotta trust me."

CHAPTER 35

Saturday morning, Craig had waited for his father to go out before retrieving the four kilos from his mother's safe. He brought the package back to his studio apartment and hid it in the best spot he could think of, in the hamper with the dirty clothes.

He and Riley were meeting the buyers in Coney Island later that night, but Craig wanted to check out the area ahead of time. Riley agreed.

Craig had a license, but didn't have a car, so they took Riley's twenty-year-old Nissan.

Perspiration accumulated on Riley's fat cheeks, just above his overgrown gray beard.

Craig asked, "Why don't you turn on the AC?"

"It don't work."

Craig was comfortable in the heat. He pointed at a couple pieces of duct tape stuck to the dashboard and asked, "What's with the tape?"

"Damn check engine lights keep flashing."

Craig laughed. "That means you're supposed to get the car serviced."

They arrived in Coney Island around lunchtime. Sun-worshippers and freaks were everywhere on Surf Avenue. Vendors selling beach balls, umbrellas, and other summer paraphernalia crowded the sidewalks.

Riley cruised as slowly as possible while he and Craig ogled young women in bikinis on their way to the sand.

Craig said, "We should take a walk on the boardwalk later. Maybe get a hot dog at Nathan's."

"Yeah. That sounds like a plan, man."

Riley turned the corner and headed up a street passing stores and a school on one side and twenty-story project buildings on the other side. He turned another corner and parked in the parking lot of a small shopping center on Neptune Avenue. The meeting was to take place in that same parking lot at 10PM tonight.

They got out of the car and walked around.

Craig glanced at the heavy traffic on the six-lane street behind them and then back at the small shopping center ahead. The projects were to the left and down the block to the right were the steel-framed, elevated train tracks above Stillwell Avenue.

Riley said, "So, this is it."

"Doesn't leave much of an escape route."

"Hopefully we don't need one." Riley adjusted his glasses. "And everyone calls me paranoid."

Craig shivered as the hot sun slipped behind a cloud. "Who are these guys again?"

"I told you, man. My dealer's connect has a cousin—"

Craig interrupted. "So, you don't really know them."

Riley hesitated, then said. "No."

"Well, I guess it's do or die." While opening the car door, Crag said, "Let's go get that frankfurter." He sat down and closed the door behind him.

Riley adjusted his glasses then got behind the wheel and started the car.

After finally finding parking, scarfing down a couple dogs at Nathan's, and going for a stroll on the crowded boardwalk, Craig and Riley sat on a wood bench overlooking the beach.

Riley said, "I'd love to light up right now."

"Not a good idea. There are cops everywhere: walking, riding those little things, and undercover too. Wait 'til we get back in the car."

"Fucking government sucks, man. Why don't they just legalize the shit already?"

Craig shook his head. "How many times do I have to tell you? The drug companies don't want weed legalized."

"Bastards."

They both looked out at the crowded beach and the calm ocean waves ahead.

Craig's spirit deflated while watching everyone enjoy their lives. His life was almost over, but he wasn't ready. He was only forty-one and he wanted to live.

His mind drifted back to a time when life was good. Before he knew he had a virus floating around in his blood. During his eight-year marriage, and even for the four years they went out before getting married, life was perfect. He and his ex-wife, Tanya, had travelled to Hawaii, The Bahamas, Italy, France, England, and Ireland.

After Tanya's thirty-fifth birthday, she stopped taking the pill. They had decided it was time to have a baby.

One year later, Craig had pains under his rib cage. At first, he thought it was just back pain, so he didn't do anything about it.

Finally, when he went to the doctor, they found his liver values off the chart. They tested him for hepatitis—twice—he was positive for Hepatitis C.

When he told his wife, Tanya, she was tested, and even though she was negative and had done her research, she still would not touch him the way she did before. She eventually stopped having sex with him altogether and then left him because she didn't want to take a chance of having children born with Hepatitis C.

After the divorce, Craig had fallen into a deep depression, but he kept going to work trying to make extra hours and save money for the medicine that his insurance didn't cover. He tried selling a little weed on the job, but he always smoked more than he sold, so he gave up on that. Now, his liver is completely scarred over and he needs a transplant.

Craig awoke from his memory when he heard a man yelling. He looked up and saw a crazy homeless man yelling at people on the beach as he waddled along the Boardwalk.

Riley had fallen asleep. The crazy man yelling woke him up.

Riley adjusted his glasses, licked his lips, and looked at Craig. "I'm dry as hell. Where was that kid selling the one dollar waters?"

"On Stillwell. Come on."

Craig and Riley bought two bottles of water from the kid on the street before heading back to Riley's car.

They drove to Bay Ridge and Riley dropped Craig off at his building.

Craig tried to take an afternoon nap, more than once, but he couldn't sleep. He wondered if he wouldn't be better off dead. At least he could finally rest in peace.

Later that night, Craig put a big coat on. He hid the four kilos in one pocket and his fully loaded 38 in the other pocket. He had wrapped all four bricks in a double layer of plastic wrap and then placed it into a black toiletries travel bag. He sat on his ancient recliner and waited.

Finally, Riley texted him.

Craig locked up his apartment and went outside while his pulse increased.

He checked his pockets about a hundred times to be sure he still had the coke and the gun while getting into Riley's car.

They sat in silence most of the way there.

Craig couldn't believe what he was doing. It wasn't supposed to be this way. Craig and Tanya should have been frolicking with their beautiful healthy children in green fields right now. Instead, Tanya was engaged to a stockbroker and Craig was risking life in prison while trying to cheat death.

They pulled into the parking lot on Neptune Avenue.

Craig knew scoping the place out earlier in the day was the right thing to do. They couldn't see much of anything now in the dark.

They were thirty minutes early. The streets and sidewalks were less populated than they'd been before. Riley backed into a parking space in front of a closed dry cleaner, next to Domino's pizza, which was still open.

They thought they would be waiting a while, but after only about ten minutes, a big black SUV with tinted windows rolled out of the driveway from the project buildings across the street.

The SUV drove through the shopping center's parking lot, then turned around and came back. Craig wondered if it was them. The SUV passed the car and stopped again before pulling into the parking space next to Riley's relic.

The driver rolled down his tinted window and peered into the car. He asked Craig, "You Riley?"

Craig looked at the big white man's ugly face and said, "No. I'm Craig. He's Riley."

The man said, "Get in. Both of you."

Craig didn't like the idea of getting into their car, but he had no choice. Riley opened the back door of the SUV and Craig slid in next to him. Craig let his jacket sleeve drape down over his hand when he pulled the door shut. He was careful not to touch anything inside the car, just in case.

A big ugly black man sitting in the passenger seat turned to Craig, who was sitting behind the driver. "Why do you look like that?"

"It's jaundice. My liver is failing. I need a transplant."

The driver said, "That shit better not be contagious."

"It's not." Craig didn't mention that his hepatitis C was contagious, but only through blood transfer. He just wanted to get the deal over with.

The black man asked, "You got the shit?"

With his hands in both jacket pockets, Craig clenched the bathroom bag with his left hand and the pistol with his right. "Yeah. You got the money?"

The white man stayed quiet while looking out the windows and watching the people outside. Riley watched the two men in the front while occasionally looking outside. The man in the passenger seat handed Craig a backpack.

Craig glanced over at Riley and then back down at the backpack in his lap. He unzipped it and looked inside at stacks of cash. He couldn't believe this was really happening. One hundred and twenty thousand dollars.

He released his grip from the gun and handed the man in the passenger seat the package.

The man handed the package to the driver.

The driver reached into the bathroom bag and opened a little piece of plastic from the corner of one brick. He scraped off a little powder with his long pinky nail and tasted it. "Very nice. Tastes like some clean shit."

Craig counted one of the stacks and then multiplied that number by how many stacks were in the bag. "It looks like there's only thirty grand here."

The driver said, "Yeah. Thirty grand. That's the price you gave us."

Riley said, "Thirty grand each. I told you thirty grand for each key. For all four kilos that's one hundred and twenty thousand dollars."

The man in the passenger seat said, "We know how to fucken

add."

Craig asked, "Then where's the rest of the money?"

The driver said, "That's all we got right now until we can sell some of this shit."

"That wasn't the deal," responded Riley.

The driver said, "That's the deal now."

"Take one kilo for now." Craig had his hand back in his jacket pocket and on his gun. He clicked the safety off while his entire body trembled. "Give me back the other three and when you have the rest of the money, we'll talk."

"Fuck that, yellow man." The driver pulled out a stiletto knife and popped the blade out. "We're taking all four kilos. You two losers better take the thirty grand and get the fuck outta here before we change our minds."

Craig was ready to shoot, but his hand was frozen. How many men was he willing to kill?

Riley raised his hands and said, "Okay man. The shit is yours." He reached for the door handle and opened the car door, ready to get out.

Craig couldn't believe Riley was going to give up so easily. Before Craig could get his pistol out of his pocket, Riley leaped forward and grabbed the coke from the man in the passenger seat.

The man in the driver's seat stabbed Riley in the side of the chest.

Craig whipped out his 38 and pulled the trigger, it was stiff, but he pulled hard and fired a slug into the driver's brain. Blood covered the leather upholstery and the windshield. The dead driver hunched over against his door.

The man in the passenger seat opened his door and slipped out with the coke.

Craig looked over at Riley. Riley wasn't moving, but he looked like he was still alive. Craig figured Riley must be in shock. He couldn't do anything about it now. He had to get the coke.

After putting the gun back into his jacket pocket and grabbing the backpack with the money, Craig climbed out of the giant SUV.

Luckily, he didn't hear any sirens yet. He watched the man dart into the projects down the block and knew he would never catch him on foot.

With his sleeve over his hand, Craig took Riley's cell phone out of his pocket and dialed 911 with his fingernails, making sure not to leave any prints. He placed the cell phone next to Riley's body and hoped someone would get there in time to save him.

After finding the keys, Craig jumped into Riley's car and zipped out of the parking lot with the lights off. Heavy traffic passed both ways on Neptune Avenue, but the smaller streets were desolate.

Craig cruised into the parking lot between two buildings and looked around. He saw a couple teenagers walking, but no big ugly drug dealers. He circled a few times, then pulled over and parked on the side.

The coke was gone and he only had thirty thousand to show for it. Not nearly enough. He knew he had to get that coke back or die trying. He felt like banging down every single door in the projects until finding the man.

After about ten minutes, sirens and lights took over the shopping center parking lot up the block. It was too late to turn back. This was now a one-way trip.

Craig stayed in the car for a little while longer. He considered going out the driveway on the other side of the projects and just cutting his losses. He had thirty grand. It was still a lot better than the three thousand it had taken him over four years to save.

Just as he started the car and decided to go home, Craig saw a big man sneaking out of a building. The man had something in his hand and was headed toward a car.

Craig pulled away from the edge and turned on his lights, illuminating the man with the bathroom travel bag in his hand. He stepped on the gas and sped forward.

The man tried to get out of the way, but he couldn't outrun a car. Craig barreled forward and slammed right into the running thief. The thump sounded like it damaged Riley's car. The body flew over the car and landed on the pavement behind him.

Craig got out of the car and hurried to the man on the ground. He picked up the bathroom bag and then checked the man's pulse. He was still alive.

After getting back in the car, Craig realized what he had to do. He couldn't leave any witnesses. The gun would be too loud. He knew the cops were still in the parking lot down the block and they would probably be entering the projects soon.

He got into the car and drove backward, over the man. He had to step on the gas harder as the little car struggled in reverse to crush a human body. Once Craig was behind him, he looked at the body on the ground. He didn't want to get out of the car again, and he still wasn't sure if the man was dead, so he decided to go over him one more time. He just hoped the cops from the parking lot weren't anywhere near.

Craig backed up a few feet and turned the wheel so he had a straight shot over the man's head. He stepped on the gas and raced forward. The front wheels and then the rear wheels pushed the car up as it rolled over the man's head and neck. Craig continued forward, out the driveway, into the street, and away from the projects.

He drove down Cropsey Avenue. It was a lot slower than the Belt Parkway, but darker. Craig didn't know how much blood, skin, or other remains he had on the car. He hoped no one would notice as he stopped for every torturous red light and waited while his entire body perspired under his clothes.

It was too risky to drive all the way home in Riley's bloody little car, so Craig drove down a quiet side street, parked, and got out.

Keeping his hands inside his jacket sleeves, he rummaged through the junk in Riley's trunk until finding some liquids that he could hopefully use to clean up his fingerprints. He looked through Riley's collection: anti-freeze, motor oil, and something he wasn't expecting to see, but was happy about, a can of black spray paint. He shook the can gently trying not to make too much noise with the little metal ball inside.

Craig opened the car door and spray painted the steering wheel, the dashboard, the door handles, and anything else he thought he might have touched. While turning his face away from the smelly fumes, he sprayed a couple marks on the outside of the car to make it look like some kids were just vandalizing.

A light came on in a house across the street. Craig almost threw the can down, but realized it had his prints on it. After stuffing the can of paint into the backpack next to the bathroom bag full of coke and the thirty thousand dollars in cash, he hurried down the block gripping his gun inside his jacket pocket.

He continued another six blocks to the train station at Bay Parkway.

Before going upstairs, Craig strolled into a Chinese food restaurant and looked at his reflection in the mirrored wall. No blood. Thank God. Just as the woman behind the counter was about to say something, Craig hurried outside onto the sidewalk and up the metal stairs to the train station above.

Even though he knew he would be in Riley's car, he had taken his Metrocard, just in case. Thankful he didn't have to waste any extra time buying one, Craig swiped his card and went through the turnstile.

He waited almost twenty minutes for the train, but it felt like twenty years.

Finally, the D-train arrived and he took it to 36th Street, where he waited another ten minutes for the R-train going the other way.

By the time he made it back home, Craig wanted to collapse on the floor. He threw the whole backpack in the closet. He was too tired to find a better hiding place. Still wearing his clothes, he lay down on his cluttered bed and stared at the ceiling while waiting for his heart rate to return to normal.

That was three now. Craig had murdered three people. He stabbed a man, shot a man, and ran a man over with a car.

He knew he was definitely going to hell. More reason to try to stay among the living as long as possible.

He also felt guilty about Riley. He knew if he had tried to help him, Riley might have a better chance of survival.

Craig closed his eyes and asked God to help Riley.

CHAPTER 36

After leaving Riker's Island on Friday, Victor and Rosie had spent the rest of that day and most of the next day at the pool hall and other areas in The Bronx looking for Nelson Kelley. Last night, their captain had told them to take Sunday off while other cops looked for Nelson.

Victor slept until 10AM and stayed in bed listening to the birds chirp until 10:30. He felt rested physically, but not mentally. The murder case, his marital problems, and of course the memory of Jennifer, all spun around in his head like a perpetual tornado. He was dying to take a pill, but he resisted.

After showering, Victor put on a pair of gray slacks and a button-down brown sateen shirt. He sprayed on some original Polo cologne, which always made his wife horny.

Evelyn had the car, so Victor took car service. While sitting in the back seat and gazing out the window of an old Lincoln, he watched the street signs. Even after living in Queens for six months, he still couldn't figure out the street naming system. There were streets, avenues, roads, places . . . and all with the same number.

Victor asked the driver, "You mind if I open the window back here?"

The driver responded with a heavy Pakistani accent, "Would you like the air conditioner, sir?"

Victor did want the air conditioner, but he didn't want to feel obligated to give the man more than a dollar tip. "The window is fine, thanks."

"Yes, my friend."

Victor rolled down the window and inhaled as the breeze cooled his face.

It was only a two-mile trip from Victor's house to the café where he was meeting Evelyn for Sunday brunch, and since there was no traffic or even pedestrians, the trip took about ten minutes. He'd originally planned to walk, but didn't want to show up with a sweat stained shirt.

After paying the driver and getting out of the car, Victor crossed the street and waited in front of a small café on the corner. He was usually late, but today he made sure to be extra early.

Within fifteen minutes, Evelyn pulled up in their blue Nissan hatchback and Victor pointed at a free spot on the avenue. Evelyn parked the car while Victor inserted some quarters into the parking machine and retrieved a stub.

He approached as she got out of the car and gave her a big hug. He held her tight, not wanting to let her go.

Evelyn said, "Polo. Are you trying to get me horny?"

Victor raised his eyebrows twice and smiled.

Evelyn said, "Fresh." She took the parking stub out of his hand, placed it on the dashboard, and closed the car door.

Inside, the beatnik-style café was almost full, so they had to settle for a small table instead of a booth.

Evelyn had a mimosa and a spinach omelet. Victor had eggs Benedict and a screwdriver.

They didn't speak while they ate. Victor was hoping the drinks would keep Evelyn calm when they did talk. She always had a quick temper. He thought about how she threw the shoebox at him and walked out the door with Sofia.

His mind also drifted back to when Jennifer turned her back on him so long ago. He knew it wasn't fair to Evelyn, always comparing her and never trusting her completely because of how Jennifer had scarred him, so he decided he needed help getting his mind right.

After their table was clear, they each ordered another drink.

Victor decided to speak first and just say what he wanted to. "I'm sorry I'm an asshole. I don't want to lose you. I hope we can go to counseling and work things out."

"You? You hate counseling."

"I hate the thought of losing you."

Evelyn just stared at Victor while the waiter brought their drinks.

Victor waited for the waiter to leave, then said, "Don't answer now. Just think about it."

They finished their drinks in silence, then Victor paid the bill.

Victor had forgotten that the building was air conditioned, but he remembered as soon as he stepped out the door and onto the sidewalk. The sun was straight overhead and the humidity was thick. People and cars now populated the lazy Sunday streets.

Evelyn stumbled a little, then leaned against Victor for support while giggling.

Victor asked, "Are you drunk?"

"Just a little." Evelyn giggled again. "Why? You gonna book me?"

"I might just handcuff you and give you an old fashioned spanking."

"Promises. Promises."

When they arrived at the car, Evelyn took the keys out of her bag.

Victor placed his hand over hers and said, "Maybe I should drive."

"You think I'm drunk, officer?"

Evelyn always loved the fact that Victor was a cop. Many nights in the bedroom began with Victor wearing his uniform.

While leaning in to kiss her, Victor said, "Maybe you need a breathalyzer test."

She didn't wait for his mouth to reach hers, she grabbed the back of his head and pulled him closer, kissing him as if she wanted to eat him.

They spent a few minutes of making out on the sidewalk like a couple of high school kids in heat, then Victor took the keys out of Evelyn's hand and helped her into the passenger seat.

He drove home in record time and double-parked. He didn't care about the parking ticket, he would take care of that later at the precinct.

They stumbled into the house and undressed each other. The first time, they did it fast, right there on the carpet. The second time, after a long playful shower, they took their time in bed and re-consummated their marriage.

Evelyn stayed all afternoon with Victor and agreed to stay the night. She called her mother and asked her to bring Sofia in the morning.

CHAPTER 37

Sunday dinner was always early at the Hill residence.

Craig was quieter than usual while his mother ate a mountain of food and his father drank a keg of beer.

While picking at the food on his plate, Craig's mother asked, "What's wrong, baby? Is it your stomach again?"

Craig's father said, "The man is forty years old and you still insist on calling him baby." He stood, grabbed a fresh beer from the refrigerator, and staggered into the living room, leaving a half-finished plate of food on the table.

Craig said, "My stomach's been bothering me a little, Ma. That's all."

"Don't eat it if it's gonna make you sick."

"I'll eat it. I just want to take my time."

"Okay, baby. You take all the time you need." She loaded her plate with another hefty serving of baked ziti and a sausage on the side.

The TV blared from the next room as Craig's father flipped through channels.

Craig was relieved that he had gotten the backpack with the coke and the money into their bedroom safe before his father had returned from the store earlier, but he was still worried that his parents could get in trouble even though they had no idea what was in their house. He had to get it out of there as soon as possible.

Craig's mother inhaled her food while Craig continued to pick at his.

The memory of what had happened last night repeated in his head. He still couldn't believe it was real. It felt almost as if it were a movie he'd watched.

CHAPTER 38

Enzo sat at his dining room table, forcing down an extra meatball while his wife, a big woman in an apron, cleared the dishes from the table and brought them into the kitchen.

The dining room was long and spacious with a black and white marble floor and wallpaper that looked like fabric. A white marble statue of David sat in one corner and a statue of the Virgin Mary sat in the other corner.

After he finished chewing his food, Enzo gulped down half a glass of soda and burped. He stood and strolled from the dining room to the living room.

His wife yelled from the kitchen, "You want the coffee up now?"

"In a while." He plopped down on his huge recliner, unbuttoned the top button on his pants, and burped. He was too stuffed for dessert.

A large Persian rug lay in the center of the polished parquet living room floor. A giant picture of Jesus hung on the back wall while two other religious paintings hung on the two adjacent walls: the last supper and the birth of Christ. Ornate white ceramic frames sat in a row on the fireplace mantle displaying a younger husband and wife with their two sons when they were growing up.

Just as Enzo was about to light a cigar, the doorbell rang. He stood, buttoned back up, and shook his head while passing the new white sofa that his wife had just bought against his wishes.

When he looked out the peephole, he was surprised to see Johnny and Peppino. He wondered why they came to his house. Did he do something wrong? He knew they had a rule about killing women, and they wouldn't kill him in front of a witness, so he felt a little better.

He opened the door.

Peppino handed Enzo a white cardboard box tied with a string and then gave Enzo a kiss on the cheek. "From Ferrara's."

"Thank you." Enzo invited them inside.

His wife came in from the kitchen. "Oh. Hello Peppino."

"Hello, Maria." He gave her a kiss on the cheek and then pointed at Johnny and said, "This is a friend of mine, Johnny."

"Nice to meet you." She shook Johnny's hand.

Enzo handed her the box. "Peppino went to Ferrara's."

"Oh, my favorite. I'll put the coffee on." She took the box into the kitchen.

Enzo sat on his recliner, but didn't recline. Peppino and Johnny sat on the new sofa. He offered them both a cigar, but both refused.

Peppino said, "I have some interesting information."

Enzo listened while lighting his cigar.

Peppino said, "I learned that internal affairs is looking into a Detective Victor Cohen. He's the homicide cop on the case and he has a history of drug use. Some black dame is going after him, I think her name was Edmunds or some shit, seems she has a real hard-on for this Detective Cohen."

The smell of fresh coffee from the other room overpowered the aroma of Enzo's cigar.

Enzo asked, "You think he's the one that took the stuff?"

"That's what I'd like to find out. I'm sure you and Johnny can come up with more information than internal affairs."

CHAPTER 39

Victor and Evelyn watched the news on TV while in bed. A reporter spoke about three murders that had happened the night before in Coney Island. Victor didn't know about it because he hadn't watched the news after getting home from the pool hall last night or while getting ready for brunch this morning.

Evelyn's eyes closed and she started snoring lightly. Victor kissed her bare shoulder.

The reporter on TV said that the man who was shot and the man who had been run over by a car, three times, were both positively identified as drug dealers. The reporter also said that the police still hadn't identified the third man, who was apparently stabbed and killed by the man who was shot. The reporter also speculated that the police were looking for at least one other suspect.

A commercial came on and Victor began to slip in and out of consciousness. His mind visualized someone in a car driving over the head and neck of another human being.

CHAPTER 40

After a night of partial sleep, tossing and turning, and violent gruesome nightmares, Craig woke up exhausted, cold, and covered in sweat.

His head hurt and his stomach felt as if it was full of acid and bile, but that was normal.

The only thing on his mind was getting the money and drugs out of his mother's safe.

He called his foreman, but the phone went straight to voicemail. Craig left a message and told him he was too sick to come in. He knew it wouldn't be a problem.

Craig didn't want to go to his parents' house while his father was there, and he knew he still had a little time before he had to get ready, so after a quick trip to the bathroom, he closed his eyes and went back to sleep. He already had a place in mind where the coke and the cash would be safe.

CHAPTER 41

Victor woke up in his shorts and undershirt freezing with the air conditioner on high. He remembered turning it off, but then wondered if he could have turned it back on in his sleep.

Evelyn slept in a fetal position under the sheet and both blankets, and on top of all that, the comforter. Even her head and face were covered.

Victor grabbed the remote control on the night table next to him and pressed the power button. The air conditioner didn't turn off. He tried again, but it still didn't turn off. He hadn't changed the batteries since he bought it two years ago, so he made a mental note to buy batteries while he was out.

He slipped out from beside his wife and tiptoed across the room to turn off the air conditioner by hand, before heading down the hall.

On his way into the bathroom, he had to sneeze, but held it in so he wouldn't wake Evelyn. He knew he was going to be sick by the way his nasal passages and throat felt.

Evelyn continued sleeping hard as Victor finished in the bathroom and then headed into the kitchen where he unwrapped and inhaled a couple Little Debbie chocolate cupcakes before setting up and turning on the coffee maker. He hoped the smell would wake his wife so he wouldn't have to. He would have let her sleep while her mother brought the baby, but Rosie had texted and said she was ready to get an early start.

Victor sipped his coffee and ate a bowl of oatmeal while watching the news on the TV in the living room. They had another report about the murders in Coney Island. Police discovered the identity of the third corpse: Riley Malone, a retired local 157 carpenter from Brooklyn. They also found his car abandoned in Benson-Hurst covered in spray paint.

The news report ended and the weather report came on: hot and sticky, as usual.

Today was the only day Victor was grateful for the summer heat. He hoped it would dry up his head cold.

He thought about the dead carpenter and for a moment wondered if it had something to do with the case that he was working on, but he knew it was probably just a coincidence.

While returning to the kitchen to wash his bowl, Victor held in another sneeze. With a paper towel, he blew his nose, then washed his hands. He was getting worse already.

Back in the bedroom, Victor put on his suit from the dry cleaner. He was ready to leave the house, so he pulled the blankets away from Evelyn's face and woke her up with a kiss.

She opened her eyes, then smiled. She puckered up and Victor gave her another kiss.

He pulled away from her offensive breath, but made sure not to let her know. "I have to run. It's early. You still have about an hour before your mother comes."

Evelyn said, "It was freezing in here last night."

"I know. I thought I turned it off, but the remote batteries are dead. My nose and throat are killing me now."

"I feel fine . . ." Evelyn looked down at the blankets on her body and then at Victor's bare side of the bed. "Did I take all the covers?"

"It's nothing."

"I'm so sorry baby."

He kissed her on the forehead. "Don't worry about it. I'll get some tea or something later. I'm just glad you're back. I missed you."

She smiled and said, "Me too."

Victor hurried out the door and onto the sidewalk.

Sunlight crept over the horizon, but the heat couldn't come quick enough.

He sneezed again, but this time he didn't hold it in. With a paper towel he'd taken from the kitchen, he wiped his nose.

On his way to the train station, Victor thought about that dead carpenter on the news. The same union, local 157 was working on The Howell Building, but Victor did remember hearing a couple years ago that a couple of different carpenters unions had merged into one. It was only on a curiosity . . . but it was a persistent one.

The closer he got to the subway, the more he thought about the murders in Coney Island. Two dead drug dealers meant drugs. But, what about the dead carpenter? What was the connection? Drugs could help explain what had happened at The Howell Building. In his mind, Victor tried to make it fit like a stubborn kid trying to force a piece into the wrong place in a jigsaw puzzle.

Just before entering the staircase to the train station above, Victor called Rosie on his cell. "Hey Rosie. You there yet?"

"Almost. Why?"

Victor sniffled and wiped his runny nose. "I'm going to Brooklyn to check something out."

"Something to do with the case?"

"Just a hunch right now." He sniffled and wiped his nose again. "Can you cover for me?"

"Yeah, sure. You sound sick. You still in bed?"

"I slept with the AC on. It's nothing. I'm at the train already. I'll see you at lunchtime."

"What do I tell Morelli?"

Victor sniffled again and wiped his nose. "I don't know. Make something up."

"Why all the secrecy?"

"Morelli doesn't like hunches. He used to always say, hunches are hard on the budget."

"Okay," replied Rosie. "I'll take care of it."

They said goodbye and hung up.

Victor put his phone into the inside pocket of his suit jacket and headed up the stairs to the station above where he swiped his Metrocard at the turnstile and made his way up another flight of stairs. The station began to vibrate as the train got closer, so Victor picked up the pace.

Panting and gasping for air, he reached the platform just as the train screeched to a stop and then opened its doors.
He squeezed into the crowded train and shivered as the air

conditioner cooled his blood.

On its way into Manhattan, the 7-train became so crowded, that some of the people trying to get on had to wait for the next train. Relieved when he finally reached his stop, Victor switched to the D-train, which then took him toward Brooklyn on the express track.

While going over the Manhattan Bridge, he called the precinct in Coney Island, but the detectives on the case were already out. Victor left a message and his cell number with the captain.

He stayed on the train as it went back underground in Brooklyn and made its stops. He thought about turning around going back to Manhattan, but he really wanted to get a look at where the crime took place, he always worked better that way.

Finally, the train went above ground and then stopped on 9th Avenue.

Victor checked his phone to see if he had a signal yet, then he checked for messages: nothing. He decided to go one more stop, then turn around if no one called.

Just before the train pulled into the next stop, his phone rang, a number he didn't recognize. The train door opened, but Victor stayed on and answered his phone. "Hello?"

It was the lead homicide detective from Coney Island. "Detective Cohen?"

"Yes."

The doors closed and the train continued on its route.

"Detective Alexander here. I'm out at the navy yard, going over the impounded car."

"The one that belonged to the carpenter?"

"Yeah. My captain says you want to check out the files. You really think it's related to your case?"

"You never know. I was hoping to check out the crime scene too."

"Nothing left there to see now. I can email you everything later, but I won't be back until well after dinner."

Victor glanced down at the houses and stores below as the train sped past them. He came all this way already, might as well go the rest of the way. He told the detective, "I'm already almost there. No point in turning back now."

"The captain will show you what we got. Call me tonight if you want to know about anything else."

"Thanks."

The two detectives said goodbye and hung up.

After only a couple stops, the train rumbled into Coney Island. The first thing Victor noticed was the Brooklyn Cyclones stadium. The train crawled to a stop and the doors opened. Victor followed a small crowd down a ramp to the station below and then out to the street.

It had been more than a few years since he'd been to Coney Island. The last time was with Jennifer. He had asked Evelyn to go a few times when they first got together, but she didn't like the beach.

The hot sun began to climb and helped dry out Victor's sinuses.

While walking along Surf Avenue past a few bars and a furniture store, all of which were still closed, Victor occasionally glanced across the street at Nathan's, the empty bumper cars, and the stores that were just opening. It was still too early for the Cyclone roller coaster and other rides to be running, but a few early joggers and sun worshippers made their way past the buildings and onto the wooden boardwalk and the sandy beach.

Victor turned the corner and crossed the street under a double-decker subway overpass before arriving at a three-story brick building that sat in the center of the block, dwarfed by so many twenty-story apartment buildings that surrounded it.

He entered the precinct and approached the desk officer who directed him to the detective unit on the second floor.

The captain met Victor and showed him all the photographs and documents on the case. There was a diagram showing where the SUV was parked and where the car ran the third man over.

Victor still would have liked to go to the scene, but the diagram told him everything he wanted to know, and he was pressed for time.

With the captain's permission, Victor made copies of everything in the file and took it with him as he headed back to the train station.

The hot sun above finished drying up his sinus.

He stopped at a newsstand in the Stillwell Avenue station and bought a package of batteries before heading up the stairs to the trains above.

CHAPTER 42

In her office, at her desk, Abby picked up her desk phone and called Rosie Li. While the phone rang, she glanced at the framed picture of Jesus on her desk.

Rosie answered, "Hello?"

"Hello, Detective Li. This is Abby Edmunds from internal affairs."

Rosie asked, "The woman from the elevator?"

"Yes."

"How can I help you?"

"First of all, I'd like to congratulate you on being the first Asian woman to make homicide detective."

"Um. Okay. Thank you."

"But that's not why I called . . . I need your help."

Rosie asked, "My help?"

"Are you with Detective Cohen now?"

"No. He went to Brooklyn."

"For something personal?"

"He didn't tell me."

Abby had a feeling Rosie was lying, but didn't want a confrontation with her now. "Well, let me be frank. I believe Detective Cohen is using drugs again. Have you ever noticed him falling asleep or reacting slowly?"

"He has a prescription for Vicoden . . . from his doctor. It's legit."

"Yes. I know about that. He also had a legit prescription three years ago, but they found him with five times that many drugs in his system."

Rosie said, "I'm sorry, but I can't help you. I don't believe he's doing anything wrong."

"At The Howell Building, he touched evidence without a glove and then failed to seal the bag properly."

"You gonna charge him for that?"

"No, but if he is using drugs again, these small mistakes will eventually lead to bigger mistakes, mistakes that could cost either of you your lives."

"I don't think he is. He takes half a pill at a time and it does not affect his work. He's a great detective with an exceptional record."

"I know he is." Abby was worried she wouldn't be able to get through to Rosie. "He's probably a great guy, too. However, that does not change the fact that he likes to feel nice from time to time. He is only human."

Rosie didn't answer.

Abby glanced back at the picture of Jesus on her desk and said, "I don't expect you to turn against your partner. Just keep an eye open. You've only known him for a short time."

CHAPTER 43

Victor made it back to his precinct by lunchtime, just as he'd told Rosie. The captain didn't say anything about his tardiness, so he knew whatever Rosie told him had worked.

"Thanks, Rosie. I owe you one." He stepped over to his desk and put his copy of the Coney Island murder file into a desk drawer.

"I got that list of the carpenters who worked that day at The Howell Building." She handed him two sheets of paper stapled together.

"I owe you two, now. Come on. I'll buy you lunch."

"How's your cold?"

"Don't worry, I won't breathe on you."

They got up and headed out to a diner for lunch, then back up to The Bronx to continue their futile search for drug dealers who would give up their comrades. Rosie seemed quieter than usual, but Victor was too busy analyzing the Coney Island murders in his head to care.

CHAPTER 44

Craig was feeling and looking better than usual due to the extra sleep he'd gotten that morning. He had already been to his mother's house and retrieved the backpack. She asked him to stay and eat, but he told her he had errands to run.

On his way home, he removed the can of spray paint from the backpack and disposed of it in a garbage can on the street.

After getting the package to his apartment, Craig separated the four bricks and wrapped them up individually. He broke off a quarter of one of the bricks and threw it into a plastic sandwich bag, which he hid in a kitchen drawer.

He then wrapped the stacks of cash in plastic wrap so it looked similar to the bricks of cocaine. He placed everything into the backpack and headed out the door.

He'd already asked his mother if he could keep his money in her safe deposit box at the bank instead of in her safe at home. Of course, she said yes. She just told him to be careful with her stuff that was already in there.

The bank was fifteen blocks away, which would have been a nice walk, but Craig didn't want to wait one second more than he had to.

He called a car service, which got him there in a matter of minutes, then he had the driver drop him off a block and a half away at a hardware store, just to be safe.

After the cab was out of sight, Craig headed to the bank.

Inside, the huge open lobby smelled of pine air fresheners and money.

Craig headed past the tellers behind their bulletproof glass, then past the desks on the side. Toward the back of the building, he pressed a button next to a steel door adorned with an engraving of a crown.

A fat impeccably dressed gay man let Craig in and asked him for his ID. Craig's mother had put all three of their names on the box, but neither Craig nor his father had ever used it. He hoped he wouldn't have a problem now.

The man scrolled through some pages on his computer, then handed Craig a sheet of paper and a pen. Relieved, Craig printed and signed his name below a list of other signatures.

The man took Craig into the vault and found his mother's big safe deposit box. He unlocked the box with two keys, slid it out, and handed it to Craig. The entire time he gave Craig bedroom eyes and laughed at every little thing he said.

Craig smiled, thanked him, and then took the big lightweight box into one of three small rooms and locked the door.

Inside the box, he found his mother's antique clock that had been in her family for over a hundred years. There was also a few envelopes that contained his parents' wills, deed to the house, and other important documents.

Just as he opened the backpack, he heard something on the other side of the door. It sounded like police radios. Craig's heart dropped. His cold flesh began to sweat.

With three and three quarter kilos and all the cash in the backpack, he zipped it up and threw it into the metal box. He closed the lid and stood next to the door listening. The sound was still there. At first, it sounded close, then far, then close again.

He knew he couldn't stay in that little room forever, but he didn't want to go out there if the cops were there.

After waiting for about five minutes, he realized that if the police were there for him, they would have already knocked on the door, or broke it down.

Craig took a deep breath and opened the door. Just as he approached the big gay man, he noticed a cute female cop in uniform with a small safe deposit box going into one of the private rooms. She didn't pay much attention to him.

The man took Craig's box, slid it back into its slot, locked it, and handed Craig his key.

Craig thanked the man and felt so relieved that he wasn't even nervous when he passed the cop's partner who was waiting for her in the lobby.

CHAPTER 45

After spending all morning fighting with himself about whether or not to do what he was planning to do, Enzo finally decided to go through with it.

After a big breakfast and a few visits to the bathroom, Enzo headed out of the house and drove to Manhattan. He drove to Abby Edmunds' office, but she wasn't in. He sat outside in his car with the air conditioner on until she returned.

She entered the building with a young white man. Enzo waited a few minutes and then went into the building after her.

In her office, Enzo introduced himself as Anthony Romano. He knew Peppino wouldn't approve of this, but he believed he was making a smart move.

"How can I help you?" Asked Abby.

"I have some information pertaining to one of your cases."

"And, how did you come across this information?"

Enzo glanced over at the young detective and then back at Abby.

Abby said, "Do me a favor, Mangano, get me a cup of coffee and a Danish."

Mangano left the room.

Abby said, "Talk to me."

"I hear you've been looking into a Detective named Victor Cohen."

"And how would you know about a police investigation?"

"I hear things."

"I don't have time for games, Mr. Romano."

"Okay, I'll tell you like it is. Someone I lent money to was robbed. The people who robbed them, made off with four kilos of cocaine."

Abby said, "I'm listening."

"The man who had the drugs last, was shot by the police in The Howell Building. My associates and I believe that the police are now in possession of the cocaine."

"One cop was killed."

"I know, but one survived. And then there's the question of Detective Cohen. I understand he has a history with drugs."

"Pills, not coke."

"All I know is that coke is worth a lot of money and all the evidence points to the cops. I'd like for us to work together."

"What makes you think I would have anything to do with drug dealing scum like you?"

"Excuse me, but I do not deal in drugs."

"You lend money to dealers. It's the same thing."

CHAPTER 46

While her daughter watched TV in the living room, Abby went into her bedroom and called Rosie on her cell phone.

Rosie answered, "I hope this isn't going to be every day."

"Sorry to bother you at home Detective Li, but I heard some interesting news today."

Rosie didn't answer.

Abby asked, "Detective, are you there?"

Rosie sighed. "I'm here. What's your news?"

"The guys wearing Hawaiian shirts took four kilos of cocaine from the dead Dominican."

"Then where's the drugs?"

"That's what I'd like to know," replied Abby.

"So, you think Detective Cohen and the two uniformed cops were in bed together and stole four kilos of cocaine from the thieves? Are you for real?"

"I don't think it happened like that at all. But I do believe Cohen knows more than he's saying."

"I think you're blinded by your hate."

"Hate? This is about justice!"

"Is it?"

Abby remembered that her daughter was watching TV in the other room and lowered her voice. "Yes. This is about justice. The Lord says that the wages of sin is death."

"Sorry Edmunds, but I'm a Buddhist."

"If you know something and you don't tell me—"

"Victor doesn't have four kilos of coke. Believe me. There's no conspiracy. I had to lend the guy ten bucks for lunch the other day."

"Well Detective, I must remind you that my inquiry into Detective Cohen is official police business and you are under orders not to speak of it with Detective Cohen."

Rosie didn't answer.

"Are we clear, Detective?"

"We're clear. Is there anything else?"

"No. Nothing else. You have a good night, Detective."

"Yeah. Whatever." Rosie hung up.

CHAPTER 47

After dinner and putting the baby to bed for the night, Victor and Evelyn made love twice and then while Evelyn lay on the bed resting, Victor bragged that he could still knock her out.

With the TV on in the background, they cuddled until falling asleep.

Victor woke up a few hours later to use the bathroom and drink a glass of water. After checking that both his wife and daughter were still asleep, he headed to the living room with the Coney Island case file in hand.

Under a small reading lamp, Victor glanced at the reports quickly, but spent a while looking at the pictures and the diagram.

He wondered how many people were there and what happened to the drugs. Like the detectives in Coney Island, Victor believed it was a drug deal gone bad. From the way things looked, it seemed that the retired carpenter was buying something from the two dealers and then a third party robbed and killed them.

A whole gang could have ambushed them, or maybe one or more of their own people robbed them. These types of cases usually ended up an inside job.

Victor wondered if that's what had happened at The Howell Building. A drug deal gone bad? Maybe the man in the Hawaiian shirt was the thief. Then where were the drugs? He hated to think of it, but he had to consider the possibility that the cop who survived could have taken the drugs.

But, what about the missing gun that had been fired? And of course, there was still the dead junkie laborer. He considered every possible theory his mind could muster up at that hour.

Victor tried to re-read the list of names that Rosie had gotten for him, but his vision blurred and his eyes began to close.

Victor went back to bed, knowing that if his wife found him working instead of sleeping, she would not be happy.

He checked Sofia once more before slipping back into bed with Evelyn. She rolled over and opened her eyes.

"Sorry to wake you, baby. Go back to sleep."

She cuddled up closer to him and slipped her hand down between his legs. "I'm not in the mood to sleep anymore."

CHAPTER 48

Craig woke up after another night of low quality sleep. He had dreams of sniffing and injecting coke, and for a moment, he was tempted to go into the kitchen and sample a little bit. But, he didn't.

He rolled out of bed and performed his morning routine before heading out to work.

Back at The Howell Building, Craig performed his job the best he could while remembering how he'd savagely butchered Robby the junkie on the first floor.

During coffee break, Craig approached two guys he knew that smoked weed and asked them if they knew anyone who did coke. One of the guys said he likes to do a little on weekends.

Craig gave him a sample, it was probably over a gram, but he didn't care. He wanted to get rid of it as soon as possible, and even if he sold it at wholesale, thirty a gram, that still added up to thirty grand for each kilo.

During lunch, the guy who Craig had given the sample to, approached with two other guys. Craig sold each of them the same amount he had given the first guy and charged them thirty dollars each. They were like kids on Christmas. He knew they'd be back for more.

CHAPTER 49

Rosie was ready to walk out the door when Victor arrived an hour late with bags under his eyes, his hair a mess, and his suit wrinkled because he didn't have time to press it.

"I'm sorry," he said. "I didn't get much sleep last night." He knew he looked terrible, but sex was always worth losing sleep for. "You mind driving?"

"Whatever." Rosie headed toward the door.

Victor followed her downstairs, out of the building, and onto the sidewalk. He caught up with her as she stood at the curb waiting for a few cars to pass. "Hey. You mad at me?"

"No. Just want to get to work. That's all."

Victor followed Rosie across the street and into the parking lot. "I have a lead."

She stopped and looked at him over the top of the car as he opened the passenger side door. "What lead?" She asked.

Victor said, "A friend of a friend told me about a barber shop where some of the Morris Park boys hang out at."

"A friend of a friend?"

"Yeah." Victor got into the car and closed the door.

Rosie got in, closed her door, and started the engine. She looked over at Victor.

"No one gets there until after twelve. We still have plenty of time."

Rosie pulled out of the parking lot and onto the street.

Victor looked over at her and said, "Unless you have a better idea?"

Rosie didn't answer, she just headed toward the expressway.

Victor asked, "That new lesbian detective find out anything about our dead junkie laborer?"

"You are so politically correct."

"What? Because I said lesbian? Or junkie?"

Rosie didn't answer, she just shook her head and stopped at a red light. "After questioning the deceased laborer's friends and family, the new female detective discovered that there's a long list of people who could have killed him."

"So, basically, no one's getting anywhere."

Rosie took the ramp up to the FDR drive and headed north as the sunlight kissed the metal and glass midtown skyscrapers ahead. "So, where are we going exactly?"

"Williamsbridge Road."

"You know how to get there?"

"I know my way around there a little bit."

"Of course."

Victor wondered what she meant by that last comment. "So, is our honeymoon period coming to a close?"

"What? Oh, sorry. Uh . . . just that time of the month. That's all."

"Oh, I see," Replied Victor. "I shall proceed with caution."

She chuckled, then said, "You really are a pig."

Victor laughed and looked ahead as traffic slowed to a stop.

It took over an hour just to get out of Manhattan and into The Bronx.

They drove past the barbershop on Williamsbridge Road, but it was still closed, so they bought lunch from a Halal cart on the sidewalk a few blocks away then ate in in the car with the air conditioner on while waiting down the block and watching the building.

Cars and people flooded the streets and sidewalks as stores opened one by one and the hot sun rose higher in the sky. Victor chewed gum while Rosie typed on her tablet.

Finally, someone approached the barbershop.

Victor and Rosie watched as the man unlocked and rolled up the steel gate, then unlocked the door and went inside.

The man was not what Victor expected: short with a big belly, a big mustache, and a limp. He looked exactly as a barber should look, but he didn't look like he'd be involved with any street gang activity.

When Victor turned to look at Rosie, he found her looking at him. "What?" he asked.

"What"

Victor said, "I'm gonna walk by and take a look inside."

"Good idea," replied Rosie.

Victor strolled down the block just behind an old woman with a walker. He glanced inside the barbershop on his way by and saw the old man preparing his chair and barber tools. Victor wondered if he got a bad tip.

He crossed the street and went back around to the car.

Inside the car, Victor said, "Looks like a normal barber."

"Okay."

"I don't know. Let's wait a while and see what happens."

They sat in silence for about twenty minutes watching the building.

Victor's eyes began to close.

Rosie asked, "Hey, you want an iced coffee?"

"That would be great. I'll get it though. You want?"

"Get me an iced tea."

"You got it." Victor got out of the car and headed the opposite way to a Dunkin' Donuts two blocks away. His bulletproof vest was heavy and hot, but he promised Evelyn he would wear it any time he questioned dangerous people.

He picked up the drinks and went back.

Inside the car, he handed Rosie her iced tea and asked, "Anything?"

"Nothing." She replied. "That old man is probably asleep in there."

They sipped their drinks for about twenty minutes and waited for another thirty minutes before three young men with goatees and earrings approached and entered the barbershop.

Victor, "Let's do this."

He and Rosie got out of the car and strolled up the block.

One of the three young men left the building alone.

Rosie asked Victor, "Should we follow him? We could talk to the other two after."

"If they're still here, that is. I'd hate to talk to one and lose two . . ."

"You're right," replied Rosie.

Victor entered first, then Rosie.

The old man sat in his chair reading the newspaper while the two young men were laughing about something. Their laughter stopped instantly when they saw Victor and Rosie.

They both showed their badges.

Victor said, "We're looking for Nelson Kelley."

The old man lowered his paper and watched.

The taller of the two young men said, "Never heard of him." He looked over at the old man. "What about you, *Tio*?"

The old man said, "Nope," then raised his paper back over his face.

Victor looked at the other young man and asked, "What about you? You know Nelson Kelley?"

"Isn't that the name of a country singer?"

The old man spoke from behind his paper, "That's Willie Nelson, *stupido*."

The tall young man laughed and said, "Sorry Officers. Can't help you. Have a nice day, though."

Victor placed his card on the counter and said, "Here's my number. Just in case."

The short man pointed at Rosie and asked, "Can I get her number?"

Victor and Rosie both ignored the comment as they turned around and headed for the door.

The tall man said, "What do you want her number for? You gonna order some pork fried rice or something?"

All three of them laughed. Rosie turned around and took a step toward them. Victor turned around to stop her.

The short man said, "I'll sue the NYPD if you try that Kung Fu shit on me."

The three of them continued laughing while Victor tried to get Rosie to ignore them.

The door opened. Everyone looked. Two other young men entered, saw Victor and Rosie, then turned around and bolted.

Victor and Rosie sprinted out the door after them.

One man dashed one way and the other went the opposite way.

Victor and Rosie split up and chased them down the crowded

sidewalk.

After a few blocks, Victor was out of breath. He bent over with his hands on his knees, panting while the young man disappeared. He hoped Rosie had done better.

Back at the car, Victor waited for Rosie and hoped she was okay.

After a few minutes, he started in the direction that she had gone. He wondered if splitting up was a mistake. He knew they probably ran because they had something on them, but you never know how a person will react when cornered.

With his handkerchief, Victor wiped the sweat from his forehead while trying to catch his breath. When he was able to speak, he called Rosie.

She answered her pone by asking, "Did you get him?"

"No. I lost him. What about you?"

"That kid was just too damn fast."

Victor said, "I'll meet you back at the car."

They met back at the car and spent the rest of the afternoon watching the barbershop, but after the incident earlier, the guys in the barbershop probably tipped off all their homeboys and told them not to come around.

CHAPTER 50

After dinner, and back at their apartment, Abby's daughter watched TV while Abby sat behind her on the sofa reading the Bible and eating chocolates from a box.

Abby glanced over to see that her laptop was fully charged, it was. She closed her bible and the box of chocolates and powered on the computer.

After logging onto Windows and checking her yahoo email, Abby logged into her police account and checked out the status of four police officers that she made a personal habit of keeping her eyes on.

Nothing interested her there, so she went straight to Victor's latest reports.

She read about Victor and Rosie's elegant police work at the barbershop in The Bronx and laughed when she read that Victor lost the man he was chasing because: he couldn't breathe anymore.

Faith laughed at the show she was watching on TV.

Abby logged out, closed her computer, and lay down next to her daughter on a throw rug on the floor.

CHAPTER 51

Enzo and Sammy sat at the same table in the back of the bar. Enzo had a drink in front of him, but Sammy didn't.

Sammy said, "No more drinking for me. That day I left here, my head was spinning. I was useless to the world. I went home, ate, and then passed out. Woke up the next morning, my head was killing me."

Enzo laughed and said, "I told you to slow down." He took a small drink from a glass of red wine and then held the glass up and said, "Everything in moderation."

Sammy nodded. "I'll try and keep that in mind."

"So, what did you find out?"

"Those cops looked for Nelson at a pool hall and at a barbershop where he hangs out sometimes. I've been looking for him everywhere. He might be long gone. I'm starting to wonder if maybe the cops really did find the shit and stashed it somewhere."

"Well, you can't follow the cops, so you're gonna have to stick with looking for Nelson."

"Did you talk to Peppino for me?"

"Yeah. He says you still have some time. He said to keep looking. I told him about your brother's crew, but he said that's an internal matter and not his problem."

"Fuck."

"Sorry, kid. I'll talk to him again when he's in a better mood. You never know."

Sammy said, "Maybe I will have that drink." He waved his hand to get the bartenders attention.

CHAPTER 52

At the precinct, after filling out their paperwork for the day, Rosie checked her computer while Victor scanned the names of carpenters on the list that Rosie had gotten him.

Victor said, "You know, I'm looking at this list here, and my eyes keep going back to the same name. A guy named Kevin Malone. Wonder if he's related to the dead guy in Coney Island, Riley Malone."

Rosie looked up from her screen and said, "Malone? Hey, I once knew a sergeant Malone when I worked in Chinatown. Maybe we should go question him, too."

"I'm gonna call the foreman." Victor took out his phone and dialed the foreman whose name and number was at the top of the list.

Victor waited as the phone rang and then went to voicemail. He left a message, "Mr. Bogues, this is Detective Cohen. I'd like to ask you about one of your employees on the list that you faxed my partner this morning. Please call me back as soon as possible."

"He probably won't call back until tomorrow."

"I don't want to wait until tomorrow." Victor pressed redial on his phone and then waited while it rang again. After the fifth ring, a woman answered. "Hello?"

"Hi. This is Detective Cohen from the NYPD. Is Mr. Bogues available?"

"He's in the shower right now. I'm his wife. Is this about the murder case?"

"Yes, mam. I'd like to speak with your husband as soon as possible."

"I'll have him call you when he gets out of the shower."

"Thank you." Victor hung up and turned to Rosie. "He's gonna call me back in a few. You go ahead, I'm gonna hit the bathroom, then hang around until he calls."

Rosie powered off her computer, then said, "Hasta *manana*."

Victor waited another twenty minutes, then decided to go home and try the foreman again later from home. He left the precinct and headed to the train station. On the way there, his phone rang.

"Detective Cohen here."

"Hello detective. This is Roger Bogues."

"Thank you for returning my call, Mr. Bogues. I was going through this list of your employees and came across a name: Kevin Malone."

"Kevin? Why do you want to know about him?"

"Has Kevin ever been in any kind of trouble?"

"Never. He's a good kid. Why? What's up?"

"Have you ever heard of him being involved with drugs?" Victor stopped at the train station and stood near the top of the staircase.

"No way. He is a model citizen. He won the regional apprentice contest a few years ago. Everybody likes the guy. He and his fiancé attend church every Sunday. I know because he invited me to his church on more than one occasion."

Victor moved out of the way as a crowd of commuters headed up the stairs and onto the sidewalk. "Do you know if Kevin Malone is related to a retired carpenter named Riley Malone?"

"Riley is Kevin's uncle. I heard about what happened to him. Do you think—?"

"Not sure what I think yet. Just going over all the bases."

"I've known Riley for twenty-five years. Whatever he was involved in, Kevin had nothing to do with it. You can be sure about that."

"Does Kevin also live in Brooklyn?" Asked Victor.

"Staten Island."

"Can you give me his number please?"

"Uh . . . I don't know if I feel comfortable giving out his

number."

"I'm a detective Mr. Bogues, and I'm investigating a murder. If you hold back any information that may—"

"Okay." Mr. Bogues gave Victor Kevin's phone number.

After ending the call, Victor called Kevin.

"Hello?"

"Kevin Malone?"

"Who's calling?"

"This is Detective Cohen from the NYPD."

"This is Kevin."

"First of all, I want to say I'm sorry to hear about your uncle. I know this is a sensitive time for your family, but I have to ask you a few questions."

"I already spoke with two detectives the day after it happened."

"I know," Replied Victor. "They're from Brooklyn. I'm from Manhattan. I'm investigating the murders that happened at The Howell Building."

"Oh. I'm not on that job anymore. I started work on a building in midtown yesterday."

"That's okay. I just need to know if your uncle knew anyone who was working at The Howell Building that day."

Kevin didn't answer.

Victor asked, "Kevin? Are you there?"

"I'm here. I guess it doesn't matter what I say now that Uncle Riley is gone."

"Please. You have to tell me what you know. Any detail, no matter how insignificant it may seem to you."

"Well. My uncle was involved in things he should not have been involved with. I just hope he repented to God for his sins before he died. I'd hate to think he's not in heaven."

"That's a little out of my jurisdiction. I just want to know what he was involved with while he was here on Earth."

"He sold marijuana, Detective. He'd been selling since I was a kid."

Victor had a hard time believing that all these murders were because of marijuana. There had to be more to the story. "Was he into anything else? Coke? Dope?"

"No," replied Kevin. "I would have known about it. His thing was pot. They said he smoked a lot of it and always had the best stuff around."

"Did you know any of his customers?"

"Yeah. About a quarter of the carpenters in our union."

"I need some names."

"I don't want to get involved."

"I can charge you with obstruction if you don't help me."

"I don't want the guys at work to know."

"I'll say I got an anonymous tip. No one will ever know we spoke."

"Well. I don't know all of his customers, and I don't remember who all was working that day. I know he sells to Big Johnny and that African guy. Oh . . . the best person to talk to about Riley's weed business would probably be Craig . . . Craig Hill. He lives near Riley and I know they hang out all the time."

"I'm not sure I remember Craig Hill. What did he look like?"

"Tall and skinny with blue eyes."

Victor thought about it for a moment, but still didn't know to whom Kevin was referring.

Kevin added, "He's all yellow from hepatitis."

Of course, Victor remembered the yellow man. He tried to stay away from him. "Yes. I remember him now. Would you happen to have his phone number?"

"No. I only know he lives close to Riley. Somewhere around 86th Street in Brooklyn."

"Thank you Kevin." Victor hung up the phone and moved out of the way for another crowd of commuters to come up the stairs.

The sun was on its way down, but the heat still lingered. He called his wife and told her he'd be later than he thought, then headed back to the precinct.

On the second floor, Victor entered his captain's office.

Captain Morelli, a short, fat man with a five 'o'clock shadow sat behind a desk eating Chinese food out of a box. He wiped his mouth and took a sip of his soda. "What are you still doing here, Cohen?"

"I just came back."

Captain Morelli burped then said, "You'd rather look at me than your wife. Don't tell me your turning faggy now, Cohen."

Victor laughed. "And people say I'm politically incorrect."

The captain took another bite of his food then spoke with his mouth full. "You gonna tell me why you're here?"

"I found a connection between a man recently killed in Coney Island and some of the carpenters working at The Howell Building."

Captain Morelli washed down his food with another gulp of soda, put down his plastic fork and asked, "What kind of a connection?"

Victor explained that Riley sold weed to some of the carpenters on the job and his death looked like it had something to do with a drug deal gone bad. He asked the captain to find out what he could about Riley's weed business from narcotics detectives in Brooklyn. He also told him he was very interested in speaking with Craig Hill, Riley's good friend who was at The Howell Building on the day of the murders.

CHAPTER 53

After work, Craig had bought a digital scale and some small jewelry bags on his way home and then bagged up a bunch of one-gram packages in his apartment.

It seemed that fifty to sixty dollars a gram was the going price. He'd decided that at thirty dollars a gram he wouldn't waste his time with anything smaller and if someone wanted a lot more, he would give them a small discount. Even if he sold everything for a hundred thousand dollars, he still had thirty more in the backpack, plus his original three.

Before he got out of the shower, his phone was already ringing. All three of the guys from work wanted more, and they had a couple friends who also wanted some.

Craig didn't want anyone to know where he lived, so he met them in an Irish pub near Sunset Park. He thought about bringing his pistol but didn't want to walk around with a smoking gun. He kept the safe deposit box key in his shoe.

At a table in the corner, Craig could smell bacon coming from the kitchen and it made his mouth water. He ordered a bacon cheeseburger and a glass of water. He was dying to have a beer, but knew his liver couldn't take it.

The guys from work came in with their friends and ordered a beer while sitting with Craig. He had brought fifty grams with him, and they bought them all, except two grams that he had put away for his cousins. He knew everyone would resell his coke at a profit, but he didn't care, he just wanted to get rid of it quick.

The men stayed until their beers were finished and then they left.

Craig still had half of his gigantic burger on his plate but was already full. He forced down two more bites, called a car service, then paid the bartender for the meal.

While waiting for his cab outside, Craig called his cousin Marie on his mother's side and left a voicemail asking her to return his call. Marie lived with her boyfriend, both of which used cocaine and pills. Craig had already tried calling her earlier, but couldn't reach her then either.

He then called his cousin Allen from his father's side. "Allen, it's Craig."

"What's up, Craig?"

"Are you busy?"

"Why?"

"I want to show you something. I can't tell you what, but I know you'll like it."

Allen hesitated for a minute, then said, "I have company."

"I'll meet you downstairs. It's important. It'll only take a minute."

A faded Lincoln pulled up to the curb. Craig jumped into the backseat.

The driver asked, "Where to, buddy?"

Craig spoke into the phone, "Allen. I just got in the car."

Allen said, "Okay. Hurry up."

Craig said to the driver, "73rd and 13th." He spoke back into the phone and said, "I'm on my way."

Craig and Allen said goodbye and ended the call as the car service driver followed hundreds of other cars up Fourth Avenue to Bay Ridge Parkway, which he then followed east.

They turned on Thirteenth Avenue passing a jewelry store, a restaurant, and a nail salon. Craig paid the driver and got out on the corner. As the car pulled away, he turned the corner onto a tree-lined street with two-story brick houses on each side. Kids were still playing outside while the sun disappeared over the horizon.

Craig hurried to the end of the block and called Allen before crossing to the other side of the crowded street.

Allen answered, "You're here?"

"Crossing 14th."

"I'm coming down."

"Okay." Craig crossed the street and waited in front of his cousin's house while watching a sexy young mother in a short skirt pushing a baby carriage.

A tall skinny man with blond hair and blue eyes came out of the four-story apartment building on the corner wearing a t-shirt, shorts, and flip-flops. He looked like a healthier, younger version of Craig. Allen worked on Wall Street and made quite a lot of money, but spent most of it on cocaine and women.

When Craig shook Allen's hand, he slipped him a gram. "Hey Allen."

Allen quickly glanced at what he was holding, then slipped it into his pocket. "Is it my birthday?"

"Just a sample. There's plenty more where that came from."

"Since when are you in the coke business?"

"It's only temporary. I know a guy who wants to unload a lot of shit. I can hook you up for thirty a gram."

"Thirty a gram? I hope it's not full of aspirin and baby laxative."

"It's clean. Real clean. Try it and let me know."

"Sorry I can't stay and chat, but—"

"That's alright. What does she look like?"

"A tight little French Indonesian."

"Nice." Craig shook Allen's hand and said, "Give her a shot for me."

Allen laughed. "I'll call you tomorrow."

Craig strolled back up to the avenue and then down two blocks to a car service. Three men were sitting in plastic chairs on the sidewalk laughing while one man sat inside the store behind a glass booth. Craig went inside and said, "85th and 6th."

The man behind the glass said, "Eight bucks. The gray car." He pointed out the window at a gray Lincoln double-parked on the street and then he tapped on the window and pointed at one of the men sitting outside.

Craig followed the man to his gray car. The sun was gone, the streetlights were on, and traffic was a little lighter. The car made it to Craig's building in just a few minutes.

Inside his apartment, Craig took off his scuffed old Nikes and turned on his computer. Before he had a chance to sit down, his phone rang. It was Allen.

Craig answered, "Hey Allen. I guess you liked it."

Allen spoke slower than usual. "I need more."

"Now? I just took off my sneakers. I'm exhausted." Craig prepared to light a joint.

Allen said, "I'll be there in a few."

"Don't you have to work tomorrow?"

"I'll pay whatever you want."

Craig didn't want to charge his own cousin more than he was charging everyone else. "I don't want more money. I'm just tired."

"Come on, man. That shit has this chick going crazy. You gotta do this, man."

"Okay, but hurry up or I might fall asleep."

"I'll be right there."

The call ended. Craig placed the joint into ashtray, put his sneakers on, then took the other gram he was saving for his cousin Marie and put it into his pocket.

He realized that Allen would probably want more than just one, so Craig took out his stash and bagged up ten more individual grams.

While putting everything away, he wiped the scale clean with his finger and then without realizing what he'd done, he licked the coke off his finger.

His lips, gums, and tongue turned numb. As the drug penetrated his nerve endings, he felt high by memory. Endorphins flooded his bloodstream.

He wanted more.

Craig opened his bag and with a quarter, scooped out a nice chunk. He sniffed it up in one shot, straight up one nostril.

It only took a second to hit him. He sniffed hard to avoid anything dripping out of his nose. With his head tipped slightly back, the numbing liquid dripped down his throat and then his brain inflated. The sound of helicopters echoed throughout his skull as his consciousness entered another plain of existence.

Craig's mouth and eyes were frozen open for at least five minutes before he realized where he was. He quickly put everything away as his heart pounded. He thought he could hear every little sound in the entire neighborhood.

Thoughts of the people coming after him continued to haunt him as he tried to clean everything up and calm himself down. He sat on the sofa and placed his hand over his heart, hoping he wouldn't die of a heart attack.

He closed his eyes, but flashes of murder kept playing like a movie on the back of his eyelids, flashes of himself killing Robby and those other two men.

It had been years since Craig had smoked a cigarette, but now he wished he had one more than ever. He opened his eyes and paced his tiny apartment waiting for Allen to get there.

CHAPTER 54

Enzo was naked and on his back while Layla, his hot mistress, was on top of him doing all the work. She threw her bleached blonde hair to the side and moaned. Enzo loved when she did that. He reached up and squeezed the implants that he'd paid for.

For the first time in his life, Enzo had recently had a problem performing, but he cured that when he bought some Viagra from a kid who comes into the bar now and then. Now his penis worked like a nineteen-year-old, but the rest of his body couldn't keep up.

Sweat poured down his fat hairy body as he panted like a dog in a desert. The air conditioner was pointed right at his face, but it still wasn't enough. He always joked with his friends about this being the best way to die, but now he had second thoughts.

Enzo's cell phone rang and at the same time vibrated across the wood end table.

"Cazzo. I thought I turned that thing off."

Layla continued riding him and said, "Leave it. Let it ring, baby."

The phone continued to ring until it finally stopped. It beeped a few seconds later to let him know he had a voicemail. A few seconds after that, it rang again.

Enzo glanced out the corner of his eye and saw that it was Johnny calling. "It's Johnny. Fuck." He reached over and grabbed the phone.

Layla stopped moving and watched as Enzo answered the call.

"What's doin', Johnny?"

"Come downstairs."

"Can you give me a few minutes?"

"Hurry. It's important."

Enzo hung up and said, "I'm sorry, baby."

She rolled off him and stormed into the bathroom, slamming the door behind her.

Enzo yelled as he struggled to get off the bed. "You know I love you for your passion, baby!" While putting on his pants, undershirt, and shoes, Enzo noticed the aroma of weed coming from the bathroom. He approached the door and yelled, "How many times do I gotta tell you to put a towel under the door when you smoke that shit?"

Layla didn't answer.

Enzo shook his head then left the apartment and took the elevator downstairs.

He wondered if Peppino found out that he'd spoken with Abby Edmunds. Now, dying under Layla's naked body did sound a lot better than dying at the end of Johnny's Glock. But, he knew he was just being paranoid. He how could they know?

Enzo saw Johnny's Camaro parked across the street. He looked around for Johnny, but didn't see him. The car window rolled down and Johnny waved to Enzo from inside the car.

He crossed the dark street, circled the car, and got in. Sitting next to Johnny, Enzo asked, "So, what's up?"

Johnny handed Enzo some official police reports. "It seems the cops like this guy Craig Hill as our boy and so does Peppino."

Enzo scanned the reports then asked, "How did yous get these?"

"Don't worry about that." Johnny took the papers back from Enzo and slipped them under his seat. "Peppino's gonna pick up this guy Hill before the cops get to him. He wants you to talk to Sammy and see if he knows anything about the guys the cops found dead in Coney Island on Saturday. He wants to know something tonight."

"Tonight?" Enzo looked at his wrist and remembered that his watch was sitting on the end table upstairs. "Okay. I just wanna get this whole thing over with."

Johnny said, "We'll talk again tomorrow."

Enzo got out of the car and headed back into Layla's building.

He planned on calling Sammy and hopefully finding out what he needed over the phone. Layla would be pissed if he couldn't stay with her tonight after promising that he would.

On his way up the elevator, Enzo's thoughts turned to those police reports. If Peppino had connections like that, he could probably find out that Enzo went to the Internal Affairs office. He just hoped that didn't happen.

CHAPTER 55

Craig's head was still ringing, but his heart had slowed. He stopped pacing, sat on the sofa, and slipped the safe deposit key into his shoe.

Inside his pants pocket, his phone rang, vibrating against his leg. Craig jumped. His heart started pounding again. He stood and took a deep breath.

He answered the phone in a low voice, "Allen?"

"I can't find a spot. Come down."

"Shit." Craig hung up, then hurried outside with a hooded sweatshirt, the hood covering his head and most of his face. His paranoia urged him to take his 38 with him, which he did.

He jumped into Allen's five-year-old red BMW.

Allen took off down the block.

Craig said, "I told you that shit was good."

Allen looked at Craig and asked, "You tried some?"

"Just a little."

"What about your liver, man?"

"I just took a taste. I'm not gonna do anymore."

Allen turned the corner and cruised slowly down the next residential street. "How much more do you have?"

"I got about ten grams on me."

"Where'd you get it?"

"I can't say. Just that it's not mine."

Allen stopped at a stop sign then turned another corner,

circling back around to Craig's street. "I'll take four. No, make that five."

After glancing out the window and then his side mirror to make sure no one was following them, Craig counted out five grams and handed them to Allen.

Allen slipped them into his pocket then took out some cash. He counted out the money and handed it to Craig.

Just as they pulled up in front of Craig's building, Craig said, "Pass my house. I wanna walk down the block."

Allen chuckled. "Paranoid already?"

"Just careful."

Allen passed Craig's building and stopped at the next corner. Craig got out, adjusted his hood, and headed back down his quiet street and then into his building.

Inside the lobby, he looked ahead realized that the door to his apartment was open. For a moment, he thought he might have entered the wrong building, but then the thought occurred that he might have really forgotten to close the door.

He had never forgotten before. He thought he remembered closing and locking the door, but then wondered if the coke was playing tricks on his mind.

As he stepped forward, Craig heard something fall, and then he heard men's voices from inside the apartment. Could it be his imagination? Auditory delusions from the coke?

He moved away from the door and stood against the wall while reaching into his sweatshirt pocket and grasping his gun. His hand trembled as he looked around the lobby wondering if anyone was looking at him through their peepholes.

The sound of cabinet doors opening and closing got louder. Craig knew someone was really in there and he knew he had to make a move. His first thought was to run, but if it were someone retaliating from the incident in Coney Island, somehow, they knew where he lived, and he knew that the next place anyone would look for him would be at his parents' house. He would not let that happen.

After taking a deep breath, Craig pulled the hammer back, then removed the gun from his sweatshirt pocket.

With both hands holding up the heavy 38, he stepped in front of the doorway and saw two big Italian men in jogging suits searching through his stuff. His bed was sliced open, his computer was in pieces, and everything else was on the floor.

One of the men spotted Craig. He showed the palms of his hands and said, "Hey. Take it easy. We're the police. Put the gun down."

Craig didn't believe they were cops. Not just because of their clothes and jewelry, but because of the way they carried themselves.

The second man said, "Let me show you my badge. Don't make any sudden moves or you might hurt someone with that thing."

Craig didn't speak, he just stood there, pointing his gun and trembling.

The second man unzipped his jacket and reached inside.

Craig alternated pointing his 38 at both men while watching every facial movement.

Even if they really were cops, Craig knew he was fucked anyway, but he had a different feeling about shooting cops as opposed to drug dealers.

When the man grabbed something inside his jacket and began to pull it out, Craig could tell by the shape and size that it was not a wallet. It was a gun.

Craig fired twice. The bullets had only a short distance to travel before propelling the man backward.

Craig spun around and fired twice at the other man, who was also reaching for something.

The man dove to the floor.

He had no idea if he hit him, but he wanted to be sure. Craig stepped closer and fired two more shots into the man's back, then turned around and bolted through the lobby and out the front door.

While running through his dark sleeping neighborhood, trying to decide where to go, Craig wondered if the two men were dead.

He only made it a few blocks then had to stop and catch his breath. He checked to be sure that he still had his cell phone and pistol, but then realized that his extra bullets were back at the apartment.

CHAPTER 56

It had taken almost the entire night with rest stops every thirty minutes, but Craig had walked all the way to Benson-Hurst. He could have taken the train or the bus, but was worried about being spotted by the cops or any other guys in fancy jogging suits.

They must be related to the guys in Coney Island somehow. After all, thirty thousand dollars was still a lot of money. He wondered how they found him and wondered how they got to him before the real cops did.

The sky was still dark, but he knew the sun would be coming up at any moment.

Across the street from his cousin Marie's basement apartment, standing in front of a closed deli, Craig called her cell phone about ten times. He wondered if she and her boyfriend Anthony were still up and too high to answer the phone or if they had already crashed. It didn't matter. There was no other place to go and he was exhausted.

He crossed the quiet street, kneeled down, and tapped on the basement window with his fingertips. It looked like the lights were off, but he could see a faint flicker of light which he figured was probably the TV.

No one answered so he tapped on the window a little louder.

Still, no one answered.

Craig stood up straight to stretch his knees and take a quick look around to be sure no one was watching. The coke had lost its effect a while ago, but he was still scared as hell.

He kneeled down once more and knocked hard on the basement window, twice.

Finally, he heard a man's voice ask, "Who the fuck?"

Craig said, "Anthony. It's Craig. Marie's cousin. Let me in."

"We're sleeping. Don't you know what time it is?"

"I just need to rest for a couple hours. I have no place to go."

Anthony started to ask something, "Rest? What—"

Craig interrupted, "I'll give you fifty bucks if you let me in."

Anthony didn't answer.

"Anthony?"

Silence.

"Anthony, I said I'll give you fifty bucks." Craig waited for Anthony to say something, but there was no response.

The first sign of sunlight began to creep into the sky from the east.

"Shit." Craig stood and stretched his knees, then, just as he was about to kneel down again, he heard a voice coming from the driveway on the side of the house.

"Yo, Craig."

Craig moved to the driveway and saw Anthony in his wifebeater and boxer shorts standing at the side door of the two-story brick house waving for him to come in.

He headed to the end of the driveway and shook Anthony's hand while slipping him fifty dollars. "Thanks."

Inside, Anthony whispered while pointing up, "Quiet. I don't want to wake my landlord." He opened one of two doors and headed down a dimly lit flight of stairs. "Close the door behind you."

Craig closed the door, then followed Anthony down the stairs into a musty, messy studio apartment with concrete floors and pipes visible along the ceiling. The only light was from the TV that played in the background with the sound muted.

Craig had only been there once, when Anthony and Marie first moved there, when it was clean and empty. They had asked him to help fix a door and a few other little handy man type things. At the time, they had said they were going to get a cheap carpet to cover the floor.

Anthony joined Marie on the bed and said, "You can take the sofa."

Craig turned and noticed the sofa covered with clothes and junk.

"Just move some of that stuff and make yourself comfortable."

Craig cleared the musty sofa, then lied down.

Marie turned her head a little, but didn't open her eyes. "Who is it, baby?"

"I told you. It's your cousin, Craig." Anthony kissed her on the forehead. "Go back to sleep."

She smiled and turned. Craig noticed that she still had her tight sexy body, even after all those years of drug use. She could have had any man she wanted, but with her coke habit, she always ended up with losers.

Craig thought Anthony was a nice enough guy, but he was still an unemployed drug addict. Thank God he had his disability checks or he'd probably start pimping out Marie like her last boyfriend did.

As he closed his eyes, the light from the television flickered against the outside of his eyelids. Craig's mind drifted from trivial matters like his cousin's lifestyle, to more important matters, like the fact that he had just shot and may have killed two more human beings.

The harder he tried not to visualize every detail of his murderous escapades, the more vivid the visualizations appeared.

He listened to the light snoring of Marie and Anthony and wished he could sleep too.

A memory came to him, a memory that came to him often, but was even more realistic now that he and Marie were in the same room. When they were teenagers, they felt each other up. They touched each other everywhere. Craig was older and wanted to go all the way, but Marie told him she wanted to remain a virgin until marriage.

Craig usually had a hard time putting that memory out of his head when it arrived, but now it was easy, memories of murder quickly took over.

CHAPTER 57

Just as Victor got out of the shower, his phone rang. He wrapped the towel around his waist and raced into the bedroom, where he grabbed the phone from the nightstand and silenced the ringer.

Evelyn rolled over in bed, but it seemed she was still sleeping.

Victor went back into the bathroom, closed the door, and answered the call. "Hello."

A lieutenant from a Brooklyn precinct asked, "Detective Cohen?"

"Yes."

"This is Lieutenant Hodges from the six eight. Your captain said you wanted some information on a Craig Hill from Bay Ridge?"

"Yes. Thanks for getting back to me so soon."

"Well detective, I have a forensics team at Mr. Hill's apartment right now."

"Why? What happened to him?"

"We have no idea where Mr. Hill is, but we have two bodies in his apartment, both connected to organized crime in Manhattan and The Bronx."

"I'll be there as soon as I can."

Victor finished getting dressed and then kissed his wife before running out the door. A cab from Queens to Brooklyn would have been too expensive, and he knew he'd have a hard time getting reimbursed from the city, so he decided to take a cab to the G-train, which would take him into Brooklyn without having to go through Manhattan.

He called Rosie and told her where he was going and why.

The trip was not as fast as he'd hoped, but fortunately, he did get to Craig's apartment before the detectives left.

After showing his badge to get in the building, Victor met with a tall, thin, balding man who led him into the apartment: Detective Trawinsky.

The bodies were already gone.

Victor looked around at the wreckage and asked, "Any sign of Hill yet?"

Detective Trawinsky replied, "Nothing. Not at his mother's or either of his sisters'. Still trying to find out who his friends were, other than that stiff from Coney Island. Seems your hunch about this kid was right."

"So, you really think Hill killed two mafia guys on his own?"

"Don't know." Detective Trawinsky pointed at numbers written in chalk on the floor. "Shells were found there, and there. Seems he wasn't even in the apartment when he started firing. My guess is he walked in on the two Guidos ransacking the place and started shooting right away. The element of surprise could be a real bitch."

Victor nodded. Everything Detective Trawinsky said made sense. "Any idea what they were looking for?"

"It seems Hill was dealing. Along with a big chunk of cocaine, we found a couple hundred small bags and a digital scale with residue on it."

In his mind, Victor tried to piece together the evidence. Cocaine certainly seemed to play a big part in what was happening now. It didn't explain the dead heroin addict back at The Howell Building, but it did hint at what had happened in Coney Island.

Detective Trawinsky said, "Sorry Detective, but my partner and I have to get back to the house and put our reports in. Can I give you a lift somewhere?"

"Thanks, but my partner is on her way to pick me up. I'll fax you everything I have on my case later."

"Sounds good." Detective Trawinski shook Victor's hand then left the building.

Making sure to stay out of the way of the people brushing for fingerprints and sifting through the rubble for evidence, Victor looked around the small dirty apartment and wondered where Craig Hill could be hiding.

CHAPTER 58

Abby and her partner had been in their office for about an hour, both of them on their computers. Mangano worked on another case while Abby once again reviewed Victor's reports.

Abby's phone rang. It was Rosie Li. Abby answered, "Hello, Detective."

Rosie said, "Hello, Edmunds. Have you heard about Craig Hill?"

"No. Should I have?"

"Victor's hunch about him was right all along. He's at Hill's apartment right now. I'm on my way to pick him up. There's two dead bodies and Hill is missing."

Abby looked away from her computer screen and noticed Mangano listening to her conversation. She kept speaking with Rosie. "Maybe Hill and Cohen are collaborating."

Rosie said, "That's ridiculous and you know it."

Abby said, "Don't be fooled, Detective. The thief comes only to steal and kill and destroy. I have come that they may have life, and have it to the full."

Rosie laughed. "You really are fucked up in the head."

Abby straightened up in her chair. She didn't like this little bitch talking to her like this. "Excuse me? You had better show me a little respect. I can cause a great deal of trouble for you too, girly."

Mangano was no longer trying to hide the fact that he was

listening. He stared right at Abby, listening to every word she said.

Rosie said, "Fuck you, Edmunds. You need professional help. Goodbye."

Abby said, "Don't you dare hang up on me . . . Detective . . . Detective?" She threw her phone to the floor. "That little bitch hung up on me. Can you believe it?"

Mangano shrugged and went back to looking at his computer screen.

Abby picked up her phone, pocketed it, and stormed out of the room.

CHAPTER 59

Craig woke up sweating, arms flailing around.

Marie grabbed his shoulders and tried to stabilize him while saying, "Craig. You're okay. Craig. Craig."

His eyes adjusted to his surroundings and he realized he was still on Marie's sofa. He had been dreaming of murder and violence, as usual, and it felt so real.

Marie said, "You don't look so good, Cuz."

"Yeah, thanks." Craig rubbed his aching head and asked, "You got any Advil or anything for a headache?" Now, in the light of day he could tell how dirty the apartment really was. Much worse than his.

She stepped to the kitchenette against the far wall and opened a cabinet above the sink full of dirty dishes. She shook some pills inside of a little orange plastic bottle with the label torn off. "I got Vicoden."

"Vicoden? You trying to kill me?"

"Sorry, Cuz. I forgot."

Craig asked, "Where's Anthony?"

"He went to get cigarettes and coffee with the money you gave him. What the hell happened anyway? You in trouble or something?"

Craig said, "Some guys found out I have some coke and they tried to rip me off."

Marie looked excited. "You have coke?"

Craig heard footsteps coming down the basement stairs and then the door opened.

Anthony came in with a brown paper bag and set it on the counter. "Finally up? You were knocked out before."

"Really?" Craig knew he slept a little but he didn't feel like it was quality sleep. Maybe he did get some good sleep after all.

Anthony took a cup of coffee and a bagel out of the bag and handed them to Marie. He gave Craig a cup of coffee and a bagel and then took out his own.

Craig placed the bagel on the counter and sipped his coffee. "Thanks."

Before opening her bagel, Marie said, "So . . . what about that coke?"

Anthony swallowed the food that was already in his mouth and asked, "What coke?"

"I'm selling some coke for a friend. Some guys tried to rob me, but I got away."

Marie asked, "You have any with you?"

"Yeah." Craig sipped his coffee. "And I'm gonna give you a sample, but I'd like to finish my coffee first."

Marie's eyes became shifty and her body became fidgety.

After chewing and swallowing another chunk of his bagel, Anthony said, "He's right, baby. You should get something in your stomach. We haven't eaten all day."

She took her bagel and coffee to the sofa and turned the volume up on the TV, which was playing the theme song to a soap opera.

Craig still hadn't opened his bagel yet, but he was really enjoying the coffee.

Anthony asked, "So . . . what happened?"

"It's a long story." Craig placed his coffee on the counter and reached into his sweatshirt pocket, which he had slept in. "I need some bullets for a thirty-eight." He showed Anthony his revolver then slipped it back into his pocket and reached for his coffee.

"I'll call my brother. He could probably get it for you."

"Thanks." Craig unwrapped his bagel and ate it. He was unusually hungry, and instead of feeling sick, the food felt good in his stomach.

He and Anthony joined Marie on the sofa and finished their breakfast. Afterwards, Anthony and Marie lit up cigarettes.

Craig hadn't smoked in years, but he wanted one. "Can I have one?"

"A cigarette?" asked Marie. "I thought you didn't smoke."

"Fuck it now."

She laughed, lit a cigarette for him, and handed it to him. As Craig smoked, Marie asked, "You got any of that good weed? Like that shit you had when you fixed the door?"

"I wish I did." Craig took a deep hit of the menthol cigarette and held it in for a second before blowing out a cloud of smoke. He reached into his pocket and pulled out one of the five individual grams he'd bagged up the night before. "I do have some of this, though."

Marie smiled and said, "That'll do."

Anthony chuckled.

Craig handed it to Marie.

She asked, "How much a gram?"

"I want thirty. You can make whatever you want on it, though."

"Thirty dollars a gram? That's it?"

Anthony asked, "Why so cheap? Is it any good?"

"My friend wants to get rid of it fast. You wanna know if it's good? Try some."

Anthony reached under the sofa and pulled out a dirty mirror with a razor blade and straw on it. He handed the mirror to Marie.

Marie extinguished her cigarette and then opened the bag and emptied its contents onto the mirror. It was chalky, yellowish, and hard to crush. She chopped it up into a fine powder with the razor and then made six lines.

Craig began to salivate as he watched Marie put the straw to her nose and sniff one line up instantly. She tipped her head back and said, "Holy shit."

Anthony took the mirror from her and sniffed a line.

Craig wanted it, but at the same time, he didn't want it. It had been so many years, so much willpower wasted just to give up now. And, it was because of this exact shit that he was now sick and dying in the first place. But, he wanted it.

"Fuck it." Craig took the mirror when Anthony handed it to him. He sniffed the third of the six lines and then held his head back and waited for it to hit him. The blood rushed to his head while he lost control of his facial muscles.

He looked at his cigarette still burning in the ashtray, and wanted to reach for it, but he was frozen. His flesh tingled while his brain inflated.

Marie's mouth was already making funny movements when she reached over for the mirror. Craig handed it to her and then forced himself to reach out for his cigarette in the ashtray while Anthony lit another.

After sniffing her second line and handing the mirror to Anthony, Marie used the remote and turned off the TV.

Just as Anthony finished his second line, the doorbell rang.

Craig's heart almost exploded as his flesh tingled. He wanted to ask if they were expecting anyone, but he was too scared to speak, so he just looked at Anthony and Marie for some kind of answer.

They didn't move. They just sat there with their mouths wide open.

The bell rang again.

Craig's heart pounded harder. His body was paralyzed.

Darkness covered the only small window in the basement apartment.

Someone knocked on the glass.

CHAPTER 60

Victor drove the gray unmarked car while Rosie sat in the passenger seat looking out the window. He had convinced her to spend a little time in Brooklyn looking for Craig Hill, even though it wasn't their case. She agreed, but only if they got back to their own case right after lunch, which they just finished eating.

"We really should get back to The Bronx and look for Nelson Kelley. There are plenty of other people already looking for Hill, and you did say only until lunch."

"I know, but they probably don't know about his cousin Marie. I just got her address from a narc here in Brooklyn. We worked together for a while in The Bronx." Victor showed Rosie the text message on his phone.

"Okay. But, if we don't find him there, we go to The Bronx."

"I promise." He turned the corner, pulled over, and double-parked in front of a two-story brick house on a quiet tree-lined residential street.

They both got out of the car.

Rosie stood on the sidewalk while watching the driveway next to the house.

Victor approached the front door and rang the basement doorbell. He waited a minute, but no one answered. He rang again. Still, no one answered. Victor rang the first floor doorbell and waited another minute.

Finally, he approached the basement window, squatted down,

and knocked on the glass. No one answered.

Rosie came toward him and said, “No one here.”

“Okay. Let’s get outta here.”

They got back into the car and headed toward the highway.

Victor said, “I’m gettin’ tired of these goose chases.”

“It wouldn’t be so bad if we stuck to one goose chase at a time.”

Victor wondered why it was so hard finding a couple amateurs like Craig Hill and Nelson Kelley. Where the hell were they hiding?

CHAPTER 61

Whoever had been at the door earlier had left a long time ago, but Craig, Anthony, and Marie stayed high and stuck to the sofa for a few more hours. They had done two more grams after the first one, then spent a couple hours smoking cigarettes and coming down.

Finally, after they were back to normal, Anthony opened a second pack of cigarettes and produced a half-empty package of cookies from a kitchen cabinet.

While all three of them devoured the cookies, Anthony's phone rang.

He looked at it and said, "My brother." He answered the phone and said, "John. What's up?" He listened for a moment, then said, "Okay. Hold on." Anthony turned to Craig and said, "He has twenty five bullets for fifty dollars."

Marie asked, "Bullets?"

Craig knew the price was steep, but he had no other choices. "I'll take it."

Marie looked at Craig, but Craig didn't say anything.

Anthony spoke into the phone. "Yeah. Where are you?" He listened for a moment and then said, "Okay. Okay. I'll see you in a few." He hung up, put his phone away, then told Craig, "He doesn't want to meet anyone. He wants me to go outside and take a ride around the block in his car."

Craig wondered for a moment if Anthony was trying to rip

him off, but he knew that he probably wasn't. He counted out fifty dollars from the money he had gotten from Allen and handed it to Anthony. "Ask your brother if he can get me anything else. I prefer revolvers because I'm not so good with guns, but I'll take whatever he can get."

Marie lit another cigarette and asked, "What? Are you going to war?"

Craig said, "Just watching my ass."

As Anthony turned for the door, Craig said, "Oh, and don't tell him about the coke yet. I still have to pick up more tomorrow."

CHAPTER 62

Instead of his favorite table in the back, Enzo sat at the bar, near the front door, and sipped a glass of wine. His phone rang. He was expecting the call. It was Sammy.

He left the bar and strolled down the street while answering the call and hoping Sammy was smart enough not to say anything incriminating over the phone.

"Enzo. I've been looking for our friend everywhere, but I can't find him."

Enzo knew Sammy was talking about Craig Hill, and he knew Sammy was smart enough to figure that Enzo was talking about Detective Cohen when he asked, "Our other friend couldn't find him either?"

Sammy responded, "Nope. Nothing."

Enzo said, "Two other friends went to look for him, but they ran into trouble."

"I know," said Sammy. "I saw."

Enzo stopped on the corner, turned around, and started back toward the bar.

Sammy asked, "What did Peppino say?"

"He said he can give you one more day, but no more than that. He wants his first payment tomorrow."

"I don't have that kind of money."

"Then you better keep looking for our friend."

"And if I can't find him?"

Before Enzo stepped out of the heat and into the air-conditioned bar for another drink, he said, "You better find him, or it could mean both of our asses."

CHAPTER 63

Still at Anthony and Marie's, Craig offered to order a pizza and give them some more coke if they let him stay the night. Of course, they agreed.

Craig called his mother and told her he was in trouble. She cried and he knew she was hurting, but he knew she would have to go through this soon anyways, if he wasn't able to come up with the transplant money.

He had the bullets in his pocket, but left the gun empty.

They ate the pizza, then sniffed the last of what Craig had on him.

After a few hours and a few Vicoden—Craig only took half a pill—Craig, Marie, and Anthony finally calmed down and drifted away to sleep.

Craig slept in his clothes on the sofa again. The only thing he removed was his shoes, but he first made sure to keep his safe deposit box key deep inside his pants pocket.

Anthony and Marie had said he could shower there, but he declined.

CHAPTER 64

The next morning, Victor knew Rosie wouldn't agree to more time looking for Craig Hill, but he wanted to try Craig's cousin Marie's house one more time.

He called Rosie. She sounded like she was still asleep. "Sorry to call so early, but I need to ask you something."

Rosie yawned, then said, "Ask away."

"Remember how yesterday you mentioned how quickly we got from Brooklyn to The Bronx because it was after rush hour?"

Rosie said, "Yeah, but I also said I don't want to spend any more time looking for Hill because it's taking time away from our own case. Remember that part?"

"Yeah. How about if I make one more stop at his cousin's in Brooklyn, you pick me up, and then we head to The Bronx. I'll be the only one wasting time. Anyway, it's better than both of us sitting in traffic going uptown."

"I don't like the idea."

"You say the word and I'll forget the whole thing, but I'd hate to see Hill get away. I know the cops in Brooklyn are on it, but I also know they're swamped."

Rosie sighed, then said, "I'll see you in Brooklyn."

"Thanks." Victor hung up.

He kissed his wife and baby while they slept and then headed out the door while the sun began to rise and illuminate a cloudy sky.

Once in Brooklyn, he approached the house and then decided not to knock on the door. Stepping toward the basement window, but being careful not to step in front of it, Victor bent over partially and listened.

A few people walking by on the sidewalk glanced over at him, but didn't say anything. Victor didn't want to draw attention to himself, so he ignored the passersby. If they stopped or said anything, he would flash his badge.

Yesterday, Victor had the feeling someone was inside. He didn't know if they were hiding Craig, or if they were just paranoid because of drugs, but he definitely had a feeling that someone was in there.

Just as he was about to walk away and call Rosie to see where she was, he heard a toilet flush in the basement. Someone was there.

Instead of ringing the doorbell and alerting them to his presence, Victor decided to go across the street and wait in front of the deli on the corner. He wasn't sure what his next move would be, but he knew he couldn't wait forever, so he called Rosie to find out where she was. "Hey. I'm here. I'm pretty sure someone's there. I heard a toilet flush. Where are you?"

"Just left the precinct. Right now I'm gassing up the car, which is customarily a man's job . . . and don't tell me about women's rights again."

"I'll make it up to you."

"Oh really? How?"

"I'll buy lunch again today."

"Keep this up and you'll be buying me lunch until I collect my pension."

Victor chuckled and then said, "Text me when you get off the expressway."

"You got it."

He hung up the phone and hurried into the deli for a cup of coffee. The smell of bacon hit him right in the face. A bacon, egg, and cheese sandwich would have really hit the spot, but he didn't want to take the chance of missing Marie, or maybe even her cousin Craig.

While waiting for the old Italian man behind the counter to make his coffee, Victor waited in the doorway and kept his eyes on the house across the street. When the coffee was ready, he asked for a blueberry muffin, paid the man, then hurried back outside.

Standing on the corner, Victor scarfed down the muffin, then began to sip the coffee. His stomach was no longer empty, but he still wanted that sandwich.

He kept looking at the time on his phone, hoping that Rosie would hit heavy traffic. He planned to wait in front of the deli in case someone came out of the house across the street. If no one showed their face by the time Rosie arrived, he would ring the bell again.

Twenty minutes passed and Victor had to pee. He wished he hadn't drank that coffee. The thought of using the bathroom in the deli occurred to him. If the old man refused him, he would just show his badge. But, he knew that within that short period of time, he could miss someone coming out of Marie's house.

Victor tried not to think about his full bladder while checking the time on his phone again and unwrapping a stick of gum.

The morning had been cool, but now the heat and humidity once again began to rise.

Another fifteen minutes passed and Rosie still hadn't texted yet, so he knew he still had some time. He was just about to give up and go into the deli to use the bathroom when he spotted someone coming out of the house across the street, a girl who fit the description of Marie Reina, slim and short with long dark hair.

With her greasy, matted hair tied into a ponytail, Marie strolled across the street wearing a pair of tattered pajama bottoms and a tiny tank top. Victor temporarily found himself hypnotized by her perfectly round breasts and firm round butt cheeks.

He watched as she headed straight toward him and then into the deli without paying any attention to him.

Victor followed her inside and waited while she ordered two egg sandwiches from the Mexican man at the grill.

"I see you're ordering two sandwiches there."

"Yeah? So what of it? My boyfriend's gotta eat, too."

"Your boyfriend? What's his name?"

"None of your fucking business, pal. That's what his name is. Now fuck off before I tell him you're bothering me."

"Take it easy, Marie."

Her eyes widened.

Just as she was about to say something, Victor said, "I thought the other sandwich might be for your cousin Craig."

She hesitated, then said, I haven't seen Craig in months. Who the fuck are you anyway? A cop or something?"

He showed his badge. "Homicide detective, Victor Cohen."

The man behind the counter finished wrapping the two sandwiches then handed them to Marie. She brought the sandwiches to the old Italian man at the register and waited for him to ring her up.

Victor put his badge away, then handed Marie his business card. "Please call me if you do hear from him."

She took his card, but didn't say anything.

Victor's phone buzzed. It was a text from Rosie saying that she had just gotten off the expressway.

He walked out of the deli and stood on the corner while Marie passed him, crossed the street, and entered the house through the side door at the end of the driveway. He looked at her perfectly round ass one more time and remembered how firm and beautiful Jennifer's ass was.

After about fifteen minutes, Rosie pulled up. Victor got in the car and began to tell her about his encounter with Marie.

Victor noticed a man coming out of the house across the street. "Look there."

"Doesn't fit Hill's description."

"No." Replied Victor. "But it does fit the description of Maries' boyfriend. I guess she was telling the truth about that other sandwich."

Rosie said, "You know, traffic was hell getting here."

"Well, in that case, what do you say we visit Hill's doctor while the rush hour traffic dies down?"

Rosie sighed, then said, "If I wasn't so fed up with sitting in traffic . . ."

"Is that a yes?"

She started the car and asked, "Where's the doctor?"

"Seventh Avenue. Not sure exactly where. Let me check." Victor checked the map on his phone since he didn't know his way around Brooklyn.

They drove to a hospital in Park Slope, an area where the hundred-year-old brownstone houses looked as if they had just been built yesterday.

Victor went inside alone while Rosie waited in the car. After using the restroom, he found a receptionist who told him that Dr.

Zimmerman had an emergency and had just left to the hospital. Victor was happy to find out that the hospital was only a block away.

He and Rosie both entered the hospital. This time, Rosie had to use the restroom.

Victor located Dr. Zimmerman and waited outside a hospital room while the doctor spoke with a big red-haired woman. A seven-year-old girl with blondish-red pigtails and yellow skin lay unconscious on the bed with wires and tubes connected to her.

When the doctor finally left the room, Victor showed his badge and introduced himself. "I'd like to ask you a few questions about Craig Hill."

"As long it doesn't violate his rights as my patient, I'll answer whatever questions I can, Detective."

"When was the last time you saw him?"

"I saw him Saturday in my office."

"Did he act any different than usual?"

"That boy is always unusual." The doctor chuckled. "He did ask quite a few questions about Deanna there." He pointed at the room with the little girl inside.

"What kind of questions?"

"Uh . . . He asked how old she was. He asked how long she had to live. I actually felt that he had a genuine sympathy for her."

"Isn't that sweet," Replied Victor. "Well doctor, I'd like to question him about a couple of homicides. Do you have any idea where I could find him?"

"Homicide? Dear God. Was he involved?"

"I can't say. Just that I need to speak with him. When is he scheduled to see you next?"

"You would have to ask my receptionist. It would be at least two weeks or more though, I did just see him."

Victor gave the doctor his card. "Please call me if he contacts you . . . or if you think of any place I might be able to find him."

CHAPTER 65

Craig had slept hard, but he was still able to get up early. He'd left Marie's apartment while her and Anthony were still sleeping. The sun wasn't even out yet.

He headed to a drug store where he bought a bottle of Advil and some water for his pounding headache, then called his boss and said he was very sick and needed a few days off.

By the time the sun did come out, clouds covered most of the sky and it smelled as if it wanted to rain. The humidity increased by the minute.

Craig thought about going to the safe deposit box first, but then decided to go see his mother first. He needed a shower and the attention that only his mother could give him.

He took two trains, and then while turning the corner onto his mother's block, he noticed a cop car double-parked a few houses away from his parents' house. The cops could have been there for him, or they could have been there for some other reason, but he wasn't taking any chances.

Craig went back to the train station and headed toward the bank.

The tellers and managers at their desks glanced over at Craig as he headed toward the safe deposit boxes in the back. He knew he looked like a bum, he just hoped he didn't smell like one, too.

Luckily, the fat gay man in the back remembered him and didn't give him a hard time.

Craig didn't even count the money he'd stuffed into the backpack. He kept a thousand dollars in his pocket for hotels, taxis, food, and clothes, then left the bank with another kilo, plus the three quarters of a kilo he'd left in there on Monday.

Even with a loaded 38 in his pocket, Craig didn't feel comfortable walking around with that much money and drugs.

On his way to Marie's place, drizzle began to fall, then quickly turned into a light but steady rain. He tried to pick up the pace.

When he was about a block away from Marie's apartment, he called her. While the phone rang, he wondered if the cops or anyone else could tap his line.

Marie answered, "Craig. Where are you?"

"I'm on my way."

"Hurry up. Anthony's waiting for you."

"I'm down the block. Wait for me at the side door."

Craig hurried to Marie's where he found Anthony outside waiting with an umbrella.

Inside, Anthony opened a shoebox and showed Craig a sawed-off double-barrel shotgun that came with about a hundred colorful bullets. "My brother said he doesn't know anyone with revolvers. He could get nine millimeters, but those are automatics, and they're expensive, and he'd need the money up front."

Marie lit a cigarette then sat on the sofa and turned on the TV.

Anthony continued, "My brother had this laying around, said he'll let the whole package go for two hundred."

Craig wondered how much of that two hundred Anthony was taking for himself. He'd asked for a revolver, but secretly was hoping for an automatic, even though he didn't know how to use one. "How much are the nine millimeters?"

Anthony said, "Five fifty."

Craig figured the fifty was for Anthony, but that didn't matter. He didn't feel comfortable looking for guns anywhere else. He counted out two hundred dollars and gave it to Anthony. "This is for the shotgun. Tell your brother I'll want one of those nines for next week."

From the sofa, Marie said, "I better not see you on the news, Cuz!"

Craig chuckled while placing the lid onto the shoebox.

He thought about all the shit in his pants and sweatshirt pockets and then looked again at the shoebox and realized he needed something better.

Craig asked, "You got a backpack or gym bag or something you could sell me?"

Anthony said, "No. Not really?"

Marie said, "What about that luggage set your mother gave you?"

"I can't sell a gift from my mother."

"Where the fuck you gonna go? Aruba? Sell him the small bag and keep the big and medium bags. She'll never know."

Anthony turned to Craig and asked, "How much?"

Craig pulled out the three quarter brick of cocaine.

Anthony's mouth dropped open. "Holy shit."

"What?" Marie asked from the next room.

They both ignored her.

Craig broke a small chunk off the corner. It didn't look like much compared to the rest of the brick, but it was at least an eight ball. Worth a hell of a lot more than part of a luggage set.

Marie came over and saw the rock on the kitchen counter. "Very nice." She turned to Anthony and said, "Go get that luggage."

She turned back to Craig and said, "You can stay here again tonight if you want, Cuz."

"Thanks. But, I have to sell some of this shit before I sniff it all. I'm supposed to be doing this to make enough money for my liver transplant."

Anthony came in the room with a set of luggage, three pieces, each with wheels.

Craig pointed at the carry-on sized bag and said, "I'll take the medium one."

"You got it." Anthony handed Craig the bag.

Craig placed the shoebox into the bag and zipped it up.

"Oh shit." Marie opened a kitchen drawer and pulled out a business card. "I forgot to tell you. A detective came around this morning looking for you." She handed him the card.

Craig took it and said, "You forgot?"

Anthony said, "Very fucking nice, Marie."

Marie replied, "Fuck you, Anthony."

Craig glanced at the card and read, Victor Cohen. NYPD. Detective.

Marie placed her hand on Craig's wrist and said, "I'm sorry,

Cuz."

"Don't worry about it." Craig slipped the card into his pocket and said, "I gotta go. I'll call you tomorrow." He kissed Marie on the cheek, shook Anthony's hand, and then headed outside into the rain with his new luggage.

CHAPTER 66

Holding his umbrella overhead to block the rain, Enzo was on his cell phone speaking with Sammy. Sammy couldn't make his first payment. Peppino said Johnny would be coming after him tomorrow, but not to kill him, because dead men can't pay.

While Sammy spoke on the other end of the phone, trying to figure out ways to convince Peppino for more time, Enzo's mind drifted. He wondered how badly Johnny was going to hurt Sammy. He felt pity for Sammy, but at the same time, he was worried about his own ass.

A gust of wind blew. Enzo held on tight to his umbrella while the rain got heavier. He wanted to get back into the bar and finish his drink. He interrupted Sammy's rambling, "Sammy. Listen to me."

Sammy stopped talking.

After a moment of silence, Enzo said, "I'm not guaranteeing it, but if you do find the coke, or enough money to make a payment, Peppino might let you off the hook temporarily. The truth is, he'd rather have the cash than the bloodshed."

"In the meantime, I can't go home? I can't see my family?"

"No. You can't." Enzo adjusted the angle of his umbrella when the wind direction changed. "But if you do like I tell you, you might have a chance. It's better than running forever . . . then you'll never see them."

There was silence on the line.

"Sammy? You there?"

"I'm here."

"Just keep trying kid. Your best bet is to keep looking for our friend. Got it?"

Sammy said, "Yeah."

"And Sammy . . . we never spoke."

CHAPTER 67

After leaving Brooklyn, Victor and Rosie drove to The Bronx with their lights on and their windshield wipers running.

They had spent the entire rainy afternoon searching in vain for Nelson Kelley or anyone who knew him, then headed back to their precinct in Manhattan to fill out paperwork.

Just as Victor and Rosie were about to leave for the night, Captain Morelli approached and said, "A member of the Morris Park gang was just picked up on his third sales charge."

Victor and Rosie looked at each other.

The captain said, "I'll put in the overtime paperwork."

Victor and Rosie headed back out into the rain and up to The Bronx where they questioned the young punk who was more than willing to make a deal to save his ass. He told them that Nelson Kelley was staying in a motel in a small city in Westchester County under his girlfriend's name.

Not wanting to step on any toes, Victor called Captain Morelli, who contacted the cops in Westchester. They picked up Nelson Kelley and held him until Victor and Rosie arrived.

Victor knew the Westchester cops had searched Nelson's hotel room without a warrant, so whatever they found in the room would probably be inadmissible in court. He knew it would be a shame for Nelson to go free, but at least he would be in custody long enough to grill him about his brother and the dead Hawaiian shirt guys.

After taking the highway north out of the city and then carefully following a long dark road through a quiet residential neighborhood with their windshield wipers and high beams on, they parked outside the suburban police station and hurried inside to get out of the rain.

The small-town police captain showed Victor and Rosie everything that his men had confiscated from Nelson's hotel room: a quarter of an ounce of coke, a little weed, and an unregistered 9mm with the serial numbers filed off. The girlfriend wasn't there.

The captain then led Victor and Rosie down the stairs to the basement where there were three large cells and one cop behind a desk.

Victor was surprised at how immaculate everything in the precinct was. Even the holding cells looked freshly scrubbed.

The captain stayed at the desk with his officer as Victor and Rosie approached the bars.

A short man with a chubby face, slicked back blonde hair, and a pencil-thin beard sat on a concrete bench in one cell while a drunken old bum slept on the floor in the next cell, snoring like a chainsaw and reeking of alcohol.

Rosie said, "You must be Nelson."

The short man spoke with a raspy voice, "You must be that hooker I ordered. I thought I said no chinks."

Victor knew Rosie was holding back her anger. He'd seen her hold it back many times, but she had never lost it. He almost hoped that she would lose her temper, just to see what she'd do. Victor stepped closer to the bars and said, "It's small towns like this where the cops get away with beating their prisoners."

"Whatever." Nelson turned toward the bum sleeping in the next cell and yelled, "Shut the fuck up!"

The bum stopped snoring, coughed, and turned on his side.

Just as Nelson sat back down, the bum rolled over onto his back and began snoring again. Nelson held his head and yelled, "Motherfucker!"

Rosie laughed.

Victor said, "You wanna get outta here for a while?"

"Forever would be nice."

Victor approached the small-town captain and asked, "Is there anywhere else we can question him? It's impossible to hear anything with that bum snoring in the next cell."

The captain chuckled and said, "You can use my office. But he stays cuffed at all times."

Victor nodded.

The small-town captain told the deputy at the desk, "Get him out."

The cop opened the cell and cuffed Nelson's hands behind his back while Victor and Rosie stood out of arm's reach.

The captain and his deputy escorted Victor, Rosie, and Nelson up the stairs and into his office.

While the captain helped Nelson sit on one of four chairs, Victor looked around at the polished tile floor and comfortable new furniture. He wondered about the salary of these small-town cops. The thought of moving his family away from the city had occurred to him many times in the past, and now he was thinking about it again.

The sound of Rosie's voice interrupted Victor's thought.

She said, "Tell us about Chris."

Victor and the captain waited silently for Nelson's response. He didn't speak, but he didn't have to. It seemed as if his mind drifted away while liquid filled his eyes.

That's when Victor realized that Chris Kelley was one of the Hawaiian shirt guys. It was like finally figuring out where that one pain in the ass puzzle piece went. "We need your help if you want to find out who killed him."

Rosie and the small-town captain both turned and looked at Victor.

Nelson said, "You got some set of *huevos*. You motherfuckers killed him, and then you robbed him. Don't tell me you didn't get a cut." He wiped the tears from his eyes.

Before Victor could speak again, Rosie spoke.

She said, "The cops didn't take the coke and you know it. Tell us the truth."

Nelson wiped his eyes again and said, "That is the fucking truth, you rat cops!"

The small-town captain said, "If you don't settle down, I'm going to be forced to get out my Taser. You ever been tased before, son? You wouldn't like it."

Victor wondered how Rosie knew there was coke involved and why she didn't tell him.

Rosie said, "As you already know, only one cop made it out

alive, and we know for a fact that he didn't take it."

"You better check again, cause we don't have it."

Rosie told the captain. "You can take him back downstairs. Thanks for your help."

"Not a problem." The small-town captain turned to Nelson and said, "Back to your cage, boy." He took Nelson out of his office and down the stairs.

Victor turned to Rosie and asked, "What the fuck?"

"Let's talk in the car."

Victor followed Rosie out of the precinct, through the rain, and into their gray car parked in the parking lot outside. He sat in the passenger seat and glared at Rosie.

"I'm sorry. Abby Edmunds ordered me not to tell you."

Victor knew she did the right thing by following orders. She could have lost her job if she didn't. However, he still felt a bit betrayed. He would have told her.

Rosie continued, "She called me up asking if I noticed anything strange about your behavior. She told me that the Dominicans were robbed of four kilos and now nobody knows where it is."

"That bitch accused me of stealing four kilos?"

"Not exactly."

"Then what?"

"She never said anything outright. I think she was throwing hints, trying to get me to talk bad about you."

Victor said, "Craig Hill."

"What?"

"Craig Hill. He was there. He probably took the drugs. Maybe he and the junkie found the drugs together. Maybe Hill killed the junkie rather than split his find with him. Hill hasn't been to work since Tuesday."

Rosie said, "It could make sense."

"And, I bet that Hill and that old carpenter tried selling the shit in Coney Island, but got robbed. Hill got away, but his buddy wasn't so lucky."

Rosie said, "So that means he still has the coke."

Victor slipped a stick of gum into his mouth and said, "He must."

"What about the two dead guys in his apartment?"

"Well, they weren't Dominican or Irish. They were Italian,

and connected. I don't know. Maybe they were trying to shake him down?"

"Didn't you say they left almost a quarter of a kilo of coke that they found?"

"That's true." Victor tried to put the rest of the puzzle together in his head.

Rosie said, "Your theory about Craig Hill makes sense. But, what about the seventh gun? There's a very good chance someone else was there."

"And that someone may have taken the drugs."

Rosie started the car and let the engine run while the wipers cleared the rain from the windshield. She looked at Victor and said, "I'm sorry I didn't tell you."

"You followed orders. Don't be sorry."

CHAPTER 68

All day, Craig had fought the urge to sniff more coke. He knew he needed a clear head for business, and was especially worried now that a detective was looking for him. And, in addition to making his liver worse, he was spending his profits.

After leaving Marie's apartment, he had stopped at a clothing store to buy a new outfit and an umbrella. His new clothes looked just like his old clothes, jeans, T-shirt, and a sweatshirt. He didn't want to waste time looking for new sneakers when the ones he was wearing were only a few months old.

With his new clothes in a bag, Craig took a car service to a cheap hotel about ten blocks away from Sunset Park. The Chinese owned and operated hotel was brand new, but already worn down. While checking in under a fake name, he wondered and hoped that the place didn't have bed bugs. The hotel rented most of its rooms by the hour, so Craig got a small discount when he paid for two full nights in advance.

As soon as he got to his room, he showered in the somewhat-clean bathroom, changed his clothes, and then went outside for something to eat and some shopping.

The sun had disappeared completely and streetlights illuminated the neighborhood. Craig opened his umbrella and thanked God that the rain was much lighter now.

Fortunately, many of the stores in the area stayed open late, especially the store that sold the things he was looking for. Craig bought a new digital scale, a thousand small jewelry bags, and two slices of pizza, all of which he took back to his room.

After eating, he got everything organized. He measured and bagged up three hundred individual grams. He loaded both guns and kept the extra bullets in the shoebox inside the luggage along with the coke and money. He pushed the luggage deep under the bed so that no one would be able to see it unless they bent over and looked directly under it.

The shotgun stayed under the mattress. The revolver as well as his safe deposit box key, stayed with him at all times.

With eighty grams, his umbrella, and his 38, Craig left the room and walked eight blocks in the rain to the Irish pub where he'd met the guys from work two days earlier. They had been calling him since then, and he finally got back to them and told them to meet him at the same place.

They brought a couple new people with them. Everyone sat at tables in the back and had a beer. Craig remembered the delicious burger he'd had the last time he was here, but he was full from the pizza.

He sold out. All eighty grams. He wished he'd brought more, but wasn't in the mood to make another trip. He was exhausted and wanted to get some rest. He told the guys he'd be back at the bar tomorrow with more.

On his way out, Craig opened his umbrella and began walking.

A man jumped in front of him. Craig stopped.

The man held a knife up and said, "Give it up."

"Give what up?" Asked Craig while looking around to see if there was anyone who could help, but it was late, and the streets were quiet due to the rain.

"I saw you in there. Everyone giving you money. I don't care what you were selling. I just want all that money." His words and breath were accented with alcohol.

"Okay. Don't stab me." Craig didn't remember the man. There were a few guys drinking at the bar, but they looked like they belonged there, so he didn't pay any attention. He felt like a fool for not keeping his eyes open.

Someone strolled along the sidewalk on the opposite side of the street. The man with the knife must have seen Craig look, because he also turned to look.

Craig stepped back, away from the knife, and reached into his pocket for his gun.

By the time the man turned back to Craig, Craig had the revolver pointed directly at the man's face. "Get the fuck outta here."

The man lowered the knife to his side, then waddled down the block.

Craig hurried a block and a half to a car service, which he then took to his hotel room.

His cell phone kept ringing, and knew he could make a lot more money tonight, but he just didn't have the strength, so he silenced the ringer.

With his safe deposit box key in his pocket and his revolver under the pillow, Craig removed his shoes and lay down on the bed with his clothes on.

He closed his eyes and fell asleep instantly.

It had only been a couple hours before the sound of a man and woman yelling at each other woke him up.

Craig got out of bed, used the bathroom, then lit a cigarette from the pack he'd bought when he was outside earlier. He smoked by the window while listening to the loud lovers quarrel. He thought about the coke and again fought the urge to touch it.

He lay down on the bed with his eyes open as the man and woman finished arguing. Finally, when the yelling stopped, he closed his eyes and hoped for sleep while trying to ignore the sound of rain against the window outside.

Between visions of murder, Craig was haunted by the memory of himself getting high.

After a couple hours of tossing and turning, unable to sleep, Craig finally gave up. He broke a chunk off the brick, chopped it up, and sniffed a nice big line. The cocaine entered his bloodstream and heightened his senses.

CHAPTER 69

Victor had gotten home before dawn while his wife was still asleep.

After a quick shower, he crawled up next to her in bed, kissed her, and closed his eyes.

The captain on duty had told him and Rosie to take half a day off, partly as a reward for uncovering the conspiracy, and partly to offset the overtime costs. Victor didn't complain. He needed the rest.

He had taken a Percocet before his shower and now he was ready to drift away into a peaceful slumber.

Evelyn's body felt good against his. He wanted to wake her up and ravage her, but he knew he would never get the rest he needed, and he still had to go into the precinct for a half day of paperwork.

While trying to figure out where the two dead Italian guys fit into the puzzle, and what happened to the seventh gun, Victor fell asleep.

CHAPTER 70

All day yesterday, Abby and her partner set up and arrested a couple cops in Queens for taking payoffs. The sting was a success, but Abby didn't care . . . all she really wanted was Victor Cohen.

Today, first thing in the morning, upon arriving at her office, Abby should have been working on her official caseload, but she wasn't, she was looking into Victor again.

Her partner knew what she was doing, but he kept his mouth shut. Abby wondered if it was out of respect for a senior officer or out of fear of a big black woman.

Abby reviewed the arrest and interrogation reports of Nelson Kelley and of the man who led them to Nelson Kelley. She then looked into Craig Hill and wondered what the connection was between him and the two dead mafia connected men in his apartment.

She was frustrated because it appeared more and more as if Victor Cohen was not involved.

Somehow, Victor's hunch about Hill was right, and she hated the fact that he was an excellent detective. It would have been nice if Cohen and Hill really were in this together, but she knew that wasn't the case. That would have been too easy.

Now what? How could she get Victor? Just wait and hope that pill popping creep slips up enough to order a drug test? That wasn't enough for Abby. She wanted a sure thing.

She decided to follow Victor and Rosie as much as she could

on her own time. She would have to tell her mother that she was working overtime.

CHAPTER 71

Victor and Rosie filed all their paperwork, then Victor explained his theory about Craig Hill to Captain Morelli. Rosie didn't say anything.

Morelli said, "Sounds logical, and we will look into it. But first, I want that seventh gun. You two better get back upstate and question Nelson Kelley again before that fancy lawyer gets him out."

Victor said, "How can we be sure the seventh gun is not at The Howell Building? There are a lot of hiding places."

Morelli replied, "We'd have to rip all the sheetrock off the walls. We'd have to—"

Victor interrupted. "The sheetrock. That's where the coke was."

Rosie said, "I thought you were talking about the gun."

The captain rubbed his temples.

Victor said, "Remember that hole in the sheetrock . . . the one that I said didn't look right?"

Rosie said, "Yeah. I remember."

Morelli asked, "Anyone gonna tell me why the hell we're talking about sheetrock now?"

Victor said, "I found a hole in the wall that looked like it was broken instead of cut. Chris Kelley could have stuffed the drugs into the wall before the cops got in the building."

Rosie added, "And you think Hill found it."

"Maybe they were watching," Replied Victor. "Hill and the junkie watched everything go down, then after everyone left, they broke the wall to get the drugs out."

Morelli continued Victor's sentence. "Then Hill got greedy, killed the junkie, and kept all four kilos to himself."

Victor said, "His doctor said he needs a transplant and some heavy duty treatment that he can't afford. He didn't make enough hours for medical insurance during the past couple years because of all the days he called in sick."

Rosie said, "Sounds like a catch twenty-two. Poor guy."

"Poor guy? Look how many people he's killed."

Captain Morelli said, "Take it easy. Your theory might make sense, but that don't mean it's true. I want you two to get back upstate. I'll talk to the guys in Brooklyn about your theory . . . and I'll send someone with a metal detector back to The Howell Building, but I can only authorize them to do the first floor."

Victor said, "I wonder if Hill saw the man with the seventh gun."

Rosie said, "There were no shells from the seventh gun inside the building."

"You two can talk about this while driving upstate."

Victor asked, "What about that info you said you had for us?"

"Oh Yeah. See, you and your theories. You made me forget what I was going to say." Captain Morelli retrieved a document from his desk and handed it to them. "Custom's records. Three men from Northern Ireland entered the country a couple days before the shooting. All three passports were fakes. Good fakes."

Victor said, "Sure. That's IRA territory."

Rosie laughed.

Morelli rubbed his temples again. "No more theories, please. Just find out who was using that seventh gun."

CHAPTER 72

Craig had slept all morning after blowing his mind out the night before. He woke up after twelve, but got ready quickly.

The bank was his first order of business. He dropped off most of the money he'd made and took the third kilo from the safe deposit box.

He thought about his mother and what she was going through. He wanted to call her, but he couldn't stand to hear her cry again. It would be better to wait and call her with good news.

After a couple hours of bagging up hundreds of individual grams in his hotel room, Craig became so good at it, he almost didn't need the scale.

With his revolver and enough individual bags to send him to prison for many years, he called a car service, which got there in about five minutes.

He went to Marie's first. She and Anthony were buying grams from Craig at thirty dollars each and reselling them for forty. She also had a couple friends there who wanted some.

Marie told Craig to be careful. She told him that a Dominican kid came around asking for Craig Hill.

Craig was tempted to stay and get high with them, especially since one of Marie's friends was a sexy little thing.

He didn't stay though. His cousin Allen was waiting for him, then he had to go back to the room and get more stuff to meet the guys from work. He got rid of almost thirty grams at Marie's and then called another car service, which took him to Allen's.

Craig got out of the car and waited about a half hour for Allen to pull up in his car.

"Sorry. I left early, but traffic was hell."

Sitting on the steps in front of Allen's building, Craig stood and approached the car.

Allen said, "Jump in. I gotta park this thing."

Craig got in and Allen started cruising the block.

"I got some friends that want some of that stuff. I hope you brought extra."

"How many do you want?"

Allen stopped at a red light and waited. "All together? I'll take thirty."

Craig took out his stash and began to count out thirty grams. Allen watched Craig count the coke even as the light changed. A car behind them beeped the horn. Allen looked up and stepped on the gas.

They circled the block again while Craig handed Allen the drugs and Allen gave Craig the money.

Allen said, "Don't turn your head, but do you remember I told you about some Dominican guy looking for you last night?"

"Yeah?" Craig didn't move his head but looked as far as he could with just his eyes.

"He just got out of that car."

Craig still tried to see what Allen was talking about without looking around. "Where? What car?"

"That little white Toyota double-parked up there."

Craig saw the car Allen was talking about.

Allen stayed back, double-parked on the same side of the street.

A thin Dominican man with a goatee and earring approached the Toyota and got in.

Craig said, "I gotta find out who he is. He was asking for me at my cousin Marie's."

"Marie? I haven't seen her in years. I'd like to get a look at her now."

Craig saw the brake lights on the Toyota light up. "Lend me your car."

"Are you crazy?"

Craig pulled about a dozen more grams from his pocket and

held them out to Allen. "Rental fee."

The Toyota pulled out into the street, but stopped behind a few other cars at the red light.

Craig said, "Come on. Hurry."

Allen took the coke and jumped out of the car. "If you fuck it up, you fix it. I know you got the money."

Craig slid into the driver's seat and pulled up behind the Toyota. Not only did he have to worry about fucking up and paying for Allen's car, he had to worry about the guy he was following spotting him. Craig had no idea who he was, but if the guy knew where Craig's cousins lived, then he was obviously a threat.

The light changed and he followed the car to the highway. It had been a long time since he had driven, but he always kept his license up to date, just in case. It felt good. It came back as soon as he grabbed the wheel and stepped on the gas.

Traffic was heavy, and the Toyota was easy to spot, so he was able to keep an eye on the car without having to stay right on his ass. Craig didn't have a plan, and he didn't even know why he was following the guy.

His phone rang a few times as he followed the Toyota into Queens and then toward the Triborough Bridge. He knew it was Allen calling, so he finally picked it up and quickly assured him that everything was okay and he had enough money to take care of any damages.

The Toyota went over the bridge into The Bronx. Craig looked at the gas gauge, which was at the one-quarter mark and hoped this guy wasn't going to Westchester.

He slowed down and passed the Toyota as the little car pulled into a spot near a bar and grill on Arthur Avenue.

The Dominican guy got out of the car and went inside.

Craig double-parked, made sure his 38 was loaded, and went inside.

The place was dark, but fancy. A few people sat at tables eating, and a few people sat at the bar drinking. The smell of cigar smoke seeped in from a backdoor that led to the garden in the backyard.

Craig approached the bar and looked around.

The Dominican man sat in the back of the room against the wall at a table with a fat Italian man wearing an expensive suit and a

Rolex.

Craig ordered a beer and left it on the bar with the change from a twenty-dollar bill. He asked the bartender for the bathroom and then headed to the back and tried to listen to what the Dominican and the Italian guy were talking about. It wasn't an intricate plan like the CIA guys in the movies, but it was the only thing he could think of. He had to find out who this guy was and why he was looking for him. These people were obviously not cops.

Craig only heard a little bit while heading toward the bathroom—just enough—they said his name, Craig Hill. Craig's heartbeat increased tenfold, but he tried not to show it and he tried not to look directly at them.

He also heard the kid call the fat man, Enzo.

They stopped talking as Craig got closer.

Inside the bathroom, Craig went inside the stall and closed the door. With his sweaty, trembling hand, he held his pistol, pulled back the hammer, and hoped those men didn't recognize him.

CHAPTER 73

Sitting at his favorite table in the back of the bar, Enzo's heart rate increased and his entire body became flush when he saw Sammy walk in. What the hell was this kid thinking? His hand trembled as he grabbed his drink downed it.

Sammy approached the table and sat down.

Enzo looked around and said, "Cazzo. You got a fucking death wish or something? Johnny just walked out here five minutes ago. He's out looking for you."

"I know," replied Sammy. "I was in my car down the block. I saw him leave, then I waited five minutes before coming in here."

Enzo kept looking around the bar, especially at the door.

"Why didn't you just call me?"

Sammy slipped a 380 semi-automatic pistol out of his waistband and showed it to Enzo on the side of the table. Was he here to rob him? Would he shoot him? Enzo wished he had his gun on him, but even if he did, he wouldn't be able to get it out on time.

Before Enzo could speak, Sammy spoke, "I need to sell this. I'll take whatever I can get. I got some cash, but not enough. If I can sell this it might add up to enough for a partial payment."

Enzo said, "I already have a gun, and I don't know anyone who's looking for one off hand. Under different circumstances, I would put the word out, but my hands are tied right now, kid. If I help you, I'm fucked, even worse than you."

When Sammy slipped the gun back into his waistband, Enzo exhaled. Times like this, anything could happen. "Please, kid. You can't stay here. Just get back to Brooklyn and find Craig Hill."

Sammy began to speak, "But Enzo—"

Enzo gestured for Sammy to wait until a man passed on his way to the bathroom. He didn't look at the man, just in case it was someone who knew him, he didn't want anyone to know that he met with Sammy.

After the man went inside and closed the bathroom door, Enzo told Sammy, "Keep the gun. You never know when you may need it."

Sammy said, "Other than being skinny and Irish with yellow skin, I have no idea what this guy Craig Hill looks like."

Enzo said, "If he's as sick as I heard, and yellow with jaundice, you'll know him when you see him." Enzo waved to the bartender to come over, then he told Sammy, "Now please, kid. You gotta get the hell outta here.

CHAPTER 74

Craig had waited in the bar bathroom for about ten minutes before deciding that it was safe to leave. He realized that if those two men had recognized him, they would have already come after him. It seemed they only knew his name, but not what he looked like. Or, maybe they just didn't get a good look at him. They probably knew he was sick, but luckily, the bar was too dark to see that his skin was yellow.

All the way back to Brooklyn, his mind raced. These guys from The Bronx couldn't have been connected with the guys in Coney Island. Could they? The guys in Coney Island never knew Craig's or Riley's last names, and they didn't seem so powerful.

He wondered how the Dominican kid and the Italian man were connected. He wondered if these were the guys who were missing the four kilos in the first place.

Craig dropped off Allen's car with a full tank of gas and enough cash to cover the parking ticket. He expected Allen to inspect the car, but by the time he got there, Allen was already floating among the clouds.

After eating Chinese food for dinner in Allen's neighborhood, Craig took car service back to his hotel room near Sunset Park.

He bagged up a more coke, and this time took a little sniff before going out.

On his way to meet the same group of guys as the night before, Craig wished he had told them to meet him somewhere else after what had happened with the guy with the knife, but it was too late to change the location now. He headed to the same Irish pub with his loaded pistol and one hundred grams.

He was high, but not enough to slow him down. He had only done a tiny bump and his tolerance level seemed to be rising. Tempted to do another on the way there, Craig resisted.

A few guys were already there drinking beers when Craig walked in. They got a table in the back and Craig ordered a soda. The others came in within the next few minutes.

After selling them most of what he had, Craig told them that he wanted to change their meeting location. He told them about what had happened the night before and how he'd scared the guy away with a gun. Part of the reason he told them this was also to let them know that he was packing.

A couple guys stayed for another beer, but most of them left after getting what they came there for.

Craig still wanted another juicy burger, but this time he was too full from the Chinese food he'd had earlier near Allen's.

He waited with the last two guys and then left with them. Although he had paid close attention and didn't see any sign of the man from last night, he still felt more comfortable not leaving the bar alone.

Outside, the night air was cool and dry and the streets were full of people walking, sitting, and just enjoying the summer.

Craig separated from the two guys he'd walked out with and headed toward a car service.

He got into the back of an old Lincoln and told the Arabic man behind the wheel where he wanted to go. The car pulled out of its spot and rolled to the corner, stopping at the stop sign. Craig watched out the window as healthy children played in the park on the corner.

The passenger door opened.

The driver said, "Hey! What are you doing?"

Craig turned forward just as the man from last night jumped into the passenger seat and slammed the door closed behind him.

This time, instead of a knife, the man had a pistol, something small, maybe a 22 or a 25. He pointed his gun at the driver and said, "Drive up to the next block and pull over."

The driver replied, "Okay, my friend. I will give you the money. Just don't shoot me."

Still holding his gun at the driver, the man said, "Shut the fuck up and drive."

Craig didn't wait. As soon as the car was halfway through the intersection, he fired three bullets into the back of the seat.

The man fell forward as blood splattered onto the dashboard.

The driver screamed and slammed on the breaks.

Craig placed the barrel of his 38 against the driver's temple and said, "Calm down and keep driving."

The man started crying as he drove forward and up the next block.

Craig pulled his sweatshirt hood up over his head and told the driver, "Pull over here and double-park."

Still crying, the man pulled the car over and parked.

Craig thought about the bad guys in the movies. They would definitely shoot this man to ensure that there were no witnesses. But, this wasn't a movie, it was real life. And Craig wasn't a bad guy, he just kept running into bad luck. For just a moment, he thought about pulling the trigger, but he just couldn't shoot an innocent man who probably had a family waiting for him at home, especially a man crying like a baby.

Craig said, "Give me the keys."

The man's trembling hand took the keys out of the ignition and handed them to Craig.

Craig quickly wiped the door handles with his sleeve and then jumped out of the car.

He sprinted two blocks until he couldn't breathe anymore, then slowed down to a stroll.

After throwing the car keys into a sewer, Craig boarded the first bus he saw and headed toward his hotel.

CHAPTER 75

After the long drive up to Westchester and an unfruitful interrogation of Nelson Kelley because his fancy lawyer was there, Victor and Rosie gave up and headed back down toward the city as the sun disappeared over the horizon.

Nelson Kelley said he didn't know anything about the whereabouts of his half-brother and he didn't know anything about The Howell Building shooting. When they asked him about the four kilos of coke, he clammed up.

Nelson's lawyer said he didn't have to answer any of their questions, especially since it had nothing to do with his case.

They knew Nelson wouldn't talk and since they couldn't use any intimidation tactics with his lawyer around, they finally gave up and left.

On their drive back to Manhattan, Victor said, "There were three fake passports from Ireland and three men in Hawaiian shirts. It only makes sense that the second gun belonged to someone with Rene Ortega. I don't think he'd be stupid enough to pick up four kilos by himself."

"Well," said Rosie. "We already questioned Ortega's family and friends, and if any of them know anything, they're not telling us."

Victor's phone rang. He answered it.

A lieutenant from their precinct told Victor about a murder in Brooklyn. The cops had found a partial fingerprint at the scene and there was a high probability that the partial belonged to Craig Hill. They also had a witness, a car service driver.

Victor wanted to go to Brooklyn to check it out, but the lieutenant told him to go back to the precinct and clock out. He said there were already enough cops in Brooklyn looking for Craig Hill, and most importantly, the captain would have his ass if he authorized any overtime that wasn't an emergency.

CHAPTER 76

Back in his hotel room, Craig paced back and forth, wearing just his underwear, socks, and sneakers. Blood dripped from his nose while he ground his jaw and looked around with bulging, dilated eyes. With both guns loaded, Craig held the sawed-off in one hand and the revolver in the other.

He'd sniffed a few grams and smoked a pack and a half of cigarettes since getting back from the pub. He hadn't been this high since he was a teenager.

Not only did flashes of murder haunt his thoughts, but now the paranoia of people coming after him began to drive him mad.

He thought about the detectives who were looking for him. He thought about the Dominican and the Italian and wondered how they knew his name. He thought about the guys in Coney Island and wondered if they knew who he was, too.

Every little sound made him jump.

He kept peeking out the windows and listening at the door.

He was ready to pull the trigger at any moment. If anyone came after him, his plan was to fire the shotgun first and then run for cover while using the revolver to pick off the rest of them.

He continued pacing, trembling, and sweating while his thoughts twisted his mind into a pretzel.

Every little shadow and fluctuation of light outside his door and window made his heart pound faster.

At first, he was scared that he'd done too much coke and

might have a heart attack, but then he began to welcome the idea.

CHAPTER 77

After work hours, and after Mangano left for the day, Abby requested and waited for a fax from the suburban police station in Westchester—copies of every document that pertained to Nelson Kelley, his arrest, and his interrogations.

She'd hoped to get to Victor's precinct before he left for the day, but she knew traffic would never let her make it on time. The next best thing was to check him out at home.

The sun retreated in the sky behind her as she sat in worse than usual rush-hour traffic, trying to get out of Manhattan.

Since she didn't know her way around Queens very well, she consulted the GPS on her phone. After taking the Williamsburg Bridge into Brooklyn, she followed the Brooklyn-Queens Expressway all the way up to Queens Boulevard, an eight-lane street flanked on both sides by apartment buildings and stores.

Abby spending almost a half hour on the gridlocked boulevard, watching day turn to night, then she finally turned onto a small tree-lined street with houses on both sides.

The quiet neighborhood only had a few lights on here and there. Abby checked the addresses while cruising by.

When she found Victor's little blue house, she passed it and pulled over across the street. All of the lights were off, except in one bedroom and in the bathroom down the hall.

After about ten minutes, the bathroom light turned off, but the bedroom light stayed on.

The loud bass from a passing car vibrated the street and at the same time, activated a few car alarms. Abby jumped in her seat and realized that she'd fallen asleep.

Victor's house was completely dark now.

Abby checked her phone, which was on silent, and saw that she'd missed a call from her daughter.

CHAPTER 78

Evelyn got out of bed and started moving around while Victor was in the shower.

When he came into the bedroom, he saw her getting her clothes ready for the day. "Why you up so early, baby?"

"I promised to drive my mother to the doctor today."

While toweling off, Victor asked, "On a Saturday? She okay?"

"She's been complaining about her foot again."

"Oh. The foot doctor." He hung up his towel, approached Evelyn, and kissed her.

She kissed him, hugged him, and said, "Happy Birthday, baby."

Victor smiled. "Thank you." He glanced over to be sure Sofia was sleeping in her crib, then he kissed Evelyn again while grabbing her thick hips. "I'd really like to unwrap my gift right now."

Evelyn stepped back, looked down at his penis, and said, "Down boy. Down."

Victor barked. Evelyn laughed. He gave her a light spank on the ass as she headed for the bathroom.

After getting dressed and waiting for Evelyn to finish her shower, Victor went downstairs to the kitchen and sat down to a cup of coffee.

Evelyn came in already dressed with the baby asleep in her car seat. She leaned over, kissed Victor, and said, "I gotta run, baby. Call you later."

"Wow. She really does have an early appointment. You're not even going to have a cup of coffee before you go?"

"I'll have coffee later." Evelyn grabbed her car keys and headed outside.

Victor finished his coffee in the living room while watching the news, then he headed out the door and toward the train station for the same commute that he did every day.

While the subway made its stops, Victor leaned against the doors, thought about that immaculate police station in Westchester, and visualized what the small town looked like during Christmas.

When he arrived at his precinct in Manhattan, Victor was surprised and a little disappointed that no one knew it was his birthday.

While Rosie was in the bathroom, Victor knocked on Captain Morelli's door, which was halfway open. He could see Morelli on the computer.

Morelli looked up and said, "Come in Cohen."

Victor entered and said, "Any news about Craig Hill?"

"None."

"Did they check his cousin Marie's?"

"More than once." Morelli opened a file cabinet and retrieved a manila folder. "You remember this case?" Morelli gave Victor the folder. "It seems the man we got convicted is up for appeal, and he claims to have some new evidence. The DA wants to talk to you about it."

Victor flipped through the pages. "This was just last year. I remember every detail."

"Maybe you should go over the file again, just in case."

"Okay, but it won't take long. What do you say after I finish, Rosie and I swing by Brooklyn and take a look for Hill one more time."

Morelli started to say something, but Victor spoke first. "I know. There's already enough cops looking for him. But, I feel like I have a connection with this guy."

"Why? Because today is both of your birthdays?"

Victor didn't answer.

Morelli said, "You think I forgot your birthday, Cohen? Pass up the chance to stuff my face?" He pointed at the door behind Victor and said, "Look there."

Victor turned and glanced out the door. He saw Evelyn holding a string with a balloon that said, Happy Birthday. Sofia sat in her car seat on a desk.

He stepped out of Morelli's office.

All the detectives yelled, "Happy Birthday!"

Rosie opened a box of donuts, took one out, inserted a candle into the dough, and lit the candle. Victor laughed.

Evelyn approached Victor, handed him the balloon, kissed him, hugged him, and whispered into his ear, "You'll get your real present tonight."

Victor hugged her while holding back a tear.

Rosie approached with the burning candle in the donut and said, "Make a wish."

Victor kissed Evelyn, then said, "My wish already came true."

The other detectives made sarcastic comments and laughed.

Victor blew out the candle. Everyone clapped their hands.

Rosie opened up the other boxes of donuts and everyone helped themselves.

They ate and drank, and for a while, Victor forgot all about Craig Hill and the trail of blood he was leaving behind him.

CHAPTER 79

Craig woke up in the afternoon. Someone was pounding on the door. At first, he thought the pounding was only in his head, then he heard the voice of a Chinese man outside his door.

He knew the man was here because it was checkout time. Craig grabbed a handful of cash and opened the door in his underwear.

The Chinese man looked at him and asked, "Rough night?"

"Tell me about it." Craig began to count out twenty-dollar bills. "I'm gonna pay you in advance for another week."

The man smiled and said, "You are good customer. Do you like I send a massage girl for you?"

Craig liked the idea. He'd been to a Chinese massage once and he enjoyed it. They treated him like a king. After washing him, they massaged him and then gave him the choice of a hand job or sex, for an extra tip of course. They even put his shoes on and tied them before he left. The only problem now was, between his condition and the cocaine, he knew he wouldn't be able to keep an erection.

"Just the room for now, but I might change my mind about the girl later." Craig handed the man the cash with an extra twenty for a tip.

The man smiled, took the money, and headed down the hall.

Craig closed his door and then took a handful of Advil for his pounding headache before tuning into some classic rock on the radio and then jumping in the shower.

While getting dressed, Craig heard the date on the radio and realized it was his birthday.

He got dressed and packed everything up except his gun and safe deposit box key, both of which he kept on him as usual.

Craig worried about the cops tapping his and his mother's phones. He'd taken a few chances with his cell phone, but kept the calls short and hoped that all the movies and TV shows were accurate about how long it took for a phone tap to kick in.

He called his mother from a pay phone.

"Oh my God, baby. Please tell me you're okay."

"I'm fine, Ma. I told you that already."

"Then why are the cops looking for you? Detectives keep coming around asking if I heard from you."

"I'm gonna talk to them soon, Ma. I just need a little more time to straighten things out. Just keep telling them that you haven't seen me, which is true anyway, so you don't have to lie."

There was silence on the line for a moment.

Craig thought he lost the signal. "Ma. You there?" Then he heard her crying. "Come on. Don't do that."

"I was going to make a cake and both of your sisters were coming with the kids."

"Make the cake. I'll try and get there, but I won't be able to stay long."

"You sure? What about the cops? They must know today is your birthday. I'm sure they'll be back around. They're very persistent."

"If it's too dangerous I won't come. But, if I do come, I won't be able to stay long." He wondered again about his mother's phone being tapped and decided to end the call. "I'm sorry, Ma. But, I gotta run."

"Okay baby. Be careful. And, happy birthday."

After speaking with his mother, Craig bought a ham and cheese sandwich and ate it back at his hotel room. He spent a few hours bagging up, resting, and resisting the urge to do any coke. He smoked a few cigarettes, but kept that to a minimum.

Riley came to mind. He had planned to find out if Riley had lived or died, but was always on the move, and at the same time scared to go to the hospital. He prayed to God for Riley's soul.

He was still very worried about the cops and the other people who were after him, but without the coke in his system, he was at least rational about it.

After a nice long refreshing nap, Craig woke up with a partial hard-on. He thought about the massage girl that he could have delivered and then he squeezed his dick to see if he could get it to work. At first, it seemed to be okay. Blood rushed through the veins and it began to grow.

Then, without warning, it went limp.

Frustrated, Craig stood and grabbed a cigarette. He steamed it down to the filter while thinking about the fact that he might be dead in a couple months and he couldn't even enjoy the last of his time on Earth.

While putting the cigarette out, he thought about his cousin Marie and her tight little body with huge breasts. He knew he shouldn't think of his cousin that way, but he couldn't help it. His penis began to grow again. He squeezed it—it felt good—then it went limp again.

That's when he realized the answer to his problem. Drugs.

Craig knew that no doctor would give him Viagra while his liver was failing, so he decided to look elsewhere.

He sent Allen a text and asked if he knew where to get Viagra. Allen texted him back saying he didn't need it and had no idea where to get it.

Craig had a feeling that Anthony could probably help him, but he didn't want Marie to know he wasn't fully functional.

Because it was his birthday and he really wanted to get laid, Craig decided to text Anthony anyway. Fuck it if Marie knew.

CHAPTER 80

Captain Morelli had let everyone relax and enjoy their donuts and coffee for almost an hour this morning, then he told them to get back to work. Evelyn had to leave because she really did have to take her mother to the foot doctor.

Victor spent a couple hours refreshing his memory on the old case that was up for appeal while Rosie caught up on some other paperwork.

Morelli stopped by Victor's desk and said, "If you want to get out of here a couple hours early, I'll put you in."

"Thanks," said Victor. "But, to tell you the truth, I'd like to swing by Brooklyn and take another look for Craig Hill."

Morelli shook his head and said, "Stubborn Fuck."

Rosie chuckled.

"You want to spend your birthday in Brooklyn? Go ahead." Morelli walked away, going toward the bathroom.

Rosie said, "Just give me another fifteen minutes. I'm almost finished here."

After finishing their paperwork and then a quick run to the bathroom, Victor and Rosie headed out to Brooklyn. First, they stopped in Benson-Hurst and waited in the car across the street from Marie's house.

About an hour later, Marie and her boyfriend left their apartment. They headed down the block and then around the corner.

Victor hurried across the street and listened by the basement window. He didn't hear anything. He waited a few more minutes before knocking on the glass. He still didn't hear anything.

While listening, he realized that Craig would probably want to see his mother on his birthday. Victor knew he would do the same if his mother were still alive.

He headed back to the car and got into the passenger seat. "I don't think anyone's there."

Rosie typed something on her tablet, then looked at her watch.

Victor said, "I say we go to his mother's for a while, then if we don't see him, we get the hell outta here."

"Good idea." Rosie put her tablet away, started the car, and took off down the block.

When they arrived at Mrs. Hill's house, Rosie double-parked and waited in the car while Victor knocked on the door.

Mrs. Hill answered the door wearing a housedress and an apron. Whatever she was cooking smelled delicious. Victor tried to get a peek inside and hopefully catch of glimpse of Craig trying to hide, but all he saw was an old Irish man asleep on a recliner chair with a collection of empty beer cans on the table next to him.

"May I help you?" asked Mrs. Hill.

Victor showed his badge. "I'm sorry to bother you, Mrs. Hill, but we're still looking for your son Craig, and I was just wondering if you'd seen him."

She shook her head. "I'm sorry, Detective."

Victor gave her his card and said, "If you do hear from him, tell him I just want to talk."

She took the card and said, "Okay, now if you don't mind. I have dinner in the oven."

"Of course." Just as Victor turned around, he caught something out of the corner of his eye, two empty metal cake pans and a big mixing bowl.

Back in the car, Victor said, "Go around the block, then park on the corner."

Rosie started the car and looked at him. "What's going on?"

Victor said, "That bitch is baking a cake."

CHAPTER 81

After a quick conversation with his mother on a pay phone, Craig learned that a detective had just been there.

Craig was about five blocks away. It was evening, but the hot sun was still overhead.

Wearing the same type of sweatshirt that he always wore, Craig also wore a baseball cap that he had just bought. He hoped the cap might disguise his face a little, especially since today his yellow skin was worse than usual.

He planned on having some cake and ice cream and then spending about an hour with his family before slipping out unnoticed. It would have been more comfortable sneaking around after dark, but his mother had already planned to have the cake in the evening so that both of his sisters could come with their kids.

As he approached his parent's block, he noticed an unmarked gray cop car parked at the corner across the street. He wasn't close enough to get a good look, but he could see a man sitting in the passenger's seat and a woman sitting in the driver's seat.

Trying to look natural and not look in their direction, he turned, crossed the avenue, and kept his gaze forward while heading the opposite way and then down another side street.

He didn't know if those were cops, but he wasn't taking any chances. He knew he needed to get the hell out of there.

On his way back to his hotel room in Sunset Park, his nerves settled enough that he decided to stop at a small diner for a cheeseburger deluxe and a piece of birthday cake.

He wondered about the other people that were after him and considered getting a room in a different hotel. But, since the hotel manager didn't ask him for ID, and he booked the room under a fake name, he felt it was safe enough to stay a while longer.

After getting back to the hotel, Craig sat on the bed with his shoes off and digested his huge meal. He turned on the TV, but nothing kept his interest, so he turned it off and put some music on.

While watching the sunset outside his window, he took a couple small sniffs and enjoyed a cigarette.

CHAPTER 82

Victor and Rosie sat in their car down the block from Craig's house. The sun was still high overhead, but it was getting late.

Rosie looked at her watch and said, "I think it's time to call it a day."

Victor agreed, "You're right, let's get the hell out of here."

"I'll drop you off at home. No point in making your wife wait any longer for her birthday boy." Rosie started the car.

Victor said, "Thanks, Ro."

Rosie pulled out of the parking spot. "Don't worry. With that patrol car coming around every half hour, there's still a good chance they can pick him up."

Victor noticed a small white Toyota pull up and double-park in front of the house. He said, "Wait. Slow down."

"Why?" Rosie slowed down while glancing out the window. "Who's that?"

"I don't know."

A thin Dominican man with a goatee and an earring stepped out of the car and hurried toward the house.

Victor said, "Holy shit. It's Sammy Ortega."

Rosie pulled the car over and double-parked.

They both got out and headed toward the house.

Mrs. Hill opened the door. They spoke, then Sammy began to yell at her.

Victor and Rosie raced to the house just as Sammy smacked

Mrs. Hill across the face. When he saw Victor and Rosie coming toward him, he pulled his 380 from his waistband and pointed it at Mrs. Hill, who was on the floor, crying with a bloody lip.

They stopped coming toward him and put their hands in the air.

Mrs. Hill begged, "Please don't shoot me."

Victor wondered if the old man inside the house was too drunk to hear what was going on. He also wondered why Sammy was here and if he really was going to shoot Mrs. Hill.

Rosie said, "Don't do it, Sammy. We can work things out."

"Oh yeah? Can you bring back my brother?"

Victor said, "Craig Hill had nothing to do with your brother's death."

Sammy's hand was shaking. His eyes were full of liquid. He fired a shot into the air.

Mrs. Hill screamed while Victor and Rosie dropped to the ground.

Sammy bolted into the house.

Victor and Rosie whipped out their guns.

Rosie said, "He's going for the back door. I'm faster. You take the car." She dashed into the house, jumping over Mrs. Hill's fat body on the floor in the doorway.

Victor raced to the car, started it up, peeled out down the block, and skidded when he almost smashed into another car while turning the corner.

The other car screeched to a stop.

Victor switched on the siren and stepped on the gas while forcing his way through traffic. The lights flashed and the siren blared as he turned another corner onto the next block. The only car on the street pulled over and let Victor by.

He spotted Sammy up ahead, running up the sidewalk.

Victor stepped on the gas, quickly getting closer.

Sammy bolted across the street, firing his gun haphazardly. People in the area screamed and ran for cover.

Victor ducked while pressing the gas pedal down even harder. He was worried about the people outside, but he was also worried about himself.

He lifted his head just in time. The car's nose was right on Sammy. He grabbed the wheel and tried to turn it, but it was too late, so he stepped on the brakes.

The wheels locked and the car skidded onto the curb, pinning Sammy's skinny body between the grill and a lamppost on the corner.

Victor got out of the car, but stayed down while retrieving his firearm. He turned and saw Rosie running up the block behind him. He pointed at the front of the car and motioned for Rosie to stay down.

She bent over while racing toward Victor and then hid next to him behind the car.

Victor said, "He was shooting at me. He's pinned against the post. I don't know if he's alive or what."

Rosie said, "Let's find out." She yelled into the air. "Sammy?"

Sammy grumbled something but they couldn't understand what he was saying.

Victor said, "He sounds fucked up."

"Let's check it out." Rosie lifted her firearm and stood.

Victor stood at the same time.

Sammy was pinned between the car and the pole. His body was twisted and blood dripped from his mouth, but he still had his gun.

Victor said, "Drop the gun, Sammy."

He didn't drop it, he just kept mumbling.

Rosie yelled, "Drop the gun or we will shoot!"

Sammy ignored them, and then, like a zombie, he began to raise his pistol real slow.

Victor fired one shot, directly between Sammy's eyes.

Sammy's hand dropped.

CHAPTER 83

Staying far away from the pub, Craig went back out to make a few deliveries. He took the bus, then the train, then after selling a couple hundred grams, he took a taxi back to his room where he met with Allen.

He was supposed to make a drop to Anthony and Marie, but was too tired, so he told Anthony he would pay his carfare if he came to the hotel to get it.

When Anthony got there, he told Craig that he wouldn't be able to get him the Viagra until tomorrow. He didn't tell Craig earlier on the phone because Craig had asked him to keep it a secret from Marie.

Anthony bought thirty-five grams, then left in the same taxi he had come in.

Craig didn't blame Anthony, but he was pissed. He was really looking forward to getting that Viagra and getting laid on his birthday. He thought about ordering a girl anyway, but knew how bad he'd feel if he couldn't perform. He decided that waiting one more day wouldn't kill him.

While watching TV, Craig sniffed a small line . . . then another small one . . . then another small one.

Before long he'd sniffed a few grams and was pacing the room in his underwear—sweating, drooling, eyes bulging, and bleeding from the nose—guns in both of his trembling hands, ready to pull the trigger.

CHAPTER 84

After a wonderful day of rides, games, and food at Coney Island, Abby and her daughter were exhausted. Upon arriving home that evening, they had cereal for dinner, then tried in vain to watch TV until finally admitting that they were too tired to stay awake. Abby tucked Faith in, prayed with her, and wished her a good night.

She went back into the living room, turned off the TV, and checked her PC to see what Victor was up to. Jackpot. She learned of Victor and Rosie's entanglement with Sammy Ortega.

Without even giving her time to change out of her pajamas, Abby dragged Faith to the car then to her mother's house.

Traffic into Manhattan was not heavy, but Abby was still worried about getting there too late. If she got there before IA sent another investigator, she could possibly get the case for herself. She turned on her siren and left it on, all the way to Manhattan, while zipping in and out of traffic.

By the time she'd gotten to the precinct, Detectives Cohen and Li had already finished writing out their reports. Fortunately, they were still there, in their captain's office.

Abby knocked on Morelli's door, then without waiting for anyone to answer, she turned the knob and opened it.

Morelli sat behind his desk talking with Victor and Rosie who were sitting in chairs opposite his desk.

Abby said, "Sorry to interrupt. I knocked, but no one answered."

Morelli was obviously annoyed. "That doesn't mean you could come in."

Abby could see that Victor and Rosie were happy with the way their captain spoke to her, but she wouldn't give them the satisfaction. She pretended not to notice Morelli's rude demeanor. "I'm here to speak with detectives Cohen and Li."

Captain Morelli said, "We're already expecting an investigator from IA. He's on his way right now." He took a sip from a can of soda, burped, and said, "No one told me anything about you being here. I'll have to hear it from your captain. Procedure . . . you know."

Abby knew there was nothing she could do but wait and hopefully help the investigating officer nail Cohen. She turned to Victor and said, "Cohen. Don't forget. If we confess our sins, he who is just will forgive us and purify us from all unrighteousness."

CHAPTER 85

After waking up and having breakfast with Evelyn, Victor went next door to do a couple errands for Mrs. Lopez.

When he got there, Alesha was in the kitchen washing dishes and Mrs. Lopez was in the living room, sitting on the sofa with the remote control in her hand.

Victor looked at the TV. It was black with white letters across it that read, no signal. "What happened?"

"I pressed something wrong, then when I tried to fix it, I made it worse. Now all I get is this no signal." Mrs. Lopez handed him the remote control and asked, "Can you fix it?"

Victor said, "I don't know. You know I'm not so good with technology. I'll try, but we'll probably end up calling the satellite company anyway."

Mrs. Lopez said, "Well, I just thought . . . as long as you're here."

Victor used the remote to power off and then back on the TV and the satellite box. "Let's see if I can figure it out."

Alesha entered the room drying her hands with a kitchen towel and asked, "Can you fix it?"

"I'm trying." Victor tried a few different things on the menu and the settings. Once he almost thought he had something, but then it went into some kind of search mode.

The doorbell rang. Alesha left the room.

Victor said, "I don't think I can fix it. I'll have to call the company and get someone out here."

"Well. I guess I'll just have to read books for a while."

Alesha came back into the room with Rosie.

Victor said, "Perfect timing." He turned to Mrs. Lopez and said, "Mrs. Lopez, this is my partner, Detective Rosie Li."

Mrs. Lopez said, "Wow. You're a cop? But, you're so pretty."

Rosie blushed. "Thank you."

Victor said, "She's great with technology." He handed Rosie the remote control and asked, "Can you take a look at this?"

She held the remote in her hand and examined it, then she looked over at the TV.

Victor said, "Thanks." He kissed her on the cheek.

Mrs. Lopez said, "Better not let Evelyn see you doing that."

Sitting on a chair, flipping through a magazine, Alesha chuckled.

Victor went into the kitchen, removed the garbage bag, tied it, and replaced it with a new one. He then took a shopping list that was hanging from a magnet on the refrigerator and slipped it into his pocket.

While passing through the living room with the garbage, Victor glanced at the TV and saw that Rosie was on the settings menu. He asked, "What do you think?"

"I'm working on it." She pressed a button that took her to another screen.

Victor took the garbage outside, put it in the pail, then came back in. After washing his hands in the bathroom, he took the shopping list from his pocket and went back into the living room.

Rosie was sitting on the sofa with the remote on the coffee table in front of her. The TV read, scanning channels, while consecutive numbers flashed on the screen. "I think I got it."

Mrs. Lopez said, "Thank you so much, honey."

Rosie smiled and said, "No problem."

While reading the shopping list in his hand, Victor asked, "No turkey this week?"

Mrs. Lopez said, "I can't take it anymore, that damn turkey almost every day."

Alesha chuckled while still flipping through her magazine.

The TV flashed and then it came on. They watched part of a car commercial, then Rosie flipped through a few channels to be sure everything was working properly.

Mrs. Lopez thanked her again, then Rosie followed Victor outside.

Victor stood on the sidewalk and glanced over at Rosie's new unmarked police car. It was double-parked next door in front of his house and it was empty.

Rosie said, "Your wife told me where you were."

Victor was still looking at the empty car. "Are they giving you a new partner?"

"They better not. And besides, you'll be back soon. Only supposed to be seventy-two hours pending a psych evaluation."

"I hope you're right." He used his handkerchief to wipe the sweat from his forehead.

"I was there. I saw everything. And I'll be with you all the way."

"Thanks."

"It's not that bad. You're getting paid to stay home and it's not coming out of your time. I'd enjoy it while I could." Rosie took out her car keys and said, "I almost forgot why I came here. I could have called, but I wanted you to see it for yourself. Check it out."

Victor followed Rosie across the street to her car. She opened the door, retrieved a document, and handed it to Victor. It was a forensics report on a gun.

Victor read it, then asked, "Sammy had the seventh gun?"

"That's right."

He gave her back the document and said, "You could get in trouble for showing me this."

"Fuck them."

Victor laughed.

Rosie said, "Come on. I'll drop you off at the grocery store."

While driving, Victor asked, "So, what happened with Hill?"

Rosie answered, "They're still looking for him."

CHAPTER 86

Sunday afternoon. Craig should have been resting up and getting ready for dinner at his parents' house. Instead, he was making cocaine deliveries all over Brooklyn.

He had sold a few hundred grams that day. Too many to count. The luggage under his bed back at the hotel room now contained many thousands of dollars. Craig wasn't sure yet how much, but he was planning on counting it before getting it into his safe deposit box tomorrow morning.

While at Marie's, Anthony quietly slipped Craig a bag of ten Viagra pills. Craig knew he only needed one, but they were only five dollars each so he decided to stock up.

He got some dinner before heading back to his room and resisted the urge to do any coke. He was worried that the coke with the Viagra would give him a heart attack or shut down his liver, especially since his skin color had been getting worse the past couple days.

Just when he was about to call the guy from the hotel and ask about the massage girl, he decided that he wanted a blonde, a busty blonde Russian girl.

CHAPTER 87

Abby ate because she was hungry, but she didn't enjoy her Sunday dinner as much as she usually did. Staring at nothing, picking at her food, Abby thought about the smug looks on their faces when she walked out of that office. They think they've won, but she wasn't going down so easily. Abby wanted to tear into Cohen more than ever now.

Her mother, both of her nieces, and her daughter were all laughing at something one of the girls said, but Abby wasn't paying attention, and she wasn't laughing.

Abby's mother stopped laughing and said, "Abby. You should go lie down a while. You're over worked."

She did not intend to lie down, she just wanted the evening to end so she could put Faith to bed and look into the killing of Sammy Ortega. There had to be something there. Something she could use. "I am tired, but I'll wait until I get home to lie down. If I fall asleep here, I won't want to get up."

Faith said, "That's what happens to me sometimes."

CHAPTER 88

Enzo sat with his wife in their elegant dining room while Frank Sinatra played from a pair of speakers in the living room. Enzo enjoyed two plates of ravioli, three meatballs, and a sausage, then smoked a cigar while his wife cleared the plates from the table and brought them into the kitchen.

He thought about Peppino's surprise visit last week and was almost expecting them to come again now.

While puffing on his cigar and leaning back in his chair, Enzo tried to relax and enjoy the music, but his mind kept drifting away. Life was great before this whole business with the four missing kilos. He just wanted things to go back to normal.

The smell of coffee began to enter the room from the kitchen, but even that couldn't keep him from obsessing about his future.

He wondered what was going to happen now that Sammy was dead. Enzo knew that more than anything, Peppino wanted his money.

CHAPTER 89

Victor and Evelyn enjoyed a delicious Sunday dinner, then spent a couple hours playing with Sofia and making her laugh while the TV rambled on in the background.

When the baby was finally tired enough to sleep, they turned off the TV, turned on some salsa music, popped the cork on a bottle of White Zinfandel, and enjoyed it in the living room while still listening to the baby monitor.

When the bottle was empty, Victor led Evelyn back up the stairs to the bedroom.

They made love and Victor forgot all about his problems at work. But, when they were finished and cuddling, the thoughts of Craig Hill, Sammy Ortega, and Abby Edmunds, once again began to flood his mind.

He headed to the bathroom to brush his teeth and urinate, then he popped an extra pill to help him sleep.

By the time he got back to the bed, Evelyn was snoring. He laughed, then curled up next to her, turned the TV on, and lowered the volume.

CHAPTER 90

After going out and buying a few sex magazines and local newspapers, Craig went back to his room and searched the ads for his dream girl.

He found a six-foot tall Russian woman with triple D breasts. He called the number and made an appointment for her to come to his room in an hour and a half, the earliest time they had available. The rate was two fifty an hour, more than most of the other ads, but she looked worth it. He hoped she would be.

Craig waited thirty minutes, then took one Viagra.

During the next hour, he smoked almost a whole pack of cigarettes while pacing back and forth. It seemed pathetic to have to pay for pussy. When Craig was in high school, he had beautiful girls falling over him, and even when he was older, up until the time he got married, he was a Casanova. Now, instead of falling over him, they either avoided him or treated him as if he had leprosy.

Finally, the hotel phone rang.

Craig picked it up. "Hello."

It was the Chinese man. "Hello, sir. You have a visitor."

"Send her up."

Craig put out his cigarette and stood in the middle of the room like a kid on Christmas waiting to open his presents.

There was a knock at the door. Craig opened it.

A tall beautiful blonde Barbie with blue eyes, wearing a tight dress and high heels stood there staring at Craig with glitter on her massive cleavage. The Viagra began to work its magic.

"Hello," he said while staring at her enormous sparkling breasts. "Please . . . come in."

She didn't move. She just squinted and spoke with a heavy Russian accent, "Why are you yellow?"

"Yellow?" Craig's heart began to race. He didn't know if it was because he was nervous or if the Viagra was working on the wrong body part. He said the first thing that came to mind, "It's probably just the lighting. Come on in."

She still didn't come in, she peeked inside the room, then looked back at Craig. "It's not the light, Honey. You are yellow. Are you sick or something?"

Craig tried to laugh it up. "Of course I'm not sick. It really is just the lighting. I'm not yellow. Come in and you'll see." He showed her a handful of cash. "I have your money right here. And a very nice tip."

"Sorry, Honey. I don't think so." She turned around and headed down the hall.

Craig yelled, "Wait! Come back! I'll pay double."

She kept going down the hall and then down the stairs.

Craig slammed the door. "That fucking bitch. Who the fuck does she think she is?" He lit a cigarette and steamed half of it down in one drag.

He forgot about the pill he had taken and started sniffing coke.

Within five minutes, he was in space.

The hotel phone rang.

Craig picked it up and whispered, "Yeah?"

The Chinese man said, "There's a big Russian man coming up to your room. I tried to stop him—"

Someone pounded on the door.

Craig hung up the phone and grabbed the shotgun from under the mattress. He held the gun down at his side, just behind his leg. His heart raced. The pressure in his veins made him feel like he would burst.

He opened the door.

A big ugly Russian man with shoulders and a head like a brick building occupied the entire doorway. "I am driver. You must pay me fifty dollars."

"But we didn't even do anything."

"I am sorry you did not like girl, but you must still pay me."

"I did like the fucking girl, Frankenstein. She was the one that walked out."

"That is not my problem. You must pay me fifty dollars."

Craig pulled back both hammers before pointing the sawed-off at the man's face. "Tell the whore to pay you your fifty dollars, Frankenstein. Now get the fuck outta here before I plaster this hallway with your big ugly fucking face."

The man raised his hands and backed up a few feet before turning around and heading for the staircase.

After the man left, Craig continued to sniff more and more coke.

It was bad enough the cops and those guys from The Bronx were after him. He still wasn't sure about the guys from Coney Island, but at least none of those people knew about this hotel room.

Now he had to worry about that big ugly Russian Frankenstein coming back. He had considered shooting him right there, but was worried about the girl. She could ID Craig and bring the cops right to him. And besides, there would be no way of hiding a shotgun blast. The people in the hotel would have called the cops even if the girl didn't. Then he would lose everything and have to spend the last couple of months of his life in jail.

After sniffing a couple more grams, Craig was back to pacing the room in his underwear—sweating, drooling, eyes bulging, and bleeding from the nose—guns in both of his trembling hands, ready to pull the trigger at any moment.

Between the Viagra and the coke, Craig's heart pounded against his rib cage.

He felt dizzy.

Everything faded to black.

CHAPTER 91

That morning, Abby arrived early at the office to check on her unauthorized phone tap of Victor's cell phone.

On Friday, she had scanned some documents that her captain had already signed authorizing a phone tap, the problem was, the documents were from another case, a closed case from last year.

Friday afternoon, she used Photoshop to alter the names and dates on the documents, then she requested the phone tap Saturday morning before heading out to Coney Island with Faith.

It wasn't until Sunday morning that the request finally went through and she had access to his phone calls. But, Victor hadn't used his phone all day Sunday.

Now that Victor was at home pending review, Abby hoped that he'd get bored or depressed and finish whatever pills he had in the house, and would have to go out for more. Her goal was to catch him red-handed buying drugs, then she might be able to talk her way around the unauthorized phone tap. Even if Victor wasn't convicted because of Abby's wrongdoing, at least she could still get him thrown off the force without a pension.

CHAPTER 92

Craig didn't know if he'd had a heart attack last night, but he did black out, and figured that probably qualified as an overdose.

He woke up on the floor and found that he had pissed on himself. After taking off his disgusting clothes, Craig took a handful of Advil for his pounding head, then took a shower. He felt hotter than usual, but decided to dress warm, just in case his temperature dropped again later.

Still feeling like shit, Craig counted his money, which was over sixteen thousand dollars. With his original three grand, and the thirty thousand from the guys in Coney Island, Craig now had about fifty grand, plus the other money that he'd just stuffed in there, maybe ten or twenty thousand, maybe more.

He took a taxi to the bank and put all the cash—minus a little spending money—into the backpack in his mother's safe deposit box. He took the last brick and headed back to his hotel room, hoping he wouldn't run into the Russian Frankenstein.

While in the taxi, even though the air was on, he began to sweat. He wondered if the temperature had gone up, or if his mini-overdose raised his body temperature permanently.

Craig thought about what he'd been doing. If he kept going the way he was going now, he would end up dead or arrested and never get to use all that money.

He decided the best thing would be to lower his prices to twenty-five a gram and try to get rid of everything as soon as possible so he could take the money, somehow sneak out of the country, and get to India for his transplant before it was too late.

After bagging up a few hundred more grams in his hotel room, Craig lay down for a nap with his safe deposit box key in his pocket, his revolver in his hand, and the shotgun under the mattress. All the coke was under the bed in the luggage that he had gotten from Anthony.

CHAPTER 93

That evening, after finishing her shift with Mangano, Abby checked Victor's phone calls and was disappointed to find that he only called two people: Rosie Li and his wife, Evelyn.

She knew it was probably a waste of time, but at this point, she was becoming obsessed. Abby called her mother, spoke to Faith, and told them she'd be working overtime again tonight.

After driving from Manhattan to Queens in the middle of rush hour traffic again, Abby parked across the street from Victor's little blue house and wondered if he was home. She sat there for about an hour before seeing Victor come out of his house.

Victor carried a plastic container that looked like it contained food to the little white house connected to his house. He rang the bell and waited a few minutes.

A black woman wearing scrubs answered the door. Victor handed her the plastic container, said something, then headed back to his house.

While Victor entered his own house, Abby decided that she should get back to hers. She waited for him to close the door behind him, then she started the car and took off toward the Brooklyn Queens Expressway.

CHAPTER 94

After eating dinner with his mistress at their favorite Italian restaurant, Enzo and Layla stepped out of the air-conditioned building and onto the steaming hot sidewalk. Enzo felt like turning around and going back in, but he wanted a cigar.

Layla smoked a cigarette, then, when it was finished, she threw the butt into the gutter and slipped a stick of gum into her mouth. "Can we get outta this fucking sauna already?"

With his cigar between his teeth, Enzo fished a small box from his pocket and handed it to Layla. "Take a look at this first."

She smiled and opened it. Inside was a pair of gold earrings with a small diamond in the shape of a heart.

Layla kissed him, hugged him, then said, "These are beautiful. Thank you. I'm gonna suck your dick extra good tonight."

Enzo smiled while puffing his cigar and anticipating his blowjob.

While strolling down the block, Enzo lost his footing. He knew he had too many drinks before dinner, but he thought he was okay. Now he was having second thoughts. The last thing he needed was extra trouble.

"Listen, sweetheart. My car's in a good spot. Let's walk one more block and grab a cab."

Layla chuckled. "You too drunk to drive?"

"Do I look drunk? I just don't wanna lose my spot."

Back at Layla's apartment, Layla tried on her new earrings,

took off her clothes, and fulfilled her promise to Enzo.

When she was done, she went into the bathroom to spit and rinse.

Enzo pulled his pants up, opened the closet, lifted up a couple blankets, and pulled out a small metal box. He opened the metal box with a key and took out a big 357 revolver, which he then loaded and placed on the bed.

After slipping the box back under the blankets in the closet, Enzo zipped up his pants and tightened his belt.

Layla stepped out of the bathroom in a sexy black nightgown and approached the bed. "Are you planning to shoot me?" She picked up the gun and looked at it.

"Don't play with that. I just loaded it." He stepped toward her, hoping she wasn't stupid enough to accidentally pull the trigger.

Layla did a gangster pose in the mirror. "I'm not gonna shoot it." She turned and handed it to him. "Don't get so nervous."

He slipped the gun into the back of his waistband, the same way he'd seen Johnny do it, then he stepped toward, Layla placed his hands on her tight little waist, and said, "You did look sexy, though. Sexy and dangerous."

"Really?" She grabbed his dick through the pants and said, "Does this gun have another shot left in it?"

CHAPTER 95

That evening Craig delivered over five hundred grams of cocaine. Every day, customers introduced him to new customers, and every day, everyone wanted more and more. They were buying big now, sometimes fifty to a hundred grams per person. He was a little worried about undercover cops, but was more worried about the cops who were already after him. And, more than that, he was worried about dropping dead within the next few weeks because of liver failure.

Craig took taxis to all his stops. Even with his revolver on him, he still felt nervous about taking public transportation with that much stuff on him.

He hadn't done any coke that night and was trying to keep it that way. He had a lot of money on him, some of it stuffed into his pants pockets, and some of it in his sweatshirt pockets along with the 38.

The sun was long gone, but the oppressive heat and humidity lingered.

Craig hadn't eaten all day, so he stopped at a pizzeria. The big glass doors were open in the front, but the breeze from outside was just hot air, and the heat from the ovens in the back wasn't helping.

After ordering one slice and a grape soda, he stood alone at the counter against the wall and ate while watching people on the Avenue outside. Most of the stores were closed, but the restaurants, Laundromats, and hair salons were still open.

On the sidewalk outside, a young woman with matted hair and dirty clothes asked a couple people for spare change, but they didn't give her anything. She noticed Craig watching her and then stepped into the pizzeria. "Could you spare a little change for something to eat?"

He noticed that under all that filth, she had a nice body. "You hungry?" He asked.

She looked at him in silence for a moment, then nodded.

Craig turned to the pizza man and said, "Another regular slice and grape juice, please." He handed the man a five-dollar bill then took the pizza and drink and placed it on the counter against the wall, next to his.

The girl looked at Craig for a moment, then tore into the pizza.

He could picture her cleaned up, naked and dripping wet after a shower. It would be nice to get some use out of that Viagra. "What's your name?"

"She answered while still chewing and without raising her head from the plate. " Courtney."

He figured that was probably a fake name, so he decided to do the same, "I'm Mike."

She didn't say anything. She just kept eating.

Craig wasn't sure if she'd heard what he said or not. He could tell she had been getting high, and he knew she would give him what he wanted for a little coke. "I have some coke if you want to party."

She swallowed what was in her mouth, then slurped down the last of her drink while staring at him.

"Well?"

Courtney nodded.

Craig led her outside and then they strolled a few blocks to his hotel, stopping at a deli on the way for a pack of cigarettes, a six-pack of beer, a big bottle of water, and some snacks.

As soon as they got to the room, Craig popped a Viagra. He needed time for it to kick in, and he didn't want to start doing coke right away, so he told her, "You can take a shower if you want." He turned the air conditioner on.

She nodded and said, "Thanks. I could use one."

He pointed to the bathroom and said, "Towels and anything else you need should be there. Oh . . . and you could use my robe, it's hanging behind the door."

Courtney smiled and headed into the bathroom.

Craig lit a cigarette and smoked it while glancing out the closed window at the streetlights below. He hoped she would take her time in the shower, not only because he needed time for the Viagra to work, but he wanted her to get cleaned up properly.

Either Courtney couldn't tell how yellow he was, or she didn't care. Craig figured that she probably just didn't care. He kept the light in the room low anyway, just to be sure.

For a moment, he wondered how many other sick men she'd been with. He knew it was disgusting and he was taking a risk, but then he remembered how the Russian call girl treated him. He couldn't even pay for pussy in his condition. He had to take what he could get, or get nothing at all.

Courtney spent about twenty minutes in the shower, then came out clean and wrapped in the white cotton hotel robe.

Craig noticed that her skin looked smooth and delicious. Her wet hair was still a matted mess, but he could get past that.

He took some coke out and gave her a rolled up dollar bill while trying to get a glimpse of her breasts from inside the robe. Courtney reminded him of his cousin Marie, and between that thought and the Viagra, his dick grew to a size he'd never known before.

They both sniffed a few lines and then smoked a cigarette while sitting on the bed.

Craig was nervous when he started touching her bare leg. She didn't look like she was enjoying it, but she didn't push him away. He caressed her flesh lightly while going a little higher each time. Finally, he opened the robe and brushed his fingertips over her pussy lips.

Courtney said, "Put some coke on my clit."

Craig liked that idea. He ripped open another gram and gave her a huge sniff before sprinkling the rest on her pussy.

He knew going down on a pig like Courtney could have him getting penicillin shots later, but between his liver failure and being wanted for murder, eating a strange pussy was the least of his worries. It had been so long, he wanted to taste her bad.

Courtney lied back and closed her eyes while Craig began to lick, kiss, and suck her pussy. He didn't like that fact that she had a hairy bush and legs like a Neanderthal, but the rest of her made it worth it.

Craig's mouth, tongue, and part of his face became numb as he went to work on Courtney's wet pussy. The more she seemed to enjoy it, the more it made his dick hard—so hard it was painful.

He couldn't take it anymore. Craig lifted his body while pulling his pants down and then he pushed his throbbing cock deep inside her.

She moaned louder and louder as he fucked her harder and harder. He blew his load in about five minutes, but that didn't matter, thanks to the Viagra, he was still as hard as a fifteen-year-old boy.

He gave her some more coke, which she sniffed while he took his clothes all the way off.

Craig only sniffed a small line before jumping back onto the bed.

He fucked her for almost an hour, but he never came a second time.

When Courtney's pussy was dry and swollen, she begged him to stop.

They sniffed a couple more grams, had a couple beers, and then, a couple hours later, they finally fell asleep.

When Craig woke up, the sunlight barely began to show itself from outside the window. It took a moment to remember that Courtney was there. He turned and didn't see her next to him. Getting out of the bed, he caught a chill, then turned the air conditioner off.

The bathroom door was closed and he could see that the light was on. His dick was still hard, and he wanted to use it one more time while he could.

Craig lit a cigarette, and instead of knocking on the bathroom door, he decided to wait until she came out.

He finished his cigarette and glanced over at the light under the bathroom door, wondering what she could be doing in there for that long.

Finally, after waiting on the bed for another fifteen minutes and almost falling asleep again, Craig decided to find out what was going on.

He approached the door and knocked. "Courtney? You okay in there?"

She didn't answer, but he could hear her moving things and

sniffing. Then he realized what she was doing . . . sniffing his coke.

The door was locked, but it was a cheap piece of shit. Craig forced the knob and angled the door to pry it open.

Courtney stood there high as a kite, holding Craig's 38. His luggage sat open and empty in the corner. She was dressed and her pockets were stuffed full. The money that didn't fit in her pockets was all over the floor along with some of his coke.

Craig knew he could stop her from leaving, but he was scared of her pulling that trigger, even if she missed, he'd still be fucked. He decided to bluff and see if it would work.

"Okay. Don't shoot. Just take what you can carry and go. I can always get more. I won't even follow you." Craig raised his empty hands and stepped out of the way for her to pass him, hoping she wouldn't pull that trigger.

Courtney didn't speak, she just stood there, pointing the gun at Craig. Finally, moving as slow as a zombie, she stepped out of the bathroom and made her way toward the front door.

When she turned to open the door, Craig reached under the mattress for his shotgun and pointed it at her back as she grasped the knob.

He wanted to blow her brains out, but he knew that would be the end of him too, he would never have enough time to get all his shit together and get away before the cops came.

Instead of shooting her, Craig smashed the back of her head with the butt of the gun.

Courtney fell sideways. Her head smacked into the TV hanging from the wall, then her limp body dropped to the floor. Blood trickled from her skull and onto the floor. Craig stared at her wondering if she was dead. He only hit her once, and he was a weak man, could he really have killed her?

Finally, after steaming down a few cigarettes and waiting for Courtney to wake up, Craig checked her pulse. He squeezed her wrist, but didn't feel anything. He had no idea how to check for a pulse, he'd only seen it done on TV. It seemed that everyone always checked the wrist or the neck.

Craig still didn't feel a pulse in her wrist, so he tried her neck, but didn't feel anything there either. After hesitating, he lifted Courtney's eyelids. Her eyes looked fake. Just as he removed his hand from her face, he felt her head drop. He picked it up and let it drop again. Her neck was broken.

How many was that now? Craig had killed so many people he'd lost count.

After taking all his money and coke out of her pockets and packing it up in his luggage, he sat next to Courtney's corpse and wondered what to do with it. At least there wasn't all that piss and shit like with Robby. Craig figured that pizza was probably her first meal in days, and after all that coke, she had to be as dehydrated as he was.

There was no way to get the body out of that hotel without anyone noticing. Even in the middle of the night, the area was full of hookers, thugs, and cops. He thought about chopping her up and removing the parts little by little. But, where would he dump them? And, how long would that take? Not to mention the mess.

He knew he was running out of time. He had to get rid of the last of that coke and get the hell out of the country quick. His only choice was to keep the body under the bed next to his stash and keep the do not disturb sign on the door for a few days until he could get away, hopefully before she began to stink.

While dragging Courtney's corpse facedown across the floor, Craig stared at the shape of her round ass through her filthy jeans. The Viagra must have still been in his blood, because his dick grew instantly. He squeezed it. It felt nice. It felt the same as it did last night when she was still alive.

Knowing that there was a good possibility he might be dead himself within a matter of days, Craig decided that he wanted to get laid one last time.

He knew it was wrong, but it didn't seem so disgusting to him. Just ten minutes ago, she was alive. It was more like she was sleeping. Technically, she was dead, but she was still fresh and pliable, and she was still beautiful. He knew it would take a while for rigor mortis to set in, and this would be his only chance.

Craig struggled to turn Courtney's corpse over and take off her clothes. When he finally had her naked, he almost changed his mind. He sat there with his chemically induced hard-on and closed his eyes, trying to clear his mind of such terrible ideas.

The air conditioner was on high, but between the heat wave and dragging a dead body across his hotel room, Craig still overheated. Sweat dripped from his head, face, and body.

For some reason, the thought of his dirty, sexy cousin Marie once again entered Craig's mind and his dick felt as if it were going to explode.

He couldn't resist. He touched her flat stomach and then spent a little time sucking and caressing her breasts. At first, he enjoyed it, but after a few minutes, he remembered she was dead. He stopped and lay down on his back. He shouldn't be doing this. She's dead.

His dick was throbbing and he knew he either had to jerk off or get over it and fuck Courtney's corpse before it hardened up. He rolled on top of her and tried to stick it in.

There was no lubrication, so Craig retrieved a small bottle of lotion from the bathroom and fucked her corpse. Because of the pill, he was nowhere near ejaculation. And looking at her expressionless dead face was beginning to turn him off. He thought about opening the eyes, but then decided that would be even creepier.

He knew he could concentrate better if he just did her from the back, so he turned the body over, raised her hips by placing a pillow under her pelvis, and then slipped it into her asshole, the one thing she would not let him do when she was alive.

Finally, after fucking Courtney's corpse like a savage animal for at least twenty minutes, Craig blew his load and rolled off her. He instantly felt guilty and sickened.

Using his feet, he quickly pushed the dead body under the bed and tried not to think about what he had just done.

Before lying down on the bed, he smoked a few cigarettes. There was no way he could sleep knowing the body was right under him. Tempted to do some coke, he resisted, knowing that getting high with a corpse in the room might drive him completely over the edge.

CHAPTER 96

Craig had laid on the bed with his eyes open for about an hour until the sun came up. His body temperature dropped significantly, so he got up and turned the air-conditioner off.

While trying to devise a plan on how to get rid of the last of the coke as quickly as possible and get out of the country without being caught, Craig began to sweat again. He thought about opening a window, but remembered the forecast said today would be even hotter than yesterday—over a hundred.

He turned the air-conditioner back on and adjusted it to seventy-four before jumping in the shower and washing his filthy sinful body. He kept forgetting which parts he already washed as his brain kept reminding itself that a dead girl was in the next room. A few times, he thought she might get up and come into the bathroom to get her revenge.

When he was sure he was done washing, he turned the water off and imagined Courtney's ghost lingering in the steam.

Craig shivered as he stepped out of the shower and reached for his towel.

It was not easy, but he forced himself to stop thinking about the dead girl in the next room and start thinking about what the hell he was going to do.

While getting dressed he devised a plan. Assuming that the Italian and Dominican guys were the ones who'd lost the coke, Craig decided to make them a deal. He would tell them that he'll give back all four kilos—untouched—for a small finder's fee. Of course, the coke was mostly gone, but they didn't know that.

He planned to lead them to The Howell Building where he knew his way around and fatal traps could be set very easily.

While thinking of ways to kill them, he realized that he could also lure the cops there, and hopefully kill everyone that was after him. Maybe he could make it look like the bad guys killed the cops. Or, maybe, he could make it look like an accident happened while the cops were taking down the bad guys. Either way, he hoped to remove suspicion from himself long enough to get away.

That still left getting out of the country. Craig decided the best way to go, would be first to make it to Mexico, then possibly get a transplant there or in Brazil. From his research, he knew the procedures would be much cheaper than in the US, but not as successful as the transplants being done in India.

He called everyone he knew and told them he had to get rid of whatever coke he had left right away. He told them it would only cost fifteen dollars a gram, but he wasn't making any more deliveries after lunch.

He bagged up the last of what he had—a little more than a quarter of a kilo—then he headed out to The Howell Building. He still had plenty of time to get there before the workers took their morning coffee break.

He sold less than a hundred grams. He knew he could have sold it all, but since the guys weren't expecting him, they didn't have that kind of cash with them. A few guys snuck out to the ATM, but the others didn't want to get stuck coming back too late.

After finishing his business at The Howell Building, Craig took the train back to Brooklyn and went straight to the bank.

He stuffed the money he'd just made into the backpack along with whatever coke he had on him, then counted out five thousand dollars and left it in the safe deposit box for his mother to find one day.

Craig left the bank and took car service back to his hotel.

In his room, he emptied the contents out of the backpack and onto the bed. After putting the coke into his pants pocket, he straightened out, organized, and counted the cash. He had eighty-three thousand dollars. And, if things worked out the way he was hoping, he would add another twenty thousand to the pot.

While retrieving the luggage from under the bed, Craig tried not to look at Courtney's naked corpse. The more he tried to look away, the more his eyes drifted back to her. His flesh tingled and his stomach churned while thinking about what he did to her. It didn't seem so bad at the time, but looking at her now, he was sickened. Her dried up skin had a blue tint to it and she didn't appear to be resting in peace. He looked away.

Craig stood with the luggage, opened it, threw the backpack into it, then pushed it back under the bed without looking.

He turned the air conditioner on maximum, hoping to help preserve the body for as long as possible, then made sure to place the, do not disturb, sign on the doorknob before leaving.

The first thing he did was go to a small cell phone store and buy two prepaid phones with GPS tracking. He told the man he wanted to know where his kid was at all the time. He paid, wrote down the numbers, then waited for the phones to be activated.

It was a long train ride from Brooklyn to The Bronx, but it was early still. Most people were probably having lunch at the time. He only had to take the R train a couple stops before transferring to the D train, which would take him all the way up to where he wanted to go.

While the train rumbled on and on along the express track, Craig hoped his assumptions about the Italian and Dominican guys being the ones who lost the coke were correct.

By the time he arrived in The Bronx, school kids were everywhere, yelling, running, and screaming. He followed a long narrow street lined on both sides by six-story brick apartment buildings until arriving at a hospital that occupied a few blocks.

He remembered that he had to go around the hospital, but he checked the map on his phone just to be sure about which direction would be quicker.

After circling the hospital property, Craig finally found Arthur Avenue, which he then followed while watching the addresses. He still had a long way to go, and he was getting tired, so he stopped for a cup of coffee at a deli.

The school kids were still out and the Manhattan commuters were still in Manhattan. Craig didn't even know if those guys would be there again, but he didn't know what else to do. If he couldn't find them, he'd have to take what cash he had and take his chances trying to get to Mexico without the cops picking him up.

After finishing his coffee, Craig headed back down Arthur

Avenue looking at all the Bakeries, Salumeria's, and other Italian stores. He'd never been here before, but he'd heard about it. This area was known as The Bronx's Little Italy. It reminded him of how Marie's neighborhood was when they were kids.

He finally found the bar and took a deep breath before entering.

CHAPTER 97

Enzo sat at his favorite table in the back of the bar while the bartender brought him a glass of soda. He was waiting for a big client to arrive, so he didn't want to have a drink before talking business.

A tall thin man in a sweatshirt and jeans entered the bar and looked around before heading towards the back.

Enzo thought the man was going to pass his table and go to the bathroom, but he didn't. The man stopped and sat down at Enzo's table. Who the fuck is this wise guy? "Excuse me," said Enzo, "But that seat is taken."

"I'll only be a minute, Enzo."

"Do I know you?" It wasn't easy to spot, but Enzo noticed a yellow tint to the man's skin and eyes. He realized it was Craig Hill.

Craig confirmed Enzo's theory. "My name is Craig Hill, and I have what you want."

Enzo sipped his soda and noticed someone else entering the bar—two men—the client he was waiting for. He motioned for them to wait a minute then he turned to Craig and said, "Some very powerful and dangerous people are looking for you."

"I know, and if you haven't heard, I'll be dead in less than two months anyway. So fuck you and your powerful, dangerous friends."

Enzo felt like slapping this man across the face, the same way he used to slap his boys when they got wise.

Craig said, “Let me make this quick. I’ll give you back your package, for a finder’s fee.”

Enzo didn’t want to bargain with this prick, but he did want to get an idea of what he wanted. He asked, “How much?”

“Ten grand each.” Craig still wasn’t sure if the man knew he was talking about four kilos of cocaine, but now he was about to find out.

“Cazzo. You want ten grand for each kilo? Forty G’s? You must be fucking nuts.”

Craig was sure that was their drugs now, so he was ready to bargain. “Okay, seven fifty.”

“I’ll have to talk to some other people about this, and I can’t go to them with a ridiculous figure like that.”

Craig said, “The lowest I’ll go is twenty. That’s five each.” He took out his 38 and showed it to Enzo on the side. “Don’t forget. I have nothing to lose.”

Enzo was tired of people pulling guns out on him, but at least he had his own gun with him now, and that gave him a little confidence. “That yellow skin scares me a lot more than that gun, kid. Put it away before you hurt yourself.”

Craig slipped the revolver back into his front sweatshirt pocket.

Enzo said, “Five each. That’s twenty grand.”

Craig said, “Agreed.”

“Now. Where is it?”

“Bring the money to the eighth floor of The Howell Building tonight at ten o’clock, and I’ll bring the stuff.” Craig handed Enzo the cell phone he’d bought earlier and said, “I’ll call you on this phone.”

Enzo looked at the phone and said, “You watch too many movies, kid.” He slipped the phone into his jacket pocket and then tapped on the heavy steel bulge in his other jacket pocket, making sure Craig knew he was not the only one with a gun. “See you at ten.”

CHAPTER 98

By the time Craig got back to Manhattan, he took the bus to the east side and stopped at a hardware store where he bought a hammer, an adjustable wrench, and a knife.

He was hungry, but he didn't want to waste time eating, so he bought a chocolate milk from a deli and chugged it while walking.

The hot sun still loomed overhead, but was on its way toward the west.

Craig hurried to The Howell Building. The crew was gone and the building was locked up. He peeked inside the temporary plywood door and saw the security guard in his booth reading a newspaper. Craig knew him, and he was happy he was on duty tonight. He didn't want to yell, but he had to get his attention. "Goose."

He banged on the plywood door twice, then waited for the guard to leave his booth and approach Craig. He was tall and wide with a booming voice. "What the hell are you doing here?"

"I was supposed to pick up my tools this morning to go to another job tomorrow, but I was sick, and I didn't come in. Thank God it's you working."

"You got any of that good weed?"

Craig remembered Goose mention once that he likes a little coke now and then. He showed Goose a couple of individually wrapped grams of coke and said, "I have some of this."

Goose looked around and said, "Put that away." He took the

keys from his belt and let Craig in. "Get in here before someone sees you."

They went inside, then Goose put the chain and lock back on.

Craig liked Goose, but he'd gone too far now to turn back, and he couldn't let any more obstacles obstruct his course. He would try to give the guy a chance, but he'd kill him if he had to. "Here, take a sample, but don't do it now, it's good shit." He handed Goose a gram, but made sure to let him see a few other grams.

Goose looked at it. "Nice and yellow." He slipped it into his pocket and asked, "It's yours?"

Craig nodded.

"How much you gettin'?"

Craig didn't want to make it sound too good to be true, so he said, "forty a gram."

"Not a bad price."

"Listen. I didn't really come here for my tools. I have a deal to make and I want to do it here. There's a cop that lives on my floor and I can't do it at my mother's house. What time you finish tonight?"

Goose shook his head while saying, Twelve o'clock, but I—"

Craig interrupted him. "I'll give you ten grams if you give me the keys to the place until eleven thirty."

"Ten grams? You trying to give me a heart attack?"

"Don't do it all tonight. What the fuck?"

"I don't know, man."

Craig didn't know if Goose was going for it, but he wanted to try a little harder before resorting to something terrible. "Listen, you take the coke, but don't do it tonight. I'll punch your little clock there every hour, then you come back at the end your shift before the next guy comes in." Craig really didn't want to kill the guy. He wanted him to take the deal. "I'll give you fifteen grams. You can't beat that."

"I don't know, man. Fifteen grams sounds real nice. But what if you or someone else gets killed in here. Not only would I be responsible for another human being losing their life, but I'd also lose my job, and if I can't pay my rent . . . fifteen grams ain't shit."

Craig waited for a definite answer.

Goose said, "I'm sorry, Craig. I can't do it."

"I understand." Craig had no choice now. This man was

standing in the way of his liver transplant. "Give me a call after you try that." He pretended to walk toward the door, then stopped and said, "You wanna smoke a joint?"

"Damn right. Just let me punch that clock real quick." Goose punched a time card machine, then began toward the stairs.

Craig knew the only way he could kill a man Goose's size was to shoot him, and he decided the best place to do that would be in the basement. "We better smoke in the basement."

"The basement? It's dark down there, and there's rats and water bugs."

Craig pointed at Goose's belt and said, "You got a flashlight. You know bugs and rats are scared of the light. Just shine it around a little."

"Why?" Asked Goose, "When we could just smoke upstairs?"

Craig had to think quickly. "They installed cameras upstairs. That's why they fired that other security guard."

"He wasn't smoking weed. He left his post and someone got in and stole all that copper."

"I know. That's why they installed the cameras. That's what I heard anyway. It might be bullshit, but it's both our asses if it's true."

Goose stared at Craig and then finally said, "Alright, let's go." He took the flashlight off his belt and moved toward the stairs.

Craig stayed behind Goose as he illuminated the way down the stairs and then into the basement. He reached into his pocket, coughed to disguise the noise while pulling the trigger back, then slipped the safety off. A month ago, Craig never would have been able to do something like this, but now killing people was a lot easier.

Goose stopped at the bottom of the stairs and shined his light around. The basement was dark, but the flashlight revealed that there were no rats or water bugs in the vicinity.

Craig followed Goose toward a huge cardboard box that stood taller than both of them.

Goose shined the light around the floor and said, "Hurry up, man. Light that thing up."

Craig almost changed his mind about killing Goose, but it was either that, or get fucked, and Craig didn't want to get fucked.

He stepped back and whipped out his 38.

He fired a single shot into Goose's forehead.

Blood and brains splattered out the back of his skull and onto the cardboard box.

The eyes never moved while the body convulsed and fell backward. Whatever was in that box was too heavy to fall over, so Goose's limp corpse slid across it, leaving blood streaks on its way down to the floor.

While reaching down to pry the flashlight from Goose's grasp, Craig wondered if anyone outside could have heard that shot. He would know soon enough.

He didn't bother wasting his energy moving the body because if his plan didn't work, then none of it mattered anyway.

Craig headed back up the stairs and peeked outside to be sure the cops weren't there, then he began his journey up the stairs to the eighth floor. Stopping a few times to catch his breath and wipe the sweat from his head and face, he wished he'd brought a couple bottles of water with him.

He checked each floor on his way up for a rope, but instead, on the third floor, he saw an old extension cord in a mini-dumpster. After getting it free of the other garbage, he coiled it loosely and brought it with him on his journey up.

Finally, when he got to the eighth floor, he sat down on a metal gang box and rested for a while with the flashlight off to conserve the batteries. The entire floor was dark because plywood covered the window openings.

He was tired already and wondered if he could have gotten the same results on the fifth or sixth floors, but he knew this would be better, he'd just have to tough it out and get it done.

After checking the time on his phone, he also checked the location of the phone he'd given Enzo. The GPS tracker showed that he was still at the same bar in The Bronx, but that didn't mean anything, only that the phone was there. Enzo could have left without it.

Craig couldn't know for sure, so he decided to continue his preparations and hope for the best. He prayed, asking God's forgiveness for murder, then asking God to help him out of this situation alive.

He placed the flashlight onto the gang box, shined it in the direction where he would be working, then started with the easy tasks first.

After removing the two-by-fours and warning signs that made

up a protective barrier blocking the open elevator shafts, he hid all the lumber behind a stack of boxes.

Sweat dripped from his head and face, he wiped it from his eyes with the back of his hand and wished he'd come better prepared. He tried to reduce his breathing and not concentrate on his dry mouth.

After a short break, Craig removed a couple sheets of Masonite from a stack and carried it to the elevator banks. He was happy there was Masonite on every floor, he didn't think he'd have the time or the strength to carry materials up and down the stairs.

The eighth floor had no sheetrock installed anywhere and only a few metal studs here and there as markers for the electricians, plumbers, and steamfitters. Most of the pipes in the walls and ceilings had already been installed and it looked as if the electrical conduits were almost finished. The floors were still bare concrete.

Craig carefully placed two thin sheets of flimsy brown Masonite onto the floor, covering the elevator shaft openings.

He found an empty cardboard box, cut the flaps off, set it upside down on the floor, then kicked it, sliding it across the Masonite toward the back wall. Fortunately, the box was light enough not to disturb Craig's false floor.

The next thing he needed was a ladder. There were plenty of ladders on the eight floor, but they were all chained up.

He made his way down to the seventh floor, which looked the same as the eighth floor, and found that the ladders there were also chained up.

On the sixth floor, there were partially built rooms with metal studs and sheetrock. The bathrooms were all tiled. Craig went in and out of every room until he finally found a ladder that someone had left opened in a bedroom, a six-foot yellow fiberglass ladder.

Once back on the eighth floor, he sat on the gang box for a few minutes with the flashlight off and caught his breath once again.

After checking the time on his phone, Craig realized it was getting late and he would have to keep working without a break. His body ached, but his mind pushed forward. He had to get the work done, and get it done right, for his plan to succeed.

He then checked the GPS again and saw that the phone he'd given Enzo was still in The Bronx, but not at the bar. Craig had no idea where the man could be, but at least he wasn't here yet, and at least he didn't dump the phone.

He placed the ladder in the center of the hallway and climbed it with the wrench in hand. He loosened the connections on the fire sprinkler pipe so that one length of pipe separated from the others.

While removing the last coupling, he wondered if Enzo could have left the phone somewhere and some kid, or maybe even a bum could have found it and is wandering around with it right now. He tried not to think about it, he tried to concentrate on the task at hand.

Craig moved the ladder, tied the old extension cord onto one end of the separated pipe, threw the cord over another pipe, and then let it hit the ground. He descended the ladder and tied the loose end of the extension cord around a horizontal drainage pipe about fifteen feet away.

After loosening the clamps from the concrete ceiling, the pipe dropped a few inches. One end wedged itself against the pipe it was just connected to while the other end hung suspended by the extension cord.

Craig made sure to stay far enough back while examining his work. He hoped that extension cord would hold long enough.

He checked the time on his phone. It was after nine.

He checked the GPS tracker on his phone. Whoever had the phone was now on the highway travelling south. It had to be Enzo. He expected everyone to arrive early, he just hoped not too early.

Craig climbed the stairs one flight to the roof and turned off the flashlight to conserve the batteries. The night air was steamy, but an occasional breeze made it bearable.

While looking at the pipe scaffolding connected to the side of the building, Craig picked up his phone and dialed the number on Victor Cohen's card.

CHAPTER 99

Victor nodded out in bed next to his sleeping wife while the TV played in the background and the air conditioner pumped the room full of arctic air.

His phone rang. He jumped.

Evelyn rolled over, but didn't wake up.

Victor didn't recognize the number, but he answered anyway. "Cohen here."

An unfamiliar voice said, "I hear you've been looking for me."

It didn't take long for Victor to realize who he was talking to. "Craig? Where are you?"

"Listen. I'm in trouble."

"I know. You have to turn yourself in."

"I can't. The guys that are after me could have me killed in jail. I need your help."

"I'm on leave . . . pending evaluation."

There was silence on the line.

"Craig, you there?"

"I'm here. Listen. I'm meeting these guys in The Howell Building at ten-thirty tonight. They said they'll let me go if I give them their stuff back, but I have a feeling they're going to kill me after they get what they want."

"Who are these guys?" Asked Victor, wondering if Craig was telling the truth.

"Big time Mafia guys. I don't know, somehow they're doing business with some Dominicans."

Victor asked, “And, what about that dead junkie?”

Craig asked, “Who?”

“That junkie laborer, Robby McPherson.”

“I’ll tell you everything tonight. I gotta run. Ten-thirty tonight . . . at The Howell Building.” Craig hung up.

Victor said, “Wait.” but it was too late. He placed the phone on the nightstand and sat on the edge of the bed wondering how much of what this guy was saying was the truth. He looked at the clock, it was 9:15.

He jumped out of bed, threw on a pair of jeans and a T-shirt, grabbed his gun, and left a note for his wife.

CHAPTER 100

Abby had tucked her daughter in at nine o'clock, then after a small snack and a few minutes of reading the bible, she checked her computer.

The first thing she checked was the phone tap on Victor. She noticed that he received a call from a number she didn't recognize—at 9:15—just ten minutes ago.

Abby's heart pounded in her chest as she typed in her password to retrieve the record of the call. Her heart pounded even harder while listening to the recorded conversation between Craig Hill and Victor Cohen. She listened to it again to be sure there was no confusion.

She grabbed her laptop and her gun, called and woke up her mother, then dragged Faith out of bed once more.

CHAPTER 101

After Enzo's meeting with Craig, Enzo had called Peppino and made it sound like the meeting was at gunpoint. Peppino said he'd be sending twenty thousand dollars with Johnny, but he wants it back, and he wants Craig dead.

Johnny drove his black Camaro while Enzo squirmed around in the passenger seat. He didn't need this shit. After getting through this, he planned to pack it up and retire to Arizona. Enzo felt a little confidence because he had his gun, but he was still scared.

Traffic on the FDR Drive in Manhattan wasn't bad, but that's because it was a Tuesday night and hot as hell. Enzo knew that the smart people were home with their families enjoying their air conditioners.

Enzo looked over at Johnny, but Johnny didn't speak or show any expression. He just drove the car like a robot on a mission.

Once they arrived at The Howell Building, Johnny passed it slowly, checking out the area, then he circled the block and did it again.

Enzo looked at his watch, it was, 9:30. He just hoped to get out of this alive and without having to spend the rest of his years in prison.

Johnny found a spot on the street, a block and a half away from the building.

As they walked, heavy gusts of wind blew garbage around in

the street.

Enzo squinted and tried not to swallow the wind as it pushed against his face and body.

Johnny, still wearing his sunglasses, crouched over slightly and marched forward.

Traffic on the streets and the sidewalks began to dwindle.

They approached the temporary plywood door. An unlocked chain dangled from it.

Enzo just hoped this kid wasn't smart enough to out-maneuver Johnny.

Johnny removed the chain and pulled the plywood door open against the wind, then, after going inside, he replaced the chain with the ends inside.

Enzo knew that to any passersby, it would seem like the door was locked. Maybe Johnny was the better man. Enzo started to feel better. He watched Johnny examine the empty security guard booth and the silent construction site ahead.

The wind outside slammed against the plywood door. Enzo jumped, sweat poured down his head and onto his face.

"Take it easy. It's just the wind." Johnny took off his sunglasses, slipped them into his shirt pocket, and retrieved a flashlight. "I need you to be alert. Now, let's find the stairs."

"Stairs?"

Johnny said, "Even if this building had a working elevator, I wouldn't take it, that's the easiest way to set someone up." With the flashlight in one hand and his Glock in the other, Johnny entered the building.

Enzo followed Johnny into the darkness while wondering if he could make it up eight flights of stairs.

CHAPTER 102

When Victor got out of the train in Manhattan, a powerful gust of wind almost blew him over. He noticed other people also trying to fight the wind. It felt like a hurricane moving in.

He didn't want to wait for the bus, so he jumped in a taxi and called Rosie.

Rosie answered after two rings, "Hey, partner. What's up?"

"Craig Hill called me. Told me he's meeting some mafia guys at The Howell Building and he wants my help."

"You think it's a trap?"

Victor said, "Could be a trap, could be the truth, could be a little of both."

"You want me to go with you?"

"I'm almost there."

Rosie said, "I'm coming. I'd tell you to wait until I get there, but I know you won't."

Victor said, "I'll see you soon."

They ended the call.

Victor stared out the car window. He could feel the wind outside pushing the taxi back and forth every time they stopped for a red light. He just hoped whatever storm was coming in, would pass quickly.

Finally, they arrived at The Howell Building. Victor told the driver to drop him off across the street, then he paid the man.

Before approaching the entrance, he looked up to see if any

lights were on inside the building. It was completely dark from the outside.

He crossed the street while checking to see if anyone was looming in the shadows, then peeked inside the skinny opening along the side of the temporary plywood door. The only thing he saw was an empty security guard booth with the light on inside of it.

With one hand on the chain, he gave it a little tug. The chain came out of its hole without any sign of a lock. Victor knew Craig Hill must already be here.

He opened the plywood door and a gust of wind almost ripped it off the hinges. Fortunately, because the only other people around were also trying to get out of the wind, no one paid any attention to Victor as he grabbed the plywood door and pulled it shut with him inside the building.

While replacing the chain just to keep the door from flying open again, Victor noticed the open lock on the floor.

He took out his firearm and the flashlight that he'd taken from home and headed into the building.

CHAPTER 103

Abby parked her car across the street from The Howell Building just in time to catch Victor going in. She watched him remove the chain, open the door, and go inside.

This bastard was involved in some shady shit, and now, Abby was going to prove it.

She stepped out of her car and fought the winds on her way across the street.

While peeking into the building, a flash of light illuminated the night sky making it look like daytime for a second. Before Abby's mind had the time to register what it was—a loud crash shook the earth—Abby jumped. Adrenaline filled her veins as car alarms blared.

She knew right away it was lightning and thunder and she should have known it was coming after watching the forecast earlier, but it still caught her by surprise.

Abby pulled the loose chain, opened the door, entered the building, and replaced the chain just as Victor did.

Inside, she glanced at the empty security booth and then at the darkness ahead. She wished she thought of bringing a flashlight.

Using her cell phone screen to provide enough light to see a foot or two in front of her, she made her way through the labyrinth of unfinished apartments and then finally to the staircase.

She looked up and saw the beam from a flashlight on the

floor above.

She knew it was Victor.

CHAPTER 104

Just as they arrived at the sixth floor, Enzo had to stop again to catch his breath. His legs and knees were killing him. He panted so loud he could barely hear the gusting winds whipping around outside.

One floor above, Johnny stopped, turned around, and said, "I'm not saying you should join a gym or anything, but at least do some walking once in a while."

Even if Enzo were able to speak, he still wouldn't have told Johnny to go fuck himself, no matter how bad he wanted to. He just raised one hand as a signal to Johnny that he's coming, then he began dragging himself up the steps once again.

The crash of thunder outside made Enzo jump. He was surprised that he even had enough energy left to be scared. His heart pounded and his lungs were working at maximum capacity, but he knew he had to keep moving.

The thought of dying under Layla's tight body occurred to him once again. It was a much more pleasant alternative to dying of a heart attack while trying to get up these damn steps.

CHAPTER 105

After checking out the second floor with his flashlight, Victor headed up the stairs to the third floor.

The wind outside howled as it passed, and sometimes the gusts were so powerful, it felt as if it would rip the plywood from the window openings.

Victor entered the third floor and turned a corner going around a finished sheetrock wall into what was to soon become a kitchen. It was exactly the same layout as the kitchen on the second floor—which was the same layout as the kitchen on the first floor—where they found Robby McPherson's bloody corpse covered in green dust.

He continued zigzagging through kitchens, bedrooms, and bathrooms looking for anything or anyone. He didn't want to waste too much time on each floor, but he still wanted to be sure no one else was there.

CHAPTER 106

Abby jumped again when thunder outside rattled the entire building. She kept telling herself to stay calm, but she was never much for calmness.

She followed the stairs as quietly as possible with her eyes on the flashlight beam above, but, as she was halfway up to the next floor, the light disappeared.

After successfully taking a couple steps in the dark, she almost tripped on the next step. She didn't want to use her phone for light again because her battery was almost gone and she knew she might need it again at a more important time.

That thought reminded her to silence her phone, which she did.

After spending a few minutes standing on the steps in the dark, the flashlight beam finally reappeared in the staircase above. It didn't illuminate where she was, but the reflective glow was enough for her to see the edge of each step as she got to it.

CHAPTER 107

Craig hid behind a stack of sheetrock near the far wall with his revolver in one hand and his new phone in the other hand.

As soon as he heard someone exit the staircase, he dialed the other cell phone.

It rang from the staircase. Craig knew it had to be the fat Italian one still making his way up, and he assumed that the first guy was that Dominican kid.

Enzo's voice answered the phone, "Yeah." He was panting so much he couldn't talk.

Craig couldn't see them yet, but he didn't want them to know that, and he didn't want to give up his position, so he whispered, "Where's the money?"

Enzo replied, "My partner has it. He's just ahead of me."

Craig whispered again, hoping the first guy wasn't looking around for him. He said, "From the top of the staircase, walk straight until you see two big closets."

"Okay. We're doing it."

Craig whispered, "Stay on the phone." He saw a flashlight beam following the length of the hallway, then he saw Enzo and another man going down the hall toward the elevator shafts.

He knew that other man was not the Dominican kid he'd seen in The Bronx, and he hoped that kid wasn't just around the corner waiting to come after him.

Thunder outside rocked the building while excitement and

fear pumped through Craig's veins. He whispered into the phone. "Stop there."

Enzo and the man stopped.

Craig said, "Let's see the cash."

Enzo's turned to the man next to him and said, "He wants to see the cash."

His accomplice opened a leather attaché case and pointed his flashlight inside of it, illuminating stacks of hundred-dollar bills rubberbanded together.

Craig said, "Close the bag and throw it toward the stairs."

Enzo repeated Craig's instructions to the man next to him.

The man did it.

Craig said, "The coke is in a cardboard box inside the closet behind you."

CHAPTER 108

On the phone, listening to Craig's instructions, Enzo turned to Johnny and said, "He says it's in a cardboard box in the closet behind us."

Johnny turned and shined his flashlight onto a small box on the floor of one of the two huge closets.

Thunder outside shook the building and made Enzo jump again. Even in the dark Enzo could tell that Johnny was getting fed up with him. Enzo said, "Let's just get the stuff and get the fuck outta here." He took a step forward, into the closet.

Something happened. It took a second for his mind to understand the actions that were under way. It felt like he was dreaming.

The floor caved in underneath him. His body fell forward while at the same time plummeting downward. Pain registered in his mind as his face smacked into the cinderblock wall in front of him. The skin burned as his face scraped the wall on its way down.

He tried to reach out and grab onto something, but there was nothing there.

He just kept falling.

CHAPTER 109

Craig watched as Enzo plummeted to his death and the man next to him didn't even try to help, he just scanned the room with his flashlight.

Thunder outside made Craig jump as he aimed his gun at the man with the flashlight. He steadied his hand, then when the man was close enough and visible, Craig fired two shots.

On his way down, the man dropped his flashlight and it rolled along the concrete.

With the security guard's flashlight, Craig illuminated the man and saw that he was shot in the torso, but still alive. The man gasped for air while Craig sent a slug into his brain.

He snatched the big gun from the man's hand, then raced to the bag with the money and grabbed it before heading back to his hiding spot behind the stack of sheetrock. He stuffed the man's gun into the bag and closed it.

If Victor was in the building, those shots would lure him up here. Craig was not only hoping for it, he was counting on it.

CHAPTER 110

While searching the sixth floor, Victor heard gunshots.

He raced up the stairs to the eighth floor, then checked the area with his firearm and flashlight in front of him.

A corpse with a bullet hole in the head and another in the torso lay on the floor in the middle of the hallway. Victor assumed this was one of the mafia guys Craig was talking about and wondered why the man would be here alone. He shined his light and held up his 9mm while looking around for more thugs.

Victor jumped at the sound of thunder outside.

CHAPTER 111

After making some noise on the third floor, Abby made sure to stay two floors behind Victor at all times. When she was on the fourth floor and he was on the sixth, she lost sight of his flashlight beam when he ran up the stairs following three gunshots.

With only the light from her phone to guide her, she finally reached the eighth floor and spotted Victor in the middle of a hallway, gun in hand, shining his light everywhere.

Another flashlight lay on the concrete floor, illuminating a dead man near Victor's feet.

Now she had him.

CHAPTER 112

Craig had waited for Victor to come up the steps and find the body, then he hid the bag of money near the stairs.

Victor was directly under the loose pipe and Craig was ready to cut the extension cord, but he couldn't, not while Victor kept shining that light everywhere.

He aimed his revolver. He was much farther away this time and was worried that he wouldn't make the shot, so he decided to get closer to the extension cord and expand his options.

When Victor shined his light the other way, Craig dashed toward the extension cord and ducked behind a stack of metal studs.

Victor's light passed his way again, but Craig was confident he could shoot the guy from this distance if he had to. It would be a shame, however, to waste a perfectly good trap.

He waited for the light to pass, then just as he was ready to peek out and shoot Victor, exploding thunder shook the building and scared the shit out of him. He ducked back down.

CHAPTER 113

Just after that last thunder, Victor heard something nearby. He shined his light everywhere, but didn't see anything. He could sense there was someone else there.

He looked twice when he noticed an extension cord coming from above and tied to a waste pipe in the wall. He followed the cord with his flashlight beam. It went up, into the ceiling, over another pipe, then it was tied around a heavy sprinkler pipe. The clamps on the sprinkler pipe were all open.

That's when he realized it was a trap.

He moved out of the way.

CHAPTER 114

Abby knew Victor didn't kill the man because the shots had already been fired before Victor ran up the stairs, but she didn't have to mention to anyone that she knew that. She knew he'd get out of the murder rap, but just his presence here, while he was supposed to be home pending evaluation, would be enough for her to order the drug test that she knew would take him down. She thanked God for giving her the strength and wisdom to dispense justice.

With her gun out, Abby stepped forward and yelled, "Drop it, Cohen!"

Victor said, "Stay back Edmunds. There's a trap." He pointed at the ceiling with his gun.

Abby wasn't falling for it. She didn't take her eyes off him. "I'm not playing, boy. Drop that gun right now, or I will shoot."

Victor said, "Okay." With one hand, he clicked the safety on and tossed his firearm a few feet away. "Now look." He turned his light and shined it where the extension cord was tied to the waste pipe in the wall.

Abby said, "Give me the flashlight, Cohen." She moved toward him.

CHAPTER 115

From behind the stack of metal studs, Craig watched as the big black woman stepped directly under the pipe. He knew he had to kill her too, and now that Cohen didn't have his gun, this was his chance.

Craig leaped up and lunged for the extension cord with the knife in his hand. The pressure that the cord had been under all this time stretched it out and weakened it, but it still took a few seconds for him to cut through it. At least it was much easier than sawing through Robby's throat.

Craig glanced up and saw Victor bolt toward the big black woman while shining his flashlight in her face. She fired at him haphazardly and missed.

Craig finally cut the rest of the way through the cord.

It snapped into the air.

Victor tackled the big black woman, knocking her to the ground and rolling out of the way with her.

The heavy pipe plummeted from the ceiling and landed with a boom almost as loud as the thunder outside.

Craig couldn't believe that stupid bastard almost took a bullet in the face and a pipe in the ass, just to save some bitch who was arresting him anyway.

He raced toward the stairs, turned off and dropped the flashlight, grabbed the bag of money, fired a couple shots in their direction, and then dashed up the stairs to the roof, where the rain and wind almost knocked him over.

Craig stood strong. He had already memorized his escape plan and the streetlights were enough for him to see what he was doing, he just hoped those two cops downstairs didn't make it up here in time to catch him. He also hoped he wouldn't slip on the wet metal, or get struck by lightning for that matter.

Blinded by the downpour, he dashed across the flat roof to the metal pipe-frame scaffolding attached to the side of the building.

He stuffed his revolver into his sweatshirt pocket, then with one hand still holding the attaché case, he placed his other hand on the mid-rail pipe. Carefully and slowly, he began to climb over, but he lost his grip, then he lost his balance and slipped. Craig went down. His back slammed against the wet wood platform below, knocking the wind out of him, but he never let go of the money.

Turning his head to avoid a mouthful of rain, he gasped for air as if he were swimming. With his free hand, Craig checked to be sure he still had his gun, then he struggled to his feet.

When he was sure no one else was on the roof, he hurried across the wood-planked platform to the metal stairs. A flash of lightning illuminated the darkness.

To avoid falling to his death, he took his time going down the slippery metal steps to the roof of the five-story building below. Craig knew that roof well. It was one of his and his buddies' smoking spots. That's how he knew the fire exit alarm on the staircase was out of order.

Thunder crashed against the night sky as Craig's trembling hands grasped the wet metal handrail even tighter as he inched his way down.

Finally, with only two floors to go, Craig picked up his speed. He slipped on the wet step below and lost his footing. He slid down the three remaining steps to the landing below and fell on his ass. His lower back throbbed when he tried to get up, but he got up anyway.

He took the last flight of stairs as slowly as he'd taken the first flight, then rested for a few seconds when he reached the bottom.

Before stepping out onto the roof next door and into plain sight, he tried to look up, but the rain felt like a power-washer on his face. He could only listen. He stood there for a few more seconds, then decided that it didn't seem like anyone was coming down the scaffold after him.

Craig dashed across the roof through the pouring rain as lightning illuminated the sky again, then he slipped into the door with the broken alarm and closed it, blocking the sound of thunder.

He tried to compose himself the best he could while making his way down the stairs and leaving a river behind him. Most of the building was quiet, but a few TV's blared here and there. He just hoped no one went in or out for the next few minutes.

The building lobby was empty and quiet. Craig kept his head down in case there were cameras, then made his way to the front door, where he looked at the rainy street outside and didn't see anyone waiting for him. He didn't see anyone at all on the streets.

Before opening the door, Craig wondered what the hell he was going to do now. He could try, but he knew that he'd never make it out of the country anyway. And if he did, he'd probably drop dead before getting his transplant.

He stepped outside onto the sidewalk and into the rain.

Another flash of lightning illuminated the sky.

The storm made Craig realize how powerless he was against the strength and the will of God. He prayed and asked God what to do.

Thunder smashed against the night sky.

CHAPTER 116

After checking the staircase and the seventh floor for Craig or anyone else, Victor returned to Abby on the eighth floor. She couldn't move her leg. They both guessed that it was broken. Victor hoped their assessment was correct, no matter how much of a pain in the ass she was, he didn't want to see her paralyzed.

Victor said, "I couldn't find him. I texted Rosie. She's on her way. I told her to keep an eye out for him."

Abby said, "Leave me. Go find him."

"He's long gone. And I'm in no shape to run after him." He reached down and tried to help her up.

"Leave me alone. I'm fine."

"You're fine? With a broken leg?" Victor once again reached down, but this time Abby didn't resist.

He helped her to her feet and then she leaned on him like a human crutch.

She was heavy on Victor's shoulder as he struggled to walk her down the stairs. They stopped to rest on each floor.

Abby checked her phone, but the battery was dead. She said, "Damn this phone. I don't understand why you won't just call for some cute, young paramedics to come and help me."

Victor asked, "You saying I'm not young and cute?"

Abby laughed.

Victor said, "If I don't find this guy and make him confess to everything, I could kiss my career, and my life, goodbye. I still might get fucked even if I do catch him, but I have to at least try."

Abby didn't say anything, but she didn't look him in the eye.

Victor hoped she felt guilty. Another man might have let that pipe kill her, but Victor couldn't do it. He said, "Come on. We have a long way to go."

He helped her back up and then they worked their way down another flight of stairs.

CHAPTER 117

Outside, the heavy rain and wind continued.

Abby still couldn't believe that Victor put his own life in danger to save hers. It would have been so much easier for him to let her fall into Craig Hill's trap.

For the first time in her life, things weren't so black and white. She realized that even though Victor had a weakness for drugs, he was still a good man, and drugs didn't define what he was.

Victor helped her to the curb and placed her in the passenger seat of Rosie's car. He got in the back seat and closed the door.

Abby looked down at her saturated clothes and felt the water draining into the upholstery.

Sitting in the driver's seat, Rosie glanced over at Abby sitting next to her, then at Victor through her rear view mirror and said, "So, you two seem to be getting along."

Abby felt worse by the minute. "I have to apologize to both of you." Before she could continue, Victor's phone rang.

Victor looked at the number and said, "It's him." He answered and said, "Hello." He stayed on the line listening for a couple minutes, then said, "Tell me where you are. I can help you. Craig . . . Craig?" He looked at his phone. "Damn it."

Abby asked, "What'd he say?"

"He said he couldn't believe I almost got killed to save a woman who was arresting me. And then he started rambling about his life being worthless anyway, and that he now wanted to save someone's life like I did. You think he's serious or just fucking with me? He sounded high as a kite."

Rosie looked at both of them then asked Victor, "You almost got yourself killed saving her life?"

Abby felt tears swell up in her eyes. "He did." She turned to Victor and said, "Thank you for saving my life."

Victor said, "I have to get to Brooklyn. I know where he's going."

Abby handed Victor her car keys and said, "Take my car."

CHAPTER 118

As Victor drove farther east into Brooklyn, the intensity of the rain decreased and the sun began to show itself over the horizon.

He hoped he was right about Craig going to the hospital to save a life, and he wished he'd taken the police cruiser rather than Abby's old jalopy.

While staring through the windshield wipers and rain at the taillights on the wet asphalt ahead, Victor realized that when he was in The Howell Building, scared for his life, he thought about Evelyn and Sofia—Jennifer Rivera never even came to mind—he only thought of his wife and daughter.

Finally, after getting off he expressway, Victor followed the streets to the hospital, parked in the garage, and called Rosie. He told her where he was and he asked her to call for backup.

Victor dashed through the rain and entered the hospital. He approached the desk and asked if there was a patient named Deanna Chapman.

There was.

CHAPTER 119

Craig left his Styrofoam coffee cup on the metal table in the desolate hospital cafeteria and slipped into the sterile bathroom to take a little sniff.

He looked around before sitting back down at the table. With three thousand dollars in his pocket, and a good amount of coke left, Craig decided the next thirty or so days of his life would consist of nothing but pleasure—unless the cops got to him first.

The coffee was too hot to drink so he just stared at it, occasionally glancing out the window at the rain outside.

When he saw Detective Victor Cohen approaching, his first instinct was to run, or to shoot, but he didn't have the strength or the will to even move.

Victor sat down at the table across from him, took out his firearm, and said, "I just came from Deanna's room. Everyone up there is celebrating a miracle."

Craig didn't say anything.

Victor said, "It seems someone anonymously donated one hundred thousand dollars . . . in cash . . . so she could get her liver transplant."

CHAPTER 120

Victor could see that Craig was high, but he waited patiently for Craig's response about the miracle donation.

Craig looked at the gun in Victor's hand, then into Victor's eyes and asked, "Would you take a miracle from a little girl?"

Victor knew that if he turned in that money it would sit in evidence forever, or at best, it would get recycled through the police department. He told Craig, "No. I wouldn't." He stood and removed a pair of handcuffs from his back pocket. "I am gonna have to take you in though."

Craig placed his hand into his sweatshirt pocket.

Victor knew Craig was going for his gun and he knew he could easily take Craig down before the gun was even visible, but he had a feeling that's what Craig wanted, and he didn't want to kill anyone today. "You'll never get it out in time. Please don't make me shoot you."

Craig bolted down the hall, pushing doctors and nurses out of the way.

Victor didn't want to shoot and put other people's lives at risk, so he chased Craig down the hall and through a door.

Craig raced through another hallway, also full of doctors, nurses, and patients.

Victor followed Craig as he made his way toward the front door and then outside.

Craig raised his gun to his temple, but before he could pull the trigger and take his own life, someone else shot him.

Victor hit the floor and looked up as SWAT team snipers from the roof across the street fired a few extra shots into Craig Hill's corpse.

The rain was gone, but a cool mist lingered as the sun began to shine bright overhead.

Books by Phil Nova:

FOUR KILOS
A novel
Internal Affairs and the mob both suspect pill-popping homicide detective, Victor Cohen, of theft and murder. Can Victor solve the murders and find four missing kilos of cocaine before it's too late?

JIHAD ON 34TH STREET
A novel
A Pakistani-American construction worker suspected of being a terrorist eludes a federal agent and tries to find the real terrorists before the feds find him.

BLACK & WHITE AND RED ALL OVER
A novella
A racist white prisoner and racist black prisoner must work together to escape after being transferred to a secret government facility for human experimentation.

THE VAMPIRE OF NEW ORLEANS
A novelette
Police in New Orleans investigate a murder that fits a pattern going back over one hundred years.

DUELING DUETS
A novelette
In this obscene, off-color parody, a fighter and a singer cross paths on their way up the ladder of success.

MAMA'S PLACE
A short story
A group of wannabe gangsters breaks into a building but only one of them comes out alive.

LAPTOP LOVE
A short story
After Alan and Tina break up, it's up to their laptops to get them back together.

JACKED
A short story
A small time mafia crew from Las Vegas hijacks a military truck coming from Roswell, New Mexico.

FREE short stories by Phil Nova:

A NEW START
A group of criminals in the future flees Earth with a fortune in diamonds and brings bad luck a new world.

ALLU
While on their way to stand trial for war crimes, a group of American soldiers in Iraq unleashes an ancient evil.

BEWARE OF GEEKS BEARING GIFTS
Government agencies investigate an outbreak of mass murders in small town America.

HOT DOG MAN
In this vulgar and offensive parody, an aged superhero comes out of retirement for one last mission.

THE DEATH OF ONE LIFE
A corrupt corporate executive makes his peace with God while dying of cancer.

Website: www.philnova.com
Email: philnova@philnova.com

20378555R00188

Made in the USA
Middletown, DE
24 May 2015